The girl looked over at me and frowned. Her dog walked over and licked my fingers.

They said dogs and owners tended to have the same personality, so I had hope for this girl.

I nodded toward the receptionist desk. "Having trouble getting out of here?"

"A bit," she said.

"Well, I just got clearance for takeoff."

She was frowning again.

"Must be nice," she said.

"Can I give you a lift?" I asked, scratching her dog's ears.

"I don't know you," she said.

"Your dog likes me," I said.

"He's not—" Her phone chimed again and she glanced at it, then lifted her gaze back to mine.

Her eyes were green. Not hazel. A deep emerald green. Mesmerizing.

I took another step forward, holding out my hand.

"I'm Wyatt," I said.

She hesitated, but then slipped her phone in her pocket and pressed her hand against mine.

She had a professional handshake. That told me a lot about her.

I grinned. "Now you know me."

She shook her head and grabbed the dog's leash with both hands.

"So can I give you a lift?"

"I don't even know where you're headed," she said.

"With this weather, I'm thinking it wouldn't matter."

I could tell she was considering it. But she was still wary. A good quality for a girl who looked like her to have.

I gave the dog another pat. "Good luck."

I turned and walked toward the door to the tarmac.

Damn. I hated leaving this girl stranded here.

But I understood where she was coming from.

She had no idea who I was.

And had no reason to leave with me.

If she were my sister, I'd commend her caution.

I reached the door and wrapping my fingers around the doorknob, prepared myself to face the air that seemed to be getting colder by the minute.

"Wait," the girl said from behind me.

SECOND CHANCE SECRETS

ALSO BY KATHRYN KALEIGH

Contemporary Romance
The Worthington Family

The Heart of Christmas

The Magic of Christmas

Second Chance Kisses

Second Chance Secrets

First Time Charm

Three Broken Rules

Second Chance Destiny

Unexpected Vows

Billionaire's Unexpected Landing

Billionaire's Accidental Girlfriend

Billionaire Fallen Angel

Begin Again

Love Again

Falling Again

Just Stay

Just Chance

Just Believe

Just Us

Just Once

Just Happened

Just Maybe

Just Pretend

Just Because

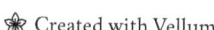

SECOND CHANCE SECRETS

THE WORTHINGTONS

KATHRYN KALEIGH

To learn more about Kathryn Kaleigh, visit

www.kathrynkaleigh.com

Kathryn Kaleigh

1

AINSLEY WORTHINGTON

I'd had better days.

I sat in a small private Cessna jet on the tarmac at a little airport just out from Aspen, Colorado.

The sun came through the windshield with a vengeance. It was hot for an October day.

A ridge of trees, flocked with shades of red, yellow, and gold started just off the edge of the runway and traveled up the mountainside until they gave way to bare rocks and finally snowcapped peaks.

A flock of birds left the trees and flew into the sky.

Yet I was left sitting here on the tarmac in this plane.

The tail of the plane wore bright red letters. Skye Travels.

One of Noah Worthington's planes.

Noah. My daddy.

Daddy was known to hire only the best pilots to fly for the company he'd built from the ground up.

It was an aviation empire now. One that rivaled some of the smaller commercial airlines.

Out of six children, I was the only one of his children who became a pilot.

Six. One brother. Three sisters. And one half-sister.

Both my half-sister and my older sister had married pilots, but that didn't count.

I had Daddy's blood running through my veins.

Yet he wouldn't hire me on until I had enough experience.

Frankly, I thought he was being harder on me than anyone else.

He'd let me haul cargo, but not people.

"Miss Worthington?" A mechanic climbed up on the wing and stuck his head through the open door of my plane.

"Did you find one?"

"I'm sorry," he said. "We have to order one from the factory. Won't be here for two days." He glanced upwards. "And with the weather they're predicting, all bets are off."

Damn.

"Is there another plane I can use?"

"You'll have to check inside. I don't have that information."

Of course he didn't.

I tossed my leather satchel over my shoulder, but left my pilot's cap on the passenger seat.

Daddy insisted that all his pilots wear a cap. He thought they added a level of distinctiveness to the pilots.

"Come on Beau," I said. "Let's get out of here."

I picked up the leash and, leaning back, hooked it on Beau's collar.

This was supposed to be a day trip. Fly up. Get the dog—a cute, friendly solid black lab—and fly back to Houston.

Simple.

But then the alternator had gone bad.

Apparently there was a shortage of alternators right now, at least for this particular plane.

And on top of that, there was a snow storm coming in.

I didn't do snow.

I was a Houston girl. Born and raised.

My older sister, Madison, lived in Denver with her fiancé. But that was about as close to snow as I got.

Though I was only picking up a dog, I was still flying a Skye Travels plane, so I was wearing part of my full uniform. White shirt. Low heels. Black jeans.

I used every opportunity to show Daddy that I was ready to fly passengers, but today seemed like a good day to bend the rules.

I had become adept at getting in and out of small planes, even wearing heels.

The big dog was a bit of a different story.

I barely had my feet on the ground before Beau jumped out, landing behind me.

He shook his whole body, fur flying, and looked at me expectantly.

I didn't know a whole lot about dogs, but I could tell Beau was still a puppy. A big gangly puppy.

Though the sun had been hot coming in through the windshield, there was a cold bite to the wind. I was wearing a little suit jacket. It wouldn't do much to keep me warm though.

"Let's go," I said, starting off across the tarmac toward the office where I'd left just an hour ago.

Beau practically pulled me along behind him.

He was being shipped from one family member to another. That's all I knew. I'm sure there was a story behind it all, but my job was just to get Beau from one airport to another.

My sister Madison would have known the whole story before she even had the flight scheduled. But she was a psychologist.

Me. I was all about the flight.

But right now I was stuck in an airport in the Rocky Mountains with a dog named Beau.

I went inside the little office and walked up to the desk.

"Hi," I said to the young lady sitting behind the desk. Her

nametag said her name was Claire. She was a tall, thin woman with short blonde hair. Her features were angular and sharp.

"Hi," Claire said with a bright smile, mostly for Beau.

"They had to order a part," I said. "for my plane."

"I know," Claire said. "I'm sorry."

"So… can you get me out of here?"

"Unfortunately we don't have any extra planes." She said it with a straight face.

"I didn't think you would," I said, plastering a smile on my face, refusing to get snippy. "Do you have access to other flights out of here?"

"I do," she said. "There's nothing. The storm."

"Right," I said. "The storm. But would you please check again?" Beau tugged at his leash and I had to catch myself to him from pulling me with him. "I have this dog I have to get to Houston."

Claire started to refuse, but I just raised an eyebrow and stood as though to say I was going to wait right here until she checked again.

Claire clicked keys on the keyboard.

Then looked back at me. "I'm sorry," she said. "There's nothing."

"Alright," I said, pulling my cell out of my pocket.

Daddy could fix this.

Claire had no idea, obviously, how to make things happen.

I shot off a quick text to Daddy.

ME: *Had to order a part. AND weather has flight delayed. Can you get me out of here?*

I walked over to one of the sofas and sat down. Beau jumped up to sit beside me.

There was only one other man in the lobby, but his back was to me. A phone was pressed to his ear.

"I don't think you're supposed to be up here," I said, pushing at Beau.

He didn't budge.

He was awfully heavy for a puppy.

DADDY: *Let me see. Hold tight. Be right back.*

Hold tight. He had no idea what he was asking.

Claire was shooting me dirty looks for having Beau on the sofa.

Well, it wasn't like I could do anything about it.

I stood up and Beau followed. We walked over to the window and turned our backs to Claire as I held my cell and waited.

Clouds had gathered around the mountain peaks. I remembered Madison talking about how the mountain peaks would disappear in a swirl of clouds when it was going to snow.

Then when clouds cleared, they would leave a layer of fresh snow.

While waiting for Daddy to get back to me, I checked the weather on my phone.

Wow. According to the projection, this whole area was going to be blanketed by snow in about… three hours.

I needed to leave. Now.

I turned and started back toward the desk, Beau in tow.

Claire saw me coming. I know she did. She stood up and disappeared into the back.

I stood in the middle of the lobby. Beau's leash in one hand. My phone in the other.

My thoughts scattered in a thousand different directions.

There was no way I was getting out of here today.

I had to find dog food for this dog. And a place to stay.

A hotel that took dogs.

I stared at my phone. Willing Daddy to write back.

The phone rang and I jumped.

"Hi Daddy," I said. I had a sinking feeling in the pit of my stomach.

2

WYATT BEAUFORT

I'd been on hold for far too long.

But it had paid off.

While I was on hold, listening to interminable elevator music, I'd watched the young lady who had come in with her dog.

I couldn't hear her conversation with Claire, the receptionist, but I could tell by Claire's smug expression and the girl's look of distress, that she was stranded here.

I stood up. Stretched. The girl was pacing and talking on her cell. She was one of those dark-haired brunettes that automatically sent my pulse racing.

But this particular dark-haired brunette had the beauty of an angel.

I didn't know who she was or where she came from. Frankly I didn't care.

I shoved my iPad into my satchel and tossed it over my shoulder.

Hanging back, I waited for her finish her call. I could hear her voice, but she spoke low, so I couldn't understand her words.

"Love you, too," she said before ending the call. I flinched.

Didn't matter. There were lots of people she could say that to. Didn't mean she was taken.

Either way, I could still help her.

Claire had disappeared into the back. I'd dealt with her before, so I wasn't surprised.

The girl stood there, looking bereft.

I walked over and stopped a few feet away.

"Hi," I said.

She looked over at me and frowned. Her dog walked over and licked my fingers.

They said dogs and owners tended to have the same personality, so I had hope for this girl.

I nodded toward the receptionist desk. "Having trouble getting out of here?"

"A bit," she said.

"Well, I just got clearance for takeoff."

She was frowning again.

"Must be nice," she said.

"Can I give you a lift?" I asked, scratching her dog's ears.

"I don't know you," she said.

"Your dog likes me," I said.

"He's not—" Her phone chimed again and she glanced at it, then lifted her gaze back to mine.

Her eyes were green. Not hazel. A deep emerald green. Mesmerizing.

I took another step forward, holding out my hand.

"I'm Wyatt," I said.

She hesitated, but then slipped her phone in her pocket and pressed her hand against mine.

She had a professional handshake. That told me a lot about her.

I grinned. "Now you know me."

She shook her head and grabbed the dog's leash with both hands.

"So can I give you a lift?"

Claire walked back out to her desk and watched us.

"I don't even know where you're headed," she said.

"With this weather, I'm thinking it wouldn't matter."

I could tell she was considering it. But she was still wary. A good quality for a girl who looked like her to have.

Claire's voice came over the loudspeaker. You'd think there was a roomful of people and not just the two of us.

"The terminal will be closing in ten minutes."

I'd been in this terminal a hundred times and I'd never even known it to have a loudspeaker.

Probably just for emergencies.

But Claire was being an ass. I'd seen it before. This was different though. She was usually a lot more subtle about it.

She smiled when she saw me looking in her direction. She raised a hand and sent me a smile.

I ignored her and turned back to the girl.

"Well," I said. "I take that as my cue to get out of here." I gave the dog another pat. "Good luck."

I turned and walked toward the door to the tarmac.

Damn. I hated leaving this girl stranded here.

But I understood where she was coming from.

She had no idea who I was.

And had no reason to leave with me.

If she were my sister, I'd commend her caution.

I reached the door and wrapping my fingers around the doorknob, prepared myself to face the air that seemed to be getting colder by the minute.

"Wait," the girl said from behind me.

3

AINSLEY

*A*s I watched Wyatt walk toward the tarmac, I felt sick to my stomach.

Weather was one thing a pilot couldn't control.

Even my daddy, Noah Worthington, couldn't control the weather.

Normally, he would have sent someone to pick me up. But with the storm coming in, it was out of his hands.

He told me to get a hotel room and wait it out.

Either the weather would clear and the part would come in or the weather would clear and he'd send someone for me.

Everything depended on the weather.

Already a few stray snowflakes were starting to fall.

Daddy had someone looking for a room in town for me, but so far everything was booked up.

Not only was it that time of the year when tourists flocked to leaf peeking, but the storm had people stranded.

And then I had this dog, so the hotel had to accept a pet.

I couldn't stay here. Claire was closing the doors, kicking me out.

I could get transportation easy enough. A cab or an uber.

But then what?

This was not a good situation.

Wherever Wyatt was going, it was out of here. If I could get away from this storm, I could get home.

And it looked like he was my last ditch choice.

He turned as I called out to him. Looked at me with a smug little grin on his face.

I shrugged.

Beau was already headed toward Wyatt. I just followed along.

"We'll come with you," I said.

"Glad I was able to twist your arm," he said, holding the door open for me.

I stepped through the door into air that colder than it had been when I'd come in.

It hadn't been that long, had it?

"Do you have luggage?" he asked.

"No."

"So no luggage."

He wasn't asking. Even though I know he wanted to.

Most people who flew had some type of luggage.

I had my satchel with my iPad and a change of clothes. I always had that with me.

But he didn't need to know that.

And I decided right then and there that I wasn't going to tell him who I was.

I'm not quite sure why. Maybe it was people I was tired of guys thinking I'd be easy to hit on because I was a pilot.

Or maybe I wanted him to think I was just a regular girl with a dog.

And not the heiress to an aviation empire.

He didn't know. And I saw no reason to tell him.

He was giving me a lift. That was all.

I had to admit though that he was good looking. He had that tall, dark, and handsome look that I was a sucker for.

He had a five o'clock shadow and a charming little sideways grin.

And those blue eyes. They seemed to just see right through me.

And on top of that, he'd come to my rescue in a time of need.

Wyatt was my knight in shining armor.

We walked across the tarmac toward a Phenom 300 private jet. I'd seen it earlier and assumed it belonged to a movie star or a corporate tycoon.

Daddy had been eyeing one of these for a while now, but there was a waiting list.

I glanced over at Wyatt.

We were definitely headed toward the Phenom.

"Are we the only ones flying?" I asked, unable to keep quiet any longer.

"Just us." He adjusted the strap of his satchel.

"You don't mind if Beau goes along?" I already knew the answer, but I was having trouble wrapping my head around getting to fly in this jet that went for millions of dollars and was hard to get.

"Why would I mind?" he asked.

I shrugged. "Not everyone likes dog hair."

Beau was running ahead of us and it was all I could do to keep him from pulling out of my hands. It was like he knew where we were headed.

"I like dogs."

He wasn't giving me any answers.

We reached the jet and he used a remote to lower the steps.

As the steps lowered, I watched him. He seemed at ease with the plane.

"Is this your plane?" I asked. Since he wasn't going to volunteer any information, I'd just have to ask.

Maybe he was like me. Maybe he figured he was giving me lift and I didn't need to know any personal details about him.

"All mine," he said.

I heard the undertone of pride that he was probably trying to hide.

He wouldn't have any way to know that I knew how hard it was to get one of these.

"You first," he said, holding out a hand toward the stairs.

It took a bit of encouragement to get Beau to go up the stairs behind me.

The plane smelled luxuriously new. Like leather and new fabric.

I wondered just how new it was. And wondered again why Wyatt was so easy about letting a stranger, much less a dog on board.

I watched as he secured the door.

"You can sit wherever you like," he said.

"Oh. Right." I'd just assumed I'd sit in the cockpit. With him.

But I wasn't telling him that I was a pilot, so it was little bit harder to explain.

I looked around. There were so many places to sit. Not just chairs. But a sofa.

Daddy had some nice planes, but this one was nicer than anything even Noah Worthington owned.

Seems my knight in shining armor was not only a pilot, but a wealthy one.

4

___

WYATT

*M*y passenger seemed reluctant to take a seat.

She was asking a lot of questions, but I didn't mind. She should ask. She was the one putting herself in a stranger's hands.

"Can I sit in the cockpit?" she asked. "with you?"

That was an interesting request. Most people, especially the ladies, liked to sit in the back and enjoy a glass of champagne during their flight.

But I didn't mind the company. In fact, I was happy to have it.

"Sure," I said.

She smiled then. For the first time.

And her smile lit up her face.

I'd thought she was beautiful before, but that smile made her drop dead gorgeous.

"On one condition," I said.

"What's that?" The wariness had come back to her eyes.

I just smiled.

"Tell me your name."

"Ainsley," she said.

"Do you have a last name?"

"Ainsley Richards."

"Well, Ainsley Richards. Welcome aboard. Unfortunately, we're under a bit of a time crunch and have to get going."

She nodded and followed me to the cockpit.

The dog, Beau, followed us.

Ainsley went straight to the copilot's seat, sat down, and buckled herself in.

I looked at her questioningly.

"What?" she asked.

"You seem to know your way around a cockpit."

"Oh," she said. "I've spent some time in planes."

I winked at her. "Good to know. You can let me know how I do."

She smiled and there was something in that smile that caught me a little off-guard. It was a secretive, knowing smile. It made me wonder if she did know enough to critique my flying.

I shook off the feeling. I knew what I was doing anyway.

I put on my headset and spoke quietly to the control tower.

A minute later, we were approved for takeoff.

I wasn't surprised since we seemed to be the last flight out of the airport.

It was irritating how quickly they'd closed everything down, but it was also impressive.

All indicators looked good, so I pushed the plane and we took off.

That moment when the wheels first left the ground was, for me, a magical time.

I glanced over at Ainsley to see how she was fairing.

She had her eyes closed and a blissful expression on her face. She looked like I felt.

Beau had laid down between us and put his head down. If I didn't know better, I think the dog was a frequent flyer.

I took us into the air and we started a slow turn north. We'd get past the mountains, and the bad weather, then head northwest.

Ainsley was staring at the computer screen, her brow creased.

Then she looked up at me.

"Why are we going to Wyoming?" she asked.

Obviously, she could read a flight plan.

"Going around the bad weather," I said.

She held up her hands and shrugged. Then pressed her button again. "Why not head south?"

AINSLEY

My phone chimed and I looked down.

I had a text message from Daddy.

DADDY: *Did you find a hotel?*

Wi-Fi? The plane had Wi-Fi?

Of course it did. Obviously satellite.

But right now I had bigger concerns.

I put on my headset and pressed the button. "Why are we going to Wyoming?" I asked again.

"Because I have to get home."

"Home." I said to myself. I hadn't bothered to ask where exactly Wyatt was taking me.

I took a deep breath. The main thing was to get away from this storm.

Once we landed in… where that airport in Wyoming was, I could find my way to Houston.

Daddy texted again.

DADDY: *Bailey hasn't been able to find anything.*

ME: *Caught a flight out. Will be in touch when I land. Sorry. It was the last flight out. Didn't have time to communicate.*

Daddy wouldn't expect to hear from again until I landed.

We always just assumed there was no cell service in the air. That cut down on a lot of worry when we didn't hear from whoever was flying.

I took another deep breath.

It served me right for not asking questions.

I'd actually never done anything like this before. But then, I'd never been in this kind of situation before either.

I practiced deep breathing. Something I would never admit to doing. It would give my psychologist sister too much satisfaction.

Closing my eyes, I pressed my head back against the headrest.

Then made a mental list of things I needed to do when we landed.

Dog food was at the top of the list.

In fact… I needed to get the dog some water. And I needed water.

"Going to the back for a minute," I said.

Wyatt nodded.

I unbuckled and went into the back. Beau stood up, shook himself, and followed me.

The fully stocked kitchen area had refrigerated water bottles and snacks and a fully stocked bar. I found a bowl big enough for him to drink from and filled it with water from one of the bottles.

Beau got artisan water today.

As he lapped up the water, I opened a bottle of water for myself and drank deeply. I hadn't realized how thirsty I'd gotten. But then flying always made me thirsty.

The plane wasn't as big as I'd expected, but it had a lot of open space and had elegant furnishings.

I sat down on the sofa to finish my water.

And I wondered just who Wyatt was.

If I had his last name, I could google him on my cell. But

without a last name, I'd be wasting my time.

Since I didn't have any other choice at this point, I'd just go along.

It wasn't like Wyatt was hard to be around.

In fact, I had a feeling he and I could be friends.

And he was nice to look at.

Besides, I was curious about who he was and what he called home.

It was possible that this wasn't actually his plane.

Some pilots went in together and bought planes. That would certainly be more feasible that just one person owning a plane like this.

Unless, of course, you were Noah Worthington. But even he didn't have this kind of airplane.

It was possible that Daddy and Wyatt knew each other.

I hadn't given Wyatt my real last name. I'd given him my mother's maiden name. Richards.

Anyone with the Worthington last name was far too easy to find on the Internet.

Especially an unusual name like Ainsley.

There was only one Ainsley Worthington in the world as far as I knew.

Feeling more centered, I put away what had become Beau's water bowl and made my way back to the cockpit.

WYATT

*A*insley stayed gone longer than I'd expected.

Just when I was about to give up on her, Ainsley came back to the cockpit, her dog at her heels.

She was most definitely a mystery.

We flew through some clouds just as she was about to sit down and hit some turbulence.

I instinctively put out an arm to steady her.

When I did, it tipped her toward me and with my arm around her, she grabbed my shoulders to steady herself.

The turbulence only lasted a handful of seconds. It was over in a blink.

But I had my arms around her and her fists were in my shirt.

She smelled like honeysuckle and vanilla.

Normally I wasn't bothered much by turbulence. I knew how to handle it. It was common in the high altitudes around the mountains, so I had a lot of experience with it.

But my heart was pounding like I'd been running a race.

Ainsley pushed back, steadying herself.

Our eyes met and for a moment, we didn't move.

It was like we were frozen there.

But in reality it only lasted a fraction of a second. She straightened and went to her seat, buckling herself in.

I adjusted the altitude to get us above the clouds.

Ainsley took out her phone and kept her gaze focused on it, thought she didn't appear to be doing anything.

Then she blew out a breath and, looking over at me, gave me a little smile.

That little smile sent my heart racing again.

I shifted in my seat.

When she'd practically been in my lap, I'd been enveloped in her scent. Something like honeysuckle and vanilla. Maybe some undertones of jasmine.

It hadn't smelled like heavy perfume at all. More like soap. Or maybe it had just been her essence.

At any rate, whatever it was, it made my thoughts foggy. That and the way she'd looked at me.

She was like some kind of mermaid calling me toward the rocks. Or whatever mermaids did.

It had been a long time since a woman had this effect on me.

But then I'd gotten good at keeping my distance. I had something one of them had described as an icy wall that I throw up in an instant.

But if anyone else had been through what I'd been through, they'd probably not only have a wall to throw up, they'd probably live behind it.

So all in all, I considered myself to be managing fairly well.

I picked up my clipboard, made a show of flipping through the pages, then casually laid it in my lap.

Just in case my cock decided to embarrass me by choosing this particular time to come alive again.

7

AINSLEY

I held my phone tightly in my hands just to keep my hands from trembling.

It wasn't the turbulence. Turbulence didn't scare me one bit.

I knew how to handle it as did any competent pilot. And Wyatt seemed more than competent.

It was way he'd looked at me. And God help me, I'd liked the feel of his arms around my waist.

I didn't date pilots.

At least, not any more.

I'd broken my own rule once and it had led to a moratorium on men.

Which I was still on, by the way.

I wasn't about to make an exception for Wyatt.

He was still a man even if he wasn't a pilot by trade. Flying a jet like this told me he wasn't.

Pilots couldn't afford this kind of plane.

He did something else for a living. Or maybe he was independently wealthy. An inheritance maybe.

Or maybe he was a high-powered executive. He didn't act like an executive. I'd seen my share of them, too.

No. Whatever he was, he was a mystery.

I tried to focus my thoughts on something else.

But sitting here in the cockpit next to this handsome pilot—and at the moment he was a pilot—there wasn't much space to think about anything else.

I wondered if I should let somebody know where I was.

I wasn't on this man's manifest. At least not under my real name.

If we crashed, no one would know I was onboard.

That thought jarred me a bit.

I clicked open my phone and put on my headset. Pressed the button to talk.

"What's our flight number?" I asked.

He rattled it off.

I typed it into a text and sent it into cyberspace.

The Wi-Fi wasn't so good right now for some reason. But I felt better just letting someone know where I was.

I sat back and forced myself to relax and enjoy the flight.

Just as my heartrate had gotten back to a steady state, Wyatt's voice came though my headset.

"Where did you need to go?" he asked.

I sighed. So much for relaxing and enjoying the flight.

"Houston," I said. Houston was a big city and wouldn't tell him much.

I wasn't so sure it mattered anyway if he knew who I was.

"I see," he said. "Guess I'm taking you in the wrong direction."

"Just a little," I said with a little smile.

It wasn't his fault I'd jumped on his plane.

He had gotten me out of a bad place. With my own plane down for who knows how long and the storm coming in, and no rooms available in town, I could have been in a mess.

"Guess we'll figure something out," he said.

"I'm sure we will," I said.

We sat in silence a few minutes.

"I just got another weather report," he said. "Looks like the storm is bigger than they'd expected. You might be stuck in Wyoming for a while."

I looked blankly at him. "How long is awhile?"

He shrugged. "A few days."

I didn't have a few days to sit in Wyoming waiting out a storm.

I had family obligations.

"I'll figure something out," I said with a bravado I didn't feel.

There were a lot of things we could control.

But weather wasn't one of them.

Weather was the great equalizer in the aviation world.

It brought pilots back down to the level of those who had to travel on the ground.

8

WYATT

A colorful radar screen was never a good thing.

But we could make it to Beaufort Valley Ranch without any problem.

Unfortunately, though, the storm had taken a turn and no one was going to be leaving by car, plane, or train anytime soon.

I told myself not to be happy about this.

But it wasn't taking. I was fascinated by the girl sitting next to me.

Her long brunette hair was pulled around to one side and she'd clipped it there. Her big green eyes were framed with long lashes. And her lips were rather pouty at the moment. I wondered what it would feel like to kiss her.

She was wearing black jeans, but otherwise, she was dressed professionally. A cute little black suit jacket. A white blouse. And I hadn't missed the red bottoms on the shoes.

This was not an ordinary girl.

She had no luggage, yet she was obviously a high class woman.

I entertained myself for a moment inventing all sorts of background stories for her.

Maybe she was a flight attendant. She knew enough about airplanes. Actually more than most flight attendants. She could read a flight plan.

So she knew too much to be a flight attendant. And her shoes didn't fit. Flight attendants didn't make enough money to buy shoes like that. Did they? Maybe I was out of touch.

Maybe she had a pilot boyfriend. Now that definitely fit. That would explain her knowledge of planes and her shoes. And she happened to be here with a dog. In a private terminal. But where was the boyfriend?

I should just ask her.

And normally I would have. I was considered by most to be a straightforward kind of guy.

But this particular situation was different.

Ainsley didn't seem to want to tell me anything.

And I felt obligated to respect that. She was a passenger. Not a date.

And that's where things got sticky.

I was actually interested in her.

And that hadn't happened to me in a really long time.

I thought I had developed an immunity to women.

I was certainly used to them throwing themselves at me.

But it wasn't happening.

Now this aloof girl had my attention and she didn't even know and didn't even seem to care.

All she wanted was to get out of Aspen and get to Houston.

It didn't seem like too much to ask. And I'd thought to put her on a plane out of there.

It occurred to me that I could turn the plane around and fly it straight to Houston.

It was possible. Hell, I had one of the best private jets on the market.

But I had an obligation. Just like she probably did.

And even if I didn't have an obligation, I secretly wanted to take her home with me.

The problem was I didn't know what I was going to do with her.

Bringing a pretty young lady home with me did not fit with my plans. Much less being stranded at the ranch with her.

9

AINSLEY

$\mathcal{W}$e were getting close to our destination. Wherever that was.

Some place in a valley. I wasn't close enough to read the screen to see that actual destination.

And my cell service hadn't come back on, so I wasn't able to look it up using the flight number.

I was flying blind, so to speak.

And depending on Wyatt to get us someplace safe.

As we began our descent, I had a good view of the land below.

It was absolutely stunning.

The green valleys were surrounded by tall majestic mountains.

As we hovered closer to the ground, I saw a herd of what looked like wild horses running below.

I'd never been a on a horse. Houston born and raised.

I'd ridden a lot of airplanes, but never a horse.

Under other circumstances, I could see this trip as being an adventure.

But instead, I was faced with uncertainty.

What was I walking into?

It could be anything.

I ruled out serial killer. Airplanes were too high profile to use for serial killings. Just didn't fit.

My best bet was that he either worked for some big company or was a high-powered mogul in his own right.

I wondered what kind of ranch he had. If he even had a ranch.

I looked over at him from beneath my lashes.

He wasn't a cowboy, at least not the traditional type.

He was wearing a pair of blue jeans. A white shirt. And a black tie. Like me, he was dressed in partial pilot's uniform. Instead of cowboy boots, he wore regular dress shoes. Like a city boy would wear.

At the moment, he was wearing dark shades and although they gave him a definite sex appeal, I was not a fan.

I liked being able to see a person's eyes.

I'd left my own shades in my plane. Hopefully they would still be there when I got back to my plane. I'd left my shades and my cap.

As we began the final descent, Beau sat up and let out a single bark.

I looked over and my gaze met Wyatt's.

I'd flown animals before, but never one like this.

Beau almost seemed to know his own way around airplanes.

In this rare moment, I really wished I was more like my sister, Madison. She would have known the dog's story.

Maybe he was some kind of special rescue dog.

I honestly had no idea. Because I hadn't bothered to ask.

I determined to work harder at finding out things about my passengers. Even if I didn't think they were any of my business. Turns out you never knew when knowledge about something might come in handy. Like now. I wanted to know about Beau, but, of course, he couldn't tell me. For all I knew, I was taking him to some little old lady in Houston or maybe to a kid with a terminal illness.

"What's his story?" Wyatt asked.

Yep. I definitely needed to make a concerted effort to get know a little more about my passengers.

10

WYATT

$\mathscr{A}$fter a smooth landing, if I did have to say so myself, I taxied to my private hangar where I kept my plane.

Though it was a bit hard to believe, Ainsley was the first woman I'd brought home with me.

I usually stayed in town. With them.

I preferred to keep my privacy private.

Yet bringing Ainsley here seemed almost natural. I actually wanted to show her my place.

Being private and living alone was nice, but sometimes it got a bit lonely.

Watching my theatre sized television alone lacked something. Namely companionship.

The thought of curling up with her on my leather sofa and watching a movie had an undeniable appeal.

She didn't say anything as we landed and I pressed the garage door app on my phone that let me into the hangar.

Once we'd taxied inside, I hit the remote on my phone again to close the door.

I wondered how she wasn't just a little bit impressed. I was still impressed and I'd lived here for over a year.

Most would consider it a long commute. But for me, getting to work was more fun than being at work. And that was saying a lot.

Not too many people got to live their dreams.

The three of us, me, Ainsley, and Beau prepared to exit the plane. Ainsley and Beau waited patiently while I went to the back and gathered up my duffle bag.

I'd asked her about Beau, but she'd just shrugged noncommittally. I don't think she knew much about him.

I decided that he was her pilot boyfriend's dog.

I'd never seen a dog who seemed so comfortable in an airplane.

So while knew absolutely nothing about Ainsley Richards, I'd invented quite a fictional life for her.

I sort of actually hoped I was close to the truth because it was a good life. Reality could be so very harsh.

I deftly batted away any negative ideas I had like maybe she was homeless and the dog had escaped from a shelter. They were helping each other survive.

Hell, even my negative ideas had a positive spin on them.

After securing the plane, I opened the door and we all three exited the plane.

It was a bit of a walk to the house, but Ainsley didn't seem to have any trouble walking in her designer shoes.

Instead, she watched the clouds over the mountains.

"It's going to snow," she said. "in the high country."

I followed her gaze. "Not just up there," I said. "It's going to snow down here, too."

"And you don't have any deicing equipment for your plane."

"Wasn't something I ever thought I'd need."

She looked me in the eyes.

"I guess you haven't lived here very long then."

Ainsley was good. I had to give her that.

We'd no more than landed and already she'd figured out that I was not a Wyoming ranch native.

Impressive.

11

AINSLEY

*T*he sprawling ranch nestled into the mountain range of western Wyoming was impressive as we flew over it.

When we landed, I expected him to get us into a car and drive us to one of the cabins up the mountain.

That was typically how it went. Momma and Daddy had a cabin in Colorado, but they had to drive about an hour or so from the airport to the house. It was a mountainous area and there was no place to park a plane.

This, on the other hand, was a flat valley area between two mountain ranges.

From the air, I'd seen one big house and several smaller cabins around it, nestled in the trees.

Again, not anything out of the ordinary.

But when we took off walking down a pebbled walkway toward the main house, suddenly nothing was ordinary about this.

So maybe he owned the plane, as he said he did, and he was using someone else's...

But he'd called this home.

If this was Wyatt's home, he was most definitely not what I expected.

A wealthy Wyoming rancher?

A little bubble of laughter escaped my lips and I quickly put a hand over my mouth to cover it.

"What?" Wyatt asked. "What's funny?"

"Nothing," I said, wiping the smile off my face. "So where are we? Exactly?"

"Home," he said, sweeping a hand around. "Welcome to Beaufort Valley Ranch."

"This is where you live?" I asked.

He grinned at me with a crooked little smile.

"Yeah. What do you think?"

I looked around. At the mountaintops hidden in the clouds.

There was a river nearby. Not only had I seen it from the plane, I could hear the rush of water.

"It's beautiful," I said. "Big."

He nodded. "Agreed."

Though Beaufort Valley Ranch was quite impressive, I was a city girl, through and through.

The thought of living in a small town was a nightmare for me.

But a ranch? I didn't even know what that would be like?

I didn't even know what kind of person would fly an airplane like that live on a ranch like this?

The whole notion was outside of my experience.

But if the cold wind blowing down from the mountains was any indication, I was about to get some sense about it.

I'd made a quick check of the weather while Wyatt had been in the back gathering up his things.

And he'd been right. There was one heck of a storm headed this way.

And no one was going to be going or coming for a while.

According to the weather report, the storm was much worse than anyone had predicted.

As we reached the front porch of the big house, Wyatt adjusted the duffle bag on his shoulder.

"I want you to feel welcome in my home," he said. "So if there's anything that you need, you have to let me know."

"Ok," I said. "I hope you have a good supply of coffee."

12

WYATT

I held the door as Ainsley stepped inside my house. The house I'd lived in for two years now. It had taken me a year before that to have it built.

I'd like to say I designed it, but truth was I'd worked closely with an architect who'd seemed to understand exactly what I wanted from the get go.

The cabin—a term I used loosely for what some called a two-story mansion—had wall-to-wall windows on every side.

It was a little bit more like a glass house than a cabin.

But no matter what time of day it was, there was some place in the house that had a perfect view.

In the summer, there were shady spots—and automatic shades—to block the sun. In winter, there were comfy chairs to sit in and soak up the warmth of the sun.

When it snowed, it was absolutely a winter wonderland outside every room.

Since I was the only person who lived around here, I didn't have to worry about privacy, but if I did want privacy, all I had to do was open an app on my phone and pick which windows to black out.

I'd always loved this house. I thought of it as a penthouse in the valley.

Instead of looking down on street caverns, I looked up at majestic mountain peaks.

But I'd never seen the house come alive as it did when Ainsley walked through it.

It was like she brought sunshine and magic with her, but she didn't even know it.

She certainly didn't make an effort to brighten any room.

She was one of the most serious women I'd met. She was quiet and obviously a deep thinker.

She rarely smiled, but when she did, it was worth the wait. Like waiting for hours to see an eagle leave its nest or waiting all year until the leaves on the aspen trees turned red and gold.

"Is Beau an inside dog or an outside dog?" I asked. But the dog was already following us around the house. So I took that as an answer. Still. I wanted to engage her in conversation, no matter how trivial.

"I don't know," she said.

That answered a lot of questions for me.

First of all, Beau wasn't her dog. Or at least hadn't been for long.

And probably didn't belong to her boyfriend.

At any rate, Beau had imprinted himself on her.

I imagined that the dog was drawn to her much like I was.

She stood in my kitchen and looked around.

I didn't cook a whole lot, but when I did, I liked a lot of space.

Space was very important to me. Without it, I couldn't think like I needed to.

I tried to see it through her eyes.

It looked more like a staged house than somebody's home.

I didn't like clutter. Hard to be creative when things were piled up and lying around. Things that had no use or purpose.

So I kept it that way.

About once a week, I gave it a good cleaning myself.

I'd hired a girl to come in and clean one time, but she'd talked so much, I couldn't stand to be in my home office while she was there.

Besides, I enjoyed it. I wasn't a messy person and I didn't have any pets, so it stayed clean.

I used the time it took to clean to think.

It usually took me two days to get the whole house cleaned because I'd come up with some brilliant inspiration and have to dash off to my computer.

"This is beautiful," Ainsley said, turning away from the kitchen island and looking at me with a glimmer of a smile on her face.

"I like it," I said.

"You actually live here?" she asked.

I smiled. "Yes, but I'm away a lot."

She turned toward one of the windows looking westward and nodded as though that explained everything.

Then she turned back. "I don't see why you'd ever want to leave."

My God. She was a woman after my own heart.

"It looks like a penthouse," she said, but it's on the ground."

I grinned. "That's exactly what I was going for."

She went over to the back door and looked out over my little garden area.

I still had some work to do there, but I didn't say anything.

Even with the work left to do, I was proud of it. I'd had the rocks delivered, but I'd arranged everything myself.

"It's starting to snow," she said with wonder in her voice.

I went over to stand next to her.

"You've seen snow, right?" I asked.

"Of course," she said, with a cross glance.

"I didn't know. Since you live in Houston and all."

Her features softened as she watched the fat flakes fall and splatter on the rocks.

"I've seen snow, but I still think it's wonderful."

I nodded. For me, snow never got old.

That's why I'd picked here to live.

It snowed just enough and was accessible enough that I could commute by plane. If I wanted to I could drive into the little town that was growing by leaps and bounds as more and more young professionals discovered it and made it their home.

I was standing close enough that I could smell her scent of vanilla and honeysuckle. So fresh and clean. It made me think about other things.

"Do you want to see your room?" I asked.

I needed to get my mind on something other than the way she smelled and the way her smile lit up the world around her.

And I had to remind myself that she wasn't here as my date or my girlfriend. She was my guest.

A guest I knew absolutely nothing about.

Other than her being from Houston, knowing a lot about airplanes, and having a dog named Beau.

13

AINSLEY

*A*lone finally, I walked from one side of the guest room to the other, looking out each window. The snow was coming down now, making a pretty picture.

Taking a deep breath, I dialed Daddy's number.

"Where the hell are you?" he asked.

Unlike Momma, he didn't feel compelled to start a phone call off with pleasantries.

"I'm in Wyoming."

"Wyoming." I heard him take a deep breath. "How was going north a good idea with this storm coming in?"

"It didn't seem like it was going to be so bad at the time," I said. "And it was the only flight out of Aspen."

"That's hard to believe," he said.

"And... there weren't any rooms. Daddy. I didn't have a choice."

"Where's the dog?"

"Sitting at my feet," I said, reaching over to pat the dog's head.

"Okay. Where are you staying?"

This was where things got sticky. I was a grown woman of

twenty-six. I had my pilot's license and was quite capable of taking care of myself.

And Daddy knew that. But I knew that he couldn't help his instinct to look after me.

I could tell him that I was at a stranger's home and he would worry.

"I'm at a small ranch," I said. "they have some rooms. And Daddy…" I said. "It's snowing."

Him being used to his kids traveling a lot along with my efforts to distract him worked. Normally Daddy was more astute, but he hadn't been feeling very well lately.

I felt a little bit guilty about telling him the whole truth, but he didn't need to worry.

We talked a few more minutes before saying good-bye.

It was sunny and ninety-three degrees in Houston.

And here it was somewhere around freezing.

But inside the house, the temperature was perfect.

After showing me to my room, Wyatt had said to come down to dinner when I was ready.

If he expected me to dress up for dinner, he didn't have his head on straight. All I had was an extra set of very casual clothes in my satchel.

Unlike my sister Brianna, who probably carried a sequined gown in her go-bag, I didn't have anything like that to wear.

So, deciding to just freshen up and wear what I had on, it was less than an hour when I headed out the door to make my way downstairs.

The house had a simple plan.

It was big and spacious. Not big and cavernous. Again, I was astounded at the similarities between it and my penthouse.

When I got downstairs, I found Wyatt in the kitchen.

He had some music on low and he was singing along to a catchy song.

He was elbow-deep in dough.

Seeing me come to the doorway, he instructed the music to stop, then simply said "hi."

"Hi," I said.

I was a sucker for a man who not only could cook, but who did cook.

My Daddy had set the bar pretty high in that department.

I'd eaten more meals cooked by him than by my mother.

Though Daddy was the entrepreneur who'd made millions, Momma was the quintessential career woman.

"I hope you like pizza," he said.

"Who doesn't?" I asked.

"Come on in," he said. "Have a seat. Do you want a glass of wine? Or a beer? Or... something else?"

I went over to the counter and sat on a bar stool so I could watch him.

"I'll have what you're having," I said.

"Good choice," he said, wiping his hands on a dish towel. "Warm or icy cold?"

"The colder the better," I said.

"A woman after my own heart," he said, pulling a beer from the fridge and twisting the top off for me. "Nothing goes better with pizza than beer."

"Agreed."

I sipped the beer. It was icy cold just like I liked it. Right at the edge of being frozen.

"Perfect," I said.

"A woman with good taste," he said, putting his hands back in the dough.

Something about him carefully kneading a bowl of pliable pizza dough made me wonder if his fingers were good at doing other things.

I sipped from the bottle again.

Not a good path to go down. I was on a dating moratorium. That meant I was keeping away from men.

All men. Even handsome man.

And, I sternly reminded myself, that including casual hookups.

Casual hookups had a tendency to get messy for me. It was probably the kind of men I picked, but my hookups tended to push me toward relationships.

And I didn't do relationships.

I'd made that decision my senior year when my heart had been broken by a college guy named Richard.

I'd fallen so hard, I was like humpty dumpty and I'd never quite gone back together just right.

He'd taken a piece of me with him.

A piece of my heart.

So I did casual dating.

But not for the last six months... and seven days...

I was shooting for a year. I'd read in one of those magazines Brianna kept lying around that although a year was a long time, it was needed for a thorough man cleansing.

So I'd set that as my goal.

I'd stay away from men for one full year, then I'd start to dip my toe back into the dating pool.

I kept up, though with what was going on in the dating world through my two single sisters and my oldest sister, Madison, had just gotten back with her college sweetheart. They'd moved in together in Denver, so I didn't see much to learn from her. She was off the market.

I had no intention of leaving the dating world for a year and coming back in cold, not knowing what had changed.

But none of this had anything to do with the handsome man spreading pizza dough onto a round iron pan.

Nothing at all.

"What do you like on yours?" he asked.

"I have green peppers, black olives, pineapple... pepperoni-."

"Just the veggies for me," I said. "Not much into meat."

I sipped my beer, not wanting it to get warm.

"A vegetarian?" he asked.

"Pescatarian," I said.

He nodded in approval. "My sister is, too. Now my brother, he'll eat anything that doesn't crawl off."

"My brother's like that, too," I said.

Now I knew that Wyatt had two siblings.

I don't know why, but I liked it that he'd told me something about his family. It made me feel closer to him.

As for why I liked feeling closer to him, I would have to figure out later.

Right now, I was just enjoying watching this very attractive man make pizza. I'd never realized how sexy a man could look in the kitchen.

14

WYATT

*A*insley was looking a whole lot more relaxed sitting in my kitchen holding a beer than she had since I'd met her.

Granted, that wasn't long ago, but, still, I found it interesting.

Was I attracted to her because it had been so long since I'd even taken the time to have a date?

It was more than that.

There was something about her that drew me to her. She was what some would call aloof. She didn't seem to have much to say, but I wanted to know everything about her.

I sprinkled chopped black olives, pineapple, and bell pepper over a crust with tomato sauce and added mozzarella cheese.

According to the news, we were going to be stuck here for a few days.

Normally when something like this happened, I would gladly hunker down and spend the time holed up at my desk working.

But I could see that wasn't likely to happen.

"How far is it into town?" she asked, swirling the beer she'd barely sipped. She shifted her gaze from watching me to the phone in her hand.

"About twenty minutes one way," I said, sliding the cast iron pizza pan into the oven and set the timer. "Why do you ask?"

She swept a hand downward. "I don't want to wear this for a week."

"Right," I said and immediately pictured her wearing one of my white button-down shirts. She'd have to roll the sleeves up and it would hang loosely down to her thighs.

All the blood rushed to my cock and I put a hand against the counter to steady myself.

"And," she said. "I need to get some dog food for Beau."

At the sound of his name, Beau sat up and barked one time.

We both looked at him, then at each other and laughed.

"You don't know anything about him?" I asked.

"Nothing," she said, reaching out to pet his head. "But he's a pretty cool little guy."

I grabbed my beer and went to sit next to her.

"You don't have any pets?" I asked.

She shook her head.

"We had a dog when I was a kid," I said. "But nothing since I moved out."

"You have something against pets?" she asked.

I glanced over at her and she was looking at me with a little smile at the corner of her lips.

"Why would you ask that?"

"Well," she said, looking toward the windows. "You live on a ranch."

"True." I reached over the counter and grabbed my phone off the charger.

"Do you have any horses at least?" she asked.

I smiled. "I have a horse."

"Then you're redeemable, at least."

"I'm glad you think so," I said, scrolling through my contacts.

"So... do you have a car?"

I stopped scrolling and looked up at her. "Of course, I have a car."

She turned and looked at me. "If we go before dark, we can back before the roads get bad."

"I don't know..." I said.

"Well, we have to get dog food."

"You're right," I said, standing up. "Hold on."

I walked toward the living room, my phone pressed to my ear.

If Ainsley wanted to go into town, we were going into town.

15

AINSLEY

We ate in the kitchen at the bar.

The pizza was some of the best.

Or maybe it was the company.

"We'll leave shortly," he said. "Head in to the general store for some dog food."

"What about some clothes?" I asked. I shuddered at an image of plaid shirts and overalls. I wasn't a fashionista like my sister Brianna, but I did have standards.

He smiled. "You'll be taken care of."

Nodding, I ate the last bit of my pizza crust.

It made sense that a man like Wyatt who owned an airplane would have some pull with the local merchants.

Wyatt took two coats from the hall closet and held one while I slipped my arms in. It was a dark gray parka and fit me perfectly. So he just happened to have a jacket that was my size. Obviously he'd had women here before.

I hadn't seen any signs that he might have a wife. He didn't wear a ring and there were no family pictures around that I'd seen.

I had a lot of questions, but I kept them to myself. It wasn't my business.

"Do we leave Beau here?" I asked. Wyatt had walked him earlier and given him some water, but I was getting concerned that the dog might starve.

Wyatt looked at the dog who was watching him with big dark eyes. "We might as well bring him," he said.

"Come on," I said, patting my leg.

Beau jumped and followed us outside. I wasn't supposed to get attached to the dog.

We went out the back door and walked a little ways to what I could only call a shed.

The snow was still coming down and the air was so cold it burned my lungs.

There was an old green Chevrolet truck. Old. Like 1970s.

I stopped and looked from the truck to Wyatt.

He was smiling at me.

"You," I said. "are an enigma."

"What?" he asked. "This is a vintage 1969 Chevrolet."

I put a hand over my mouth and nodded slowly.

Wyatt was such a typical guy.

It was funny that he owned a brand-new Phenom airplane *and* a 1969 Chevrolet truck.

And he seemed to be just as proud of his truck as his airplane.

I looked around, but this was the only vehicle I saw.

I guess he had to cut corners somewhere.

He opened the door. "You ready?"

Beau jumped inside first. Then I shrugged and climbed inside the cab.

The inside had been modernized. New gray leather seats. And it even had seatbelts.

He came around and climbed into the driver's side. We both buckled up, Beau sitting between us.

"Here we go," he said. "We have to make sure we're back before they close the roads."

"They actually close them?"

He put the truck in reverse and backed out.

"They have to close them," he said. "Or people..." he glanced at me. "will find all kinds of excuses to get out and put themselves at risk."

I just shrugged. And looked out the window at the snow coming down like rain.

However dangerous this might be, for me, it was absolutely beautiful.

And any girl who flew airplanes almost every day couldn't possibly be afraid of a little snow.

16

WYATT

I knew better than to drive to town with a storm on the way.

First of all, I was from Denver. And second, I'd lived out here long enough to learn the rules.

A pilot who didn't obey the rules ended up in trouble.

But Ainsley had looked at me with those big green eyes and I couldn't say no to her.

She was the mermaid on the rock, calling out to me.

And I was the hapless sailor who risked everything to get to her.

The town would be closing soon to give everyone time to get ready for the storm.

But I'd talked to my buddy Johnny who ran the General Store in town. He was staying open for a while yet so people could pick up supplies and things that they needed.

The general store had everything, even a little café.

If I'd known we were going into town, we would have eaten there at the café instead of me making pizza, but that was just how it went sometimes.

"How far is it?" she asked, warming her hands on the heat blowing out of the vents.

"We'll be there in a few minutes," I said.

I was honestly worried about the roads.

I'd heard of people who hadn't heeded the warnings. Things would freeze up and black ice was deadly.

But right now, while it was still daylight, the snow was still melting on the roads.

And it was almost worth it to see Ainsley's flushed cheeks as we traveled through the snow.

As we neared the downtown area, we passed a lot of houses, mostly new construction. And most of them had smoke coming from their chimneys.

I was a little bit jealous. I didn't have a wood burning fireplace. It was something I hadn't thought I'd needed. But now I was thinking how nice it would be to sit with Ainsley in front of warm fire.

I parked on the edge of the street and turned off the motor.

"This is it?" she asked, trying to see the building through the falling snow.

"Yep," I said. "Not too bad, huh?"

"Not bad at all."

"Come on Beau," I said, opening my door.

"We're taking him inside," she asked when I came around and opened her door.

"They don't mind," I said. "Besides, the owner is a buddy of mine."

SHE PULLED the hood up over her head as we made our way toward the door. We passed half a dozen people heading out, their arms loaded with paper bags.

"I hope there's something left," she said.

"Oh yeah," he said. "Johnny stays prepared for bad weather like this."

She nodded. "Kinda like a hurricane in Houston."

"Kind of, I guess." I held the door open for her, Beau at her heels.

If that dog didn't belong to her, he sure gave a good impression of being her dog.

"So whose dog did you say this is?" I asked.

"I don't know. My job was just to pick him up."

I didn't say anything.

Johnny waved to me from behind the counter. "Never expected to see you out in weather like this," he said. Then he looked at Ainsley and grinned. "But then again..."

"Shut up, Johnny," I said.

Johnny said something to the young lady running the counter and came over to give me slap on the shoulder and a quick hand shake.

"Looking for anything in particular?" he asked, looking at Ainsley.

I shot down the surge of jealousy. After all, I'd told him that I was bringing in a friend to pick up some essentials. I hadn't said girlfriend.

"I need some clothes," she said.

He nodded, a curious look on his face.

"I got stranded," she said. "in the weather."

Johnny looked at me as though he didn't believe a word of what she was saying.

"We have a section over there," he pointed across the store. "T-shirts. Sweatpants. That sort of thing. Lots of casual clothes."

"Perfect," she said and took off in that direction.

"A girl with a dog?" Johnny said. I wasn't sure if it was a question or a statement.

"Like she said, she got stranded."

"I believe you," he said. "It's just... she doesn't look like your sister."

"Never said she was."

Johnny held up a hand. "Just saying. I've never known you to bring a girl home with you."

"There's always a first time," I said. "Besides, it isn't like I brought her home. She got stranded. I was being a good Samaritan."

Johnny burst out laughing. "Keep telling yourself that. Any red-blooded American male would do the same."

I just glared at my friend.

"Maybe you'll start a new trend," he said.

Before I could answer, his cashier called out to him and he left with a quick "see you later."

Johnny was wrong. I wasn't starting a new trend. I wasn't going to just start bringing girls home.

Home was my private place. A place where I could work uninterrupted.

When I needed people around, I went into Aspen or even Denver, though I preferred Aspen better.

The office there was more peaceful and I could walk wherever I needed to go.

A lot of people complained about all the tourists, but I didn't mind. To me they brought life to the little town.

17

AINSLEY

*L*eaving Wyatt and his friend to hash whatever they had going on, I followed Johnny's direction over to the clothing section.

I saw nothing I would normally wear. No designer jeans. No silk tops.

This was definitely time to call in the big guns.

I sent my sister a text.

ME: *Are you busy?*

BRIANNA: *Not so much. What's up?*

ME: *Need some fashion help.*

While I waited for Brianna to respond, I could almost feel her excitement radiating through my phone. Brianna was the fashion expert of the family.

BRIANNA: *Where are you?*

ME: *A little town in Wyoming.*

Brianna didn't bother texting back. She facetimed me.

"You're where?" she asked when I answered the call.

I held my phone up and shrugged at my sister's perplexed expression.

"There was a weather thing."

"Oh," she said.

She shouldn't be the least bit surprised. As pilots, both Daddy and I were always traveling to different places. She should be used to it.

"It was supposed to be a day trip," I said. "but it looks like it's going to be more like a week and I only have one change of clothes."

She shuddered. "How awful. So where are you shopping?"

I turned around so she could see the clothing section.

"It's a little general store," I said. "and café and grocery store."

"Goodness," she said. I could feel her rolling up her sleeves and getting ready to do some serious work. "So show me what we're dealing with."

I gave her a quick scan.

"Is that it?" she asked.

"Hey. It's not Nordstrom's."

"I can see that. Where do you want to start?"

I looked around. Found a gray t-shirt that had *Wyoming* plastered across the front.

"This one looks good," I said, holding it out for her.

She put a palm against her forehead.

"A hoodie? Really?"

"What? It doesn't have a hood."

Brianna rolled her eyes. "What else do they have?"

"How about a t-shirt?" I pulled a light gray t-shirt off a shelf. "This one matches the sweatshirt."

"Why did you even call me?" she asked.

"There isn't that much to choose from." I said. "Sweatpants or…" I looked around. "sweatpants?"

Brianna laughed. "I guess I'd go with sweatpants."

"It's not like we'll be going out or anything. It's a snowstorm."

"Hey Ainsley?" Wyatt asked from behind me. "You finding anything?"

"Yeah," I said. "I'll just be another minute."

"Who's that?" Brianna asked.

"That's the guy I'm staying with," I said without thinking.

"You're staying with him?" Brianna asked. "Whoa. Maybe you should back up a bit."

"He just gave me a ride."

Brianna lifted her eyebrow. "Let me see again. He's hot."

"No," I said, turning around. "It's not like that."

"Well, maybe it should be like that," she said.

"I have to go," I said. "Talk later."

I disconnected with my sister and grabbed enough sweatpants, t-shirts, and underwear to last me a few days.

With my arms full, I walked back toward Wyatt.

He smiled when he saw me and rushed to take the armful of clothes from me.

"We can wash, you know."

I shrugged. "This way I didn't have to choose."

18

WYATT

I put Ainsley's stack of clothes on the counter with the bag of dry dog food and box of canned dog food.

"What kind of snacks do you like?" I asked, looking around the rows of chips, nuts, and candy bars.

"Fruit," she said.

Fruit. Of course. A girl who looked like her would naturally eat fruit. It made sense.

The store was starting to clear out now. We made our way over to the produce section.

Ainsley grabbed some strawberries, bananas, and tomatoes.

There wasn't much to choose from, but it was still an odd assortment.

"Anything else?" I asked, taking the packs from her hands.

"No. That should do it."

We walked back to the counter where Beau was waiting.

A pretty little girl was on her knees, petting him.

Beau looked like he was in doggy heaven.

A harried looking man saw us and quickly apologized.

"I hope you don't mind," he said. "they just seemed to take to each other."

Ainsley quickly put the man at ease.

"Don't worry," she said. "He's loving it."

"Yeah, he's good with kids." The man said, putting a bag of chips and a loaf of bread on the counter.

"How many kids do you two have?" he asked, looking back at us.

Neither one of us answered. We both just stared at him. Fortunately, the man didn't seem to notice.

Ainsley glanced at me, then was the first to respond.

"None, yet," she said.

"Well, when you do," the man said. "your dog here is going to be great."

"He's a good dog," Ainsley said.

"Come on, Kitty Kat," the man said, calling his daughter.

"Can't we stay just a little bit longer?" the girl pleaded.

"Your momma's gonna be afraid we got lost in the snow if we don't hurry up and get back."

"Okay," Kitty Kat said with a cute little pout.

"You've got your hands full," I said, pulling myself out of my stupor.

"You got that right," he said. "I've got a fifteen-year-old girl at home. It does not get any better."

Ainsley and I both laughed. The man quickly checked out and with a bag in one hand and the girl's hand in another, he dashed outside.

"See you later," he said. "Be safe out there."

"You too," Ainsley said.

I watched Ainsley as the cashier rang up our purchase.

Ainsley went to pull open her wallet, but I held up a hand.

"No need," I said. "I've got this."

"Want me to just put it on your account, Mr. Beaufort?" the cashier asked with a smile.

Ainsley didn't say anything, but I could tell by her

expression that she was only agreeing because she didn't want to make a scene.

At least that's what I got out of it.

Right now, I was hoping that my old truck could get us home.

And I didn't need Ainsley to be worried about that. Worrying about who was paying for what was a much safer distraction.

19

AINSLEY

We were one of the last ones to leave the General Store and by the time we got loaded up in the truck with Beau between us, the snow was coming down so hard we could barely see.

It was getting dark, too.

I thought about saying something to Wyatt about paying for the stack of clothes I'd bought, but decided it wasn't worth the effort. I was so beholden to him already that I just mentally added it to what I figured I owed him.

He pulled out onto the street and started toward his house.

I didn't have a lot, any really, experience with snowstorms, but for the first time I was feeling a tingle of nervousness in my stomach.

The heat blared from the vents, but still it was freaking freezing. I was literally shaking inside the coat. What if this old truck couldn't make it home? We'd freeze out here in the dark.

Beau nudged at Wyatt's arm. The little traitor.

"Don't worry little guy," he said. "We got you plenty to eat. It won't be long."

Wyatt, however, seemed to have no concern about it his truck making it home.

We were just on the outskirts of town when we saw flashing lights up ahead.

Dread washed over me. Had someone already crashed in this storm?

Wyatt had been right to be nervous about getting out in this weather.

I should have listened to him.

Wyatt slowed down as we approached and saw that a police car was blocking the road.

A policeman stepped out and walked up to Wyatt's window.

"Evening Wyatt," the policeman said.

"Good evening, Eric. What's going on?"

"Had to close the road."

"Just snowing so far," Wyatt said.

"Got reports of ice on the bridge."

Wyatt stared straight ahead. Tapped a finger against the leather steering wheel.

"Guess we're not going home then."

"There are still a couple of cabins available over at the town square."

Wyatt nodded. "Got it. Thanks."

"Drive safe," the policeman, Eric said.

"Will do."

Wyatt backed up into a driveway I could barely even see and turned the truck around.

"What's the town square?" I asked.

Wyatt was leaning forward to see out the windshield.

"I don't know why they call it that," he said. "It's more like a cluster of cabins around the hotel they call the Town Square House."

"Well, that's fortunate," I said. A couple of cabins would be just fine. In fact, it would probably be better than me staying in

Wyatt's house. I wondered why he didn't put me up in one of them to begin with. It would have made more sense than him bringing a stranger to his house. Of course, there was the weather issue.

Wyatt pulled into a gravel parking lot and put the truck in park.

The Town Square House looked a lot like The Stanley House in Estes Park. Not a normal hotel at all. More like a stately lodge.

"If you want to stay here, I'll go inside and check us into the cabins."

The idea of going back out into the cold gave me shivers.

"Ok," I said, holding my hands up to the meager heat that was finally warming up the truck cab. I gave him a quick smile. "I'll wait."

I didn't even bother to offer him my credit card.

He was already stepping out of the truck. "Be right back," he said.

I pulled up the collar of the downy coat and snuggled deeper into it as the cold air swirled inside from the open door.

This was kind of unfortunate. I'd been enjoying Wyatt's company and had been thinking that it might be fun to spend some time with him.

My sister was right as much as I hated to admit it.

Wyatt was hot.

Yes, I decided. It was definitely better that we each got our own cabins here.

A couple of minutes later, Wyatt came back and climbed into the truck.

"It's getting colder by the minute," he said, rubbing his hands together.

"Glad we were able to get a place to stay," I said. I was almost back to where I started this morning. Stranded with no place to go.

"Yeah," he said, backing out of the parking spot and heading around the hotel where the cabins must be.

"It's really pretty here," I said.

Wyatt pulled up in front of one of the little cabins and put the truck in park.

Then he turned, scratched Beau behind the ears, and looked at me.

"There's just one thing," he said.

"What's that?" I put my purse over my shoulder in preparation to get out into the blistering cold.

"They only had one cabin left."

20

WYATT

The one-room cabin was cozy and romantic.

It actually felt more homey than my own house. My house had been built to be everything modern.

This place had been designed for coziness.

It was technically three rooms, if you counted the bathroom and little galley kitchen.

There was a wood burning fireplace and a bundle of wood sitting next to it. That was convenient.

Ainsley took her bags, sat on the sofa, and sorted her new clothes.

At least one of us had something to wear.

When the girl at the check-in desk had told me there was only one cabin left, I hid my joy. I'd even done my due diligence by asking if there were any room available in the hotel itself.

But she'd immediately told me that the one cabin was all they had left.

I was more than ok with that.

The thought of being in separate cabins was not something I'd liked the idea of.

I liked the idea of spending time with Ainsley.

While Ainsley sat on the sofa, Beau jumped onto the bed.

"Looks like Beau's going to be using the bed," I said.

"Looks like it," she said, taking her clothes and putting them in one of the little dresser drawers.

Then she turned around and faced me.

"Where are we supposed to sleep?"

It was the first thing she'd said in acknowledgement that we were in something of a predicament.

"You can have the couch," I said in jest. Of course I expected her to take the bed.

"What about you?" she asked.

I couldn't tell if she was serious or not, but I went along with it.

"I don't know. There's no bathtub."

"Maybe they have some extra blankets," she said. "you could make a pallet on the floor."

"I'll have to check," I said with a straight face. "Maybe I'll get a fire going fire to add some warmth in here."

"Good idea," she said, pushing off the dresser.

While I bent down to get a fire started, she wandered into the kitchen area.

With a lot of patience, I had a little flame going by the time I saw her walk back out of the corner of my eyes.

She came and stood next to me.

"Nice fire," she said. "I found something in the kitchen."

"Thanks." I looked up.

She was holding a bottle of wine and two wine glasses.

"I knew I was going to like this place," I said, dusting my hands and standing up.

She handed me the bottle of wine and opener, then went to sit on the sofa.

Beau jumped off the bed and came over to put his head in her lap.

Lucky dog.

Things were just getting better and better.

21

AINSLEY

*H*aving a glass of wine with a good-looking man was not breaking my moratorium on men.

There were exceptions to everything.

And being stranded in a snowstorm in Wyoming had to count as exception.

Any reasonable person would agree.

Besides… we didn't know each other.

We didn't travel in the same part of the country.

And we'd never see each other again after I got out of here.

Justification was my forte, after all.

While Wyatt worked on uncorking the wine, I got a text from my sister, Madison, who lived in Denver.

MADISON: *Heard you were stuck in this snowstorm.*

ME: *I'm in some little town in Wyoming.*

MADISON: *So who's the guy?*

ME: *What guy?*

MADISON: *The hot guy waiting for you in the store.*

ME: *Going to kill Brianna.*

I glanced up at Wyatt and smiled.

He poured wine into one of the glasses and handed it to me.

Our fingers brushed for just a second as I took the glass from him.

"Thank you," I said.

"Everything all right?"

"It will be after I kill my sister."

MADISON: *Come on. At least give me his name.*

Wyatt sat down beside me, holding his own glass of wine.

He held up his glass.

"To snowstorms," he said.

I clinked my glass against his.

Snowstorms indeed.

I hadn't known what I'd been missing by living in the humid heat of Houston, Texas.

ME: *Wyatt.*

I seriously expected that to be the end of my conversation with Madison tonight.

As a younger sister, she was obligated to give me a hard time. I didn't mind. It was part of the closeness of family.

I set my phone aside.

"I think Beau especially likes cold weather," I said, rubbing his ears.

"I think somebody is going to miss this little guy."

I smiled at him again. There was something about him that tripped up my heart rate.

With the fire roaring in the fireplace and the snowflakes falling silently outside and the warmth of the wine… this was a perfectly romantic setting.

Another text came in.

I picked up my phone and turned it over.

MADISON: *Kade wants to know if it's Wyatt Beaufort.*

22

WYATT

*T*he flames licked at the dry logs in the fireplace.

At this rate, I would have to go in search of more firewood before the evening was over.

Maybe tomorrow I could walk over to the General Store and get Johnny to sell me some firewood.

The store was within walking distance. Maybe…

As I took a sip of wine, I glanced over at Ainsley. She had nearly dropped her phone and now she was looking at me with a deer in headlights expression.

She was looking at me with her exquisitely green eyes. Eyes that I could fall into get lost in.

"Something wrong?" I asked.

"No," she said quickly and, turning her phone over, set it aside.

Something was definitely up. But it wasn't my business.

She was a stranger to me, mesmerizing green eyes or not.

"You sure? You look a little… out of sorts." Even though my head told me to leave it alone, I couldn't resist.

The more I knew about this girl, the more I wanted to know about her.

I nodded and tapped the glass of my wine glass.

"So…" she said. "besides being a pilot, do you do something else?"

Since I didn't have anything to hide, I didn't mind her asking and I didn't mind telling her.

"I'm a graphic designer."

So maybe I didn't just jump right in there and tell her everything. Sometimes, in my experience, it was better to leave a few things to the imagination. Especially things that might sway her opinion one way or the other.

There were two other ways I could have gone with my answer, but they both held completely different connotations. In order to give her a complete answer, I would have to tell her too much. And I wasn't ready to do that.

Graphic designer was the safest answer.

"Really? My sister is a graphic designer."

Uh oh. That meant I was going to have to tell her more about what I did than what I had planned.

"Small world," I said. I really didn't want to go into this topic with her, but it seemed rather rude not to.

"What does she do?"

"She mostly makes book covers and designs ads for authors. I'm sure she does more than that, but she lives in California, so I don't see her all that often. She's actually my half-sister."

So she has a half-sister. That was another piece of the puzzle that was Ainsley Richards.

"So it's just the two of you?"

She looked at my sideways as though she was trying to decide how to answer and took another sip of her wine.

"I have four sisters, including her, and a brother."

"Wow. Big family."

"Yeah," she said, but her tone suddenly turned wistful and she leaned back against the sofa staring at the flames while she rubbed Beau's ears.

I'd never wanted to be a dog before, but right now, I wanted to be where Beau was.

With my head in her lap and her hands rubbing my ears.

Or maybe there were other things...

I shifted, adjusting my suddenly too tight pants.

23

AINSLEY

*O*MG.

I pulled the blanket up to my chin and tucked my feet beneath Beau who had taken his place across the bottom of the full-sized bed.

The fire was still blazing, but I'd pleaded fatigue, changed into my pajamas, and crawled into bed.

Wyatt was sitting on the sofa, so I could only see his profile from here.

My sister's boyfriend knew Wyatt.

That put a whole new spin on things.

My idea that I was stranded in a cabin during a snowstorm with a complete stranger wasn't true.

And for all I knew, my half-sister Danielle knew him, too. I didn't know how big the world of graphic design was, but at this point, I didn't rule anything out.

I watched as Wyatt adjusted his pillow and pulled the blanket over him.

Now that he was lying down, I couldn't see him at all.

If I closed my eyes I could forget that he was here.

Almost…

Not really...

Brianna's words replayed in my head. *He's hot.*

Hot was an understatement.

He was freaking on fire.

Broad shoulders, but not too broad. Lean, but not skinny.

He was about a head taller than me and I had a feeling I could cuddle up to him like a big teddy bear.

He had that whole tall, dark, and handsome thing in the bag.

His hair was short, just brushing the collar of his shirt. And I didn't have to touch it to know that it was soft.

A lock of hair kept falling over his forehead and he had to keep sweeping it back. He wasn't one of those guys who glued their hair down like a Ken doll.

And his eyes. His bright blue eyes were like the clearest blue ocean water I'd ever seen. Kauna'oa Bay, Hawaii specifically came to mind. There was so much mystery behind those eyes.

He was a pilot. The owner of a Phenom 300 airplane.

He drove an ancient green truck.

And he was a graphic designer.

Who lived in a huge glass cabin in the middle of a valley in Wyoming.

There was so much more to learn about his man.

And yet all I really wanted to find out was how his lips felt on mine.

I wanted to curl up on the sofa in his arms in front of the fireplace and spend hours kissing him.

He'd entwined himself into my head and I couldn't stop thinking about him.

And I didn't even want to stop thinking about him.

There was no way I was going to get any sleep tonight.

24

WYATT

I put my hands behind my head and stared at the flames in the fireplace.

Something seemed to have changed while we talked.

Actually, I think it had something to do with a text message that had come in on her phone.

Maybe her boyfriend... or husband... was upset with her right now.

Surely she hadn't told anyone that it was just the two of us staying in a cottage alone. Especially not the man in her life.

Or, hell, it could have been anything.

I was making assumptions about someone I was just getting to know. And in all truthfulness, I knew very little about her personal life.

I was learning things slowly, though. I now knew that she was from a big family.

That was a different experience from how I'd grown up.

Would I be a different man if I'd grown up in a big family?

With more than just me and my sister?

Dad worked all the time and our mother was a nurse, so she'd worked long hours.

My sister had been and still was a bookworm, so I'd been left with endless hours to spend however I wanted to.

And it just so happened that I chose to spend a ton—far too many—of those hours playing video games.

There was nothing I could do about it now.

If I'd known... maybe I would have done something different. Tried a little harder.

I liked to think that it had paid off for me. I knew video games inside and out. I knew what I liked and I knew what worked.

Since I'd been expected to go to college, I'd majored in graphic design. Neither one of my parents seemed to notice, much less to care.

I'm not sure they even to this day really knew what I did for a living.

They lived in a retirement community in Florida.

Happy as clams. Their son flew down to visit once a month or so.

But as far as they knew, I flew like everyone else. On someone else's airplane.

I'd tried to explain to them several times what I did. I'd even tried to explain to them once that I owned my own airplane, but the conversation had been interrupted by the dinner bell and the conversation had faded into nothing.

They'd apparently forgotten all about it and that's when I'd stopped even trying to tell them anything about my personal life.

It was so outside their realm of reality anyway.

I wondered how it was with Ainsley and her family.

I wondered if they knew and cared what she did.

Hell, I wondered what she did.

How had I spent the better part of a day with someone and not gotten to know them well enough to find out what they did.

Because I was trying to let her maintain her privacy.

As long as I didn't pry into her life, I didn't have to talk about mine.

Not that I had anything to hide.

I sighed.

Tomorrow was another day. Tomorrow we would start again.

And maybe this time I'd go about things a little bit differently.

Maybe.

It was probably the only way I was going to find out what her lips felt like on mine.

25

AINSLEY

I woke sometime in the middle of the night.

The only sound was from a log falling in the fireplace. The fire had burned down to almost just embers, but it was cold.

And quiet.

I was used to spending the night in hotels, so I was quick to orient myself.

But that wasn't the problem.

The problem was that it was too quiet. There was no hum of a furnace. The only sound was Beau snoring at the foot of the bed.

It was dark. The only light came from what was left of the fire in the fireplace.

And I was cold. I burrowed my feet beneath him and rolled over to tap my phone screen.

It was two twenty. The middle of the night.

I blinked and looked more closely at my phone.

The power had gone out.

And apparently there was no generator to kick in and warm things up.

I needed to go to the bathroom and grab a bottle of water.

I put my feet on the cold floor and almost changed my mind.

I had some socks but they were across the room. I'd be better off just hurrying.

Grabbing my phone, I turned on the flashlight.

Darting across the room, I took care of business, then went into the kitchen to grab a bottle of water.

Just as I went through the door that led into the main cabin, I bumped into someone.

Wyatt.

I yelped.

He put his hands on my arms to steady me.

And probably, I thought with a little laugh to myself, to keep me from hitting him, thinking he was an intruder.

I knew exactly who he was. I'd just been startled.

"Hi," he said. "It's me."

"I see that." I took a step back to go around him. "I was just getting some water."

"Me too," he said, but he still had a hand on my right arm.

"The power went out," he said.

"I see that." I stopped trying to walk around him and just stood there. My feet were freezing on the cold floor.

"What are we supposed to do?" I asked. "Call someone?"

"Not likely," he said. "The power crews can't get out in this to do anything."

"So… we're just going to freeze to death."

I saw a hint of a smile flash across his lips and I was glad he couldn't see my cheeks flush in the dim light as a brief notion of how we might keep each other warm crossed through my mind.

"I'll go out in the morning. See about getting some more firewood."

I nodded and tried to go around him again.

This time he let me go.

I was a bit disappointed.

"Ok then," I said. "My feet are freezing. So…" I pointed in the general direction of the bed.

"Right," he said. "Good night."

"Good night." I dashed toward the bed and dived back under the covers.

Beau opened one eye and looked at me, then went back to snoring.

I turned off my phone's flashlight and stared in the direction of the ceiling.

I heard Wyatt walk across the floor and get himself nestled back beneath his blanket on the sofa.

I snuggled beneath the blanket, tucking my feet beneath Beau.

But I was still shivering.

Yep. We were going to freeze.

26

WYATT

There was no way we were going to freeze to death.

I'd find us some firewood if I had to go out and chop it myself.

Besides, there were other ways to stay warm.

I was pretty sure we could figure this out.

But at the moment, Beau had the best deal of all.

That dog had made himself a place in the bed with Ainsley.

I'd never been envious of a dog before.

But I guess there was a first time for everything.

I wondered how long a guy was supposed to wait before he suggested body heat as a means of survival. Was there protocol for this sort of thing?

As a resident of Wyoming, I should know the answer to this. Unfortunately I kept my head stuck in a computer screen when I wasn't flying my airplane or riding my horse or tinkering with my old truck.

Of course, surviving in a snowstorm without heat was something I'd never had to worry about since I had my own whole-home generator. I could go a good two weeks without power. More with a propane refill.

Power outages had never been a problem for me.

And I wasn't inclined to let them start now.

I just wish I knew the protocol.

I mentally ran through my list of buddies who might know the answer.

Then I laughed at myself.

They'd laugh their asses off if I called and asked about a protocol for sharing warmth with a woman.

I worked hard to hide my nerdiness beneath dark aviator glasses and interesting vehicles from an old green truck to a bright red Lamborghini.

No one had called me a nerd to my face since ninth grade.

That's when I'd taken over the yearbook and suddenly became the cool guy who had control of which images people went down in history with.

I attributed that one computer skill to being the beginning of my success.

So. No. I would figure this thing out for myself.

Besides, the power would probably be back on in the morning.

I'd get up early, like I always did. Take a walk downtown. Find out what was going on.

How long the power was going to be off. Buy some firewood.

I'd be back by the time Ainsley woke up.

Then we'd figure out how to spend the day.

I had some ideas about that.

Ideas that I had a feeling she wouldn't go for.

But who knows, stranger things had happened.

And I might just develop a fondness for snowstorms.

I had most definitely developed a fondness for a particular reticent petite southern girl with long brunette hair.

27

AINSLEY

*W*hen I woke the next morning, sunlight streamed in through the window behind the bed.

Beau wasn't at my feet anymore and Wyatt wasn't on the sofa.

In fact, the blanket was neatly folded and left on the back of it, the pillow tucked somewhere out of sight.

And there was a blazing fire in the fireplace.

But the bed was far enough away that it was still cold in the bed. And the power was still off.

I grabbed my phone, went over to the sofa, and wrapped the blanket around me.

At least we weren't going to freeze to death. At least not for a little while.

I had a ton of text messages that had come in while my phone was on *do not disturb.*

I checked Momma's first.

MOMMA: *Good morning. Ainsley.*

Momma seemed to think that text messages had a formality of communication to them. She couldn't seem to grasp that text messages were by nature quick and to the point.

MOMMA: *Hope you're staying safe in that snowstorm. Don't try to fly until it's safe.*

Being married to a pilot, Momma should know that I couldn't fly even if I wanted to until it was safe to do so.

But, then again, she was married to THE Noah Worthington of Skye Travels, so if Noah wanted to get out there and fly his plane on an icy pond, I doubted that anyone would say a word to him.

MOMMA: *Let me know you're safe. Madison said you're with an old friend of Kade's.*

And with that, things were suddenly weird.

I'd liked the idea of being hunkered down with a good-looking mysterious Wyoming man. But the good-looking Wyoming man was a friend of sister's boyfriend.

What were the odds?

ME: *I'm safe Momma. Please don't worry.*

She'd used the word safe three times in two text messages. She may be a psychologist, but she had her own anxiety issues.

The next message was from my sister.

MADISON: *I know you didn't ask. And you may not even need to know this, but Kade says Wyatt is a good guy.*

MADISON: *They did some kind of two-week flight training together, but don't worry, Wyatt isn't a full-time pilot. So if you want to date him, you can. ;)*

I rolled my eyes. Madison, like everyone else in my family, knew that I didn't date pilots. Not since that one time, anyway.

ME: *Thanks for the info. But I'm not dating anyone.*

Madison wrote right back.

MADISON: *Right. Forgot about the moratorium. Well... too bad.*
ME: *Shouldn't you be teaching a class or something?*

Anything besides harassing me about my love life.

MADISON: *Storm has us closed down, too. Kade just beat me in a game of Monopoly.*

ME: *Monopoly? Seriously? Can't you think of something better to do?*

MADISON: *Taking a break.*

Geez. Ever since Kade had come back into her life, my sister was ridiculously in love.

ME: *TMI*

MADISON: *LOL. You're the one who asked.*

The door opened and Wyatt, his hands full, walked in with Beau at his feet.

I laid my phone down as though I'd been caught doing something I shouldn't have been doing.

What was wrong with me?

To make up for it, I smiled. "Hi."

Wyatt smiled back. "Good morning."

He set his bags on the coffee table.

"I bribed my buddy to open the café."

"Seriously? They're open?"

If the café was open, there was hope that we could get out of here soon.

"No," he said, looking at me sideways. "I seriously bribed him."

He held up two disposable coffee cups. It wasn't Starbucks but I wasn't complaining.

"Didn't know how you liked your coffee. Or if you even drank coffee. But I brought a latte and a black."

"The latte," I said.

He handed me one of the cups.

"That's what my money was on," he said. "And... since I couldn't get him to cook anything, I brought muffins."

"Muffins are perfect," I said, sipping the hot coffee. I hadn't even thought about food until know, but I was suddenly starving.

"Are we going to have power back on soon?" I asked, peeling the paper wrapper from one of the blueberry muffins.

"The whole town is out. And the roads are like glass." Sitting down next to me, he started eating a muffin himself.

"They're saying we might be stuck here for a…" he glanced over at me. "few days."

"A few days?"

I should have felt panicky.

I normally would have at not being able to fly home.

I loved, loved flying. But one thing I loved most about it was it that it gave me the freedom to get around.

Being stuck somewhere, like in Aspen yesterday, left me feeling trapped. Why else would I have hopped the first plane to anywhere?

But oddly enough, even though I waited for it, the panic didn't come.

Instead, I felt almost a little bit… relieved.

I sipped the coffee and tried to sort that out.

I was actually ok with being stuck here with Wyatt.

Oh. My. God.

I liked Wyatt.

He was getting past my moratorium walls.

I was in trouble.

28

WYATT

I should have brought two lattes.

I took a sip of the black coffee and tried not to make a face.

If I had to drink black coffee, I'd just stop drinking the stuff altogether.

Fortunately, I'd had a good cup of coffee with creamer while I sat with Johnny for a few minutes.

If Ainsley knew how much this coffee had cost me, she'd probably think I'd lost my ever-loving mind.

And I just might have.

She had herself so wrapped into my brain, that I'd paid Johnny three times what he normally got for this coffee and the food I'd bought from him.

I was lucky he'd been willing to walk over and open the store for me.

And he'd sworn me to secrecy. If it got out, he'd be opening up for the whole town.

If it had been me, I would opened up my store, but Johnny was enjoying the time with his family. He had a six-year-old who wanted to go sledding.

I got it.

But he'd instructed me to just go to his house if I needed anything else.

He'd also given me unrestricted access to his firewood stash. I think it was so I wouldn't try to bribe him again.

I didn't even want to think about what that was going to cost me before this storm was over.

Fortunately, I didn't care. I just found it interesting.

It had been a long time since I'd been so enchanted this much with a girl.

I'm sure there had been other girls I'd dated that I liked, but I couldn't stop thinking about Mary Beth in second grade.

I'd followed her around the school yard like a puppy.

She moved away with her family at the end of the school year.

Thinking back on it, I hoped I didn't have anything to do with that decision her family made.

"You don't like black coffee, do you?" Ainsley asked, sitting forward and looking at me.

"Not really," I admitted. "How did you know?"

She shrugged. "Both my mother and my sister are psychologists. I pick things up. Besides, you just made a face."

I laughed. "A face?"

"Yeah. Like you just ate green beans."

"What's wrong with green beans?"

She scrunched up her nose to make a face. "Slimy," she said.

I grinned at her. "I'll remember to never try to feed you green beans."

She grinned back. "Thank you."

I set my coffee down. At least now I didn't have to pretend to like it.

"So…" she said, taking a bite of her muffin. "What do people do during snowstorms?"

I had a whole lot of things race through my head, but I didn't dare share any of them with her.

It was actually a really good question.

29

AINSLEY

I sat back and watched Wyatt's reaction.

I'd asked him a leading question on purpose.

A question I knew didn't have an easy answer.

Even though I'd never been locked down in a snowstorm for days, there had been days here and there when the roads in Houston had iced over and we were stuck at home.

Typically we'd read books or play games.

But I wasn't looking for that kind of answer from him.

He didn't answer me.

Instead, as much as I knew he didn't like it, he picked up his black coffee and sipped it.

That told me the question made him uncomfortable.

And I was sort of enjoying it.

He seemed so confident and sure of himself.

And I wasn't really happy with the fact that I seemed to like him.

"We could play a game," I said, answering my own question.

He nearly spit out his coffee.

He sat it down again. "This stuff is awful," he said, then

looked at me with a smile playing about the corner of his lips. "What kind of game?"

I hesitated. If I went down this direction, I was going to learn more about him, but he was also going to learn more about me.

I wasn't sure how much more I could or even wanted to keep private from him.

I actually wanted to get to know him.

Moratorium be damned.

"We can play Would you Rather."

"I don't know that game," he said.

"It's easy," I said, pulling my feet up under me.

"Okay," he said. "Do we need my iPad?"

I shook my head. "Nope. Just questions."

"What are the rules?"

Did it have rules? I didn't even know.

"You have to answer honestly," I said.

"I see. Okay."

"I'll go first." I sipped my coffee to give myself time to think.

He stretched out his legs and seemed to get comfortable.

We were sitting on opposite ends of the couch, sort of facing each other now.

Beau jumped up between us and put his head my lap. I scratched his ears.

I came up with an easy question to start.

"Would you rather go fishing or go shopping."

"Go shopping," he said.

"You're supposed to be honest," I said.

"That is honest. I like to go shopping."

I nodded. "Okay." Maybe he was a little like my brother Quinn. But it was much too soon to make assumptions.

"So now what do we do?" he asked.

"You get to ask me one."

"Would you rather..."

I waited. What would this handsome man ask me. Out of an infinite number of choices, what would he want to know.

"Would you rather eat chocolate ice cream or vanilla ice cream?"

I put a hand over my mouth and laughed.

"Chocolate," I said. "What about you?"

"Wait," he said. "Is it allowed to ask the same question back?"

"You can." I shrugged. "If you want to."

"Vanilla," he said. "So would you rather go fishing or shopping?"

It was my rule to be honest.

I thought about my sister Brianna. She'd kill me, but…

"Go fishing," I said.

"You would not," he said.

"Why wouldn't I?" I asked, trying to keep a straight face.

"Because you bought out the General Store. I don't think they have any smalls left."

"That was guy shopping. My sister would have had to try everything on first."

"Okay," he said, watching me carefully. "Have you ever been fishing?"

I smiled. "Maybe."

He looked at my sideways. "I think you're breaking your own rules."

"Obviously you didn't grow up with a big family."

"Obviously." He waited a second. "Who's turn is it?"

"Would you rather fly a kite or build something with Legos?"

He shook his head. "I can't answer that."

"Why not?"

"Because I like them equally."

"Right. I get that you're a pilot. I thought you'd say fly a kite."

"I also like to... build things. Is there a list of questions somewhere? Because I don't think you're supposed to ask questions if you already know the answer."

"I didn't know the answer," I said. "But okay. You don't seem to like this game. Your turn to pick the game."

Really. I hadn't expected Wyatt to be so testy.

Didn't he know that games were supposed to just be for fun?

30

WYATT

"I need to take Beau out for a walk," I stood up abruptly and grabbed the dog's leash from the end table.

He jumped down, barked once, and sat on his haunches while I snapped the hook on his collar.

The cold air hit me like a slap in the face.

I hadn't realized just how warm the fire was. But then I'd been sitting with back to it.

Beau didn't really need to go for a walk, but he hadn't turned down the chance to come outside.

He stood next to me, patiently waiting while I decided which way I wanted to go.

Mostly, I'd just needed some air.

Most of the time, I handled things fine. Thanks to years of therapy.

But now and again, a stray image would slip past my walls of defenses and nearly bring me to my knees.

Not wanting to see anyone, I led Beau away from town. We walked slowly, our warm breath sending little gusts of fog into the air.

I'd been fine until Ainsley had said something about coming from a large family.

I'd already known it. She'd told me how many brothers and sisters she had. So it shouldn't have come as a surprise.

And it wasn't a surprise.

It was just one of those things that struck me wrong.

It happened on occasion and it was always out of the blue.

The psychologist had told me it was just something I'd have to live with. That the memories were scattered all through my body and that I would never be completely rid of them.

They were a part of me.

We'd worked through the guilt.

That it hadn't been my fault.

And on a cognitive level, I got that.

But on an emotional level, I would never forgive myself.

How many seventeen-year-old girls died from a heart attack?

They said it was congenital. That there was nothing I could have done.

And I believed them.

That wasn't where the guilt came from. The guilt came from not pushing my sister harder to spend time together.

As I walked, I realized that sitting on the sofa playing essentially a child's game with Ainsley and talking about family had been a trigger.

The thing I regretted the most was not hanging out with my older sister more.

Not just playing games and talking.

I'd been fourteen. She had been seventeen.

And when we got home from school that day, she'd gone to take a nap and I'd gone to play a video game.

I think that's when I really retreated into my own head.

Since I hadn't given my sister time, how could I in good conscience give attention to anyone else?

I took a deep breath, letting the cold air burn my lungs.

And talked myself through it. Just like my psychologist had taught me.

It wasn't my fault.

And Ainsley wasn't my sister.

It was okay to spend time with someone else.

Beau and I turned around and started walking back to our cabin.

Now I had to go back try to make amends with Ainsley.

I liked her. I liked spending time with her.

All I had to do was get past my own tortured brain cells.

I distracted myself by imagining what it would feel like to kiss her.

Once I was able to separate thoughts of family away from thoughts of Ainsley, I'd be okay.

In fact, trying to steal a kiss from her would be a good distraction. And would once and for all separate her from my own regrets about family.

31

AINSLEY

*A*fter Wyatt left with Beau, I walked around the little cabin, idly straightening up as I tried to sort out what had happened.

I might be a pilot, but I'd also grown up with a psychologist for a mother. And a sister, too.

So I was more attune to human suffering than most people.

Couldn't live in the same house with a psychologist and not pick things up.

And since my younger sister and mother were always having conversations that involved things psychological, I was double exposed.

I didn't mind.

Sometimes it would have been nice to be able to ignore things about other people, but other times, like now, it was what kept me from taking Wyatt's leaving personally.

Whatever he had going on in his mind was his business.

And he obviously knew enough to take a walk to clear his head.

I wouldn't ask him about it or make a big deal out of it.

I would just act like nothing had happened. He could talk to me about it or not. It was up to him.

I'd say I'd probably never see him again after this trip, but he was Kade's friend. I could see him anywhere. He'd probably even be at my sister's wedding.

So all the more reason to leave him alone.

I finally sat on the sofa, in Wyatt's place, with the fire to my back, wrapped the blanket around me and sent my father a text.

ME: *Are you working?*

He didn't like us asking how he felt, so us girl had to find other ways to find out in a round about way.

DADDY: *Not today. In my woodshop.*

When Daddy worked in his woodshop, it was always a good sign.

As the oldest and Daddy's favorite, I checked on him probably more than I should have.

ME: *Sounds fun. Making anything interesting?*

DADDY: *Working on making something new. But I can't tell you what it is. It's a surprise.*

I smiled to myself. Daddy was making something for me. Or maybe Momma. Or even one of my sisters.

ME: *Enjoy yourself.*

DADDY: *You too.*

I laughed to myself. Daddy didn't even know what I was doing, but he was always telling us to have fun.

Was I? Having fun?

I could be.

Wyatt was a handsome man. And kind.

He had some issues going on, but who didn't.

Was it time to call off my moratorium on dating?

The warm blanket still wrapped around my shoulders, I got up and went to stand at the window.

Wyatt was walking back with Beau beside him.

He said something to Beau and the dog turned and looked at him.

I laughed.

It was too bad I didn't even know who the dog belonged to. I was going to miss him.

But still. It was sweet watching the way Wyatt and the dog were bonding.

Beau walked over to a tree and stopped to do his business.

Wyatt waited patiently for him.

His actions toward Beau gave me a lot insight into him as a man.

Animals could tell these things.

And if Beau believed that Wyatt was a good man, then I would put money on it.

That was one thing I'd learned. Unlike people, animals didn't lie.

Just looking at Wyatt caused my heart to swell. I felt like the damn Grinch when his heart swelled up and he became a happy citizen of Whoville.

My heart was swelling up and bursting out of the seams the constraints of my self-imposed moratorium.

So this was how the Grinch felt.

Free. And happy.

I felt free and happy.

Free to enjoy Wyatt's company. No pressure. No commitment.

Just good clean fun.

Then he turned and looked in my direction.

He saw me standing at the window watching him.

I lifted a hand in greet and he did the same.

My heart had butterflies. Or maybe the butterflies were in my stomach.

At any rate, I was a mess.

Just giving myself the freedom to enjoy my time with Wyatt without having to worry about my own restrictions was incredibly freeing.

Then he smiled.

And I knew I was in trouble.

32

WYATT

"Come on, Boy," I said. "Ainsley is waiting for us."

Beau kicked up dirt with his back feet and trotted to catch up.

If I didn't know better, I'd swear the dog understood English.

I'd started off well enough with Ainsley.

But that was typical. I was good at holding it together for a little while.

Then something would happen like it had with Ainsley and I'd fuck it all up.

Usually by the time that happened, I was ready to end the relationship anyway.

But it was different with Ainsley.

Not only was I just getting to know her, she was the kind of girl a man wanted to keep around. The kind of girl a man could take home to his parents.

Not that I'd done that since high school, but then I'd moved out when I started college. So there had been no reason to bring a girl home.

Occasionally my mother would ask if I was dating anyone.

I always said no, even if I was. Because I didn't want to take any of the girls I was dating home. I told myself I didn't want to subject a girl to them, but that wasn't always the truth.

Oddly enough, when I thought about taking Ainsley with me to Florida to see my parents, the image seemed natural.

As Beau and I walked toward the cottage, I decided the cold must be messing with my head.

I should be thinking about getting her out of her pants, not taking her home to meet my parents. Besides, I'd been overly testy when I'd stormed out. She might not even be talking to me anymore.

I stopped in front of the door and knocked the snow off my boots. Beau shook himself as though to do the same.

I patted him on the head. "You're a good boy," I said. "Maybe I should keep you. Do you want to stay with me?"

Beau barked once and I swear he was smiling as we went inside.

While I closed the door, locked up, and tugged my boots off, Beau darted over to where Ainsley was back to sitting on the sofa. She had my spot with her back to the fire, by the way.

Beau jumped up into her lap. She laughed and wrapped her arms around him, kissing him on the top of his head.

A girl who wasn't afraid of dog germs.

Well, I was just about to declare her the perfect woman for me.

And the fact that she didn't even seem upset about me getting testy earlier sealed the deal.

"Hi," I said. "I don't recommend getting outside if you don't have to."

She glanced down at the blanket.

"You're not going to get an argument from me on that one."

I rubbed my hands together. "Do you want some hot chocolate?"

"You have some?" she asked.

"Of course. Can't make a store run in a snowstorm without bringing home hot chocolate.

"Sure," she said.

I walked into the kitchen and turned on the gas stove. At least we had that going for us. Then went back to the door.

"Thought you didn't like chocolate." She was looking up at me from beneath those long dark eyelashes of hers.

"I like vanilla ice cream. Hot chocolate is in a whole different realm."

"I see," she said, leaning forward.

I'd wondered if she'd get up and try to help me with making the hot chocolate. But she surprised me and didn't. She hadn't tried to help with pizza last night.

I went back inside the kitchen.

I was impressed.

I liked a woman who didn't automatically think her place was in the kitchen.

My mother was like that. She'd shoo my father out of the kitchen before he even had a chance.

I liked the opportunity to take care of my woman.

I scoffed at myself.

My woman.

If Ainsley even suspected I was thinking of her that way, she'd probably slap me across the cheek.

Hmm.

I opened the packets of chocolate and dumped them into the mugs I found in the kitchen.

Maybe I should tell her and see what happened.

There was nothing wrong with a little passion now and then to get things heated up.

Geez. Cold air and my brain did not appear to be compatible.

I stayed in the kitchen while the water heated.

I wasn't sure how I wanted this to go.

It really had been going well.

There was no reason to mess with something that was working.

Even if I was thinking about getting her out of those sweatpants.

We'd be so much warmer if we slept in the same bed.

Focus.

Get the brain in the right place.

She wasn't some random girl I'd picked up—even though technically she was, she was actually my friend Kade's girlfriend's sister.

Wasn't there some kind of rule about that being off-limits?

Or was that just some irrational thought coming out of my frozen brain?

Maybe I just needed to drink something hot and warm up my brain cells before I started getting crazy thoughts about her.

33

AINSLEY

*A*s I sipped the hot chocolate, I watched Wyatt as he stoked up the fire and added another log.

I was considering the puzzle of why he had to be so handsome as he stood up and dusted his hands.

His cell rang and he went back to the kitchen to answer it.

I realized this was the first time I'd seen him texting or using his phone since I'd met him.

I heard his muffled words, but couldn't make them out.

He listened more than he talked until the end of the conversation.

When he came back, I decided to hit the problem head on.

"Girlfriend?" I asked with what I hoped was a carefree tone.

He glanced at me. "No. Work."

I waited for him to say more, but he just sat down on what was now his end of the sofa.

Beau had gone back and taken his place in the bed.

"What about you?" he asked. "Boyfriend?"

I froze with my mug halfway to my lips. That was about the last thing I expected him to ask me.

"No," I said. "No boyfriend."

He looked at me, a bit bemused. "Why not?"

"What do you mean why not?" He was sounding a bit like my sister Madison.

That was the kind of thing she would ask me.

"Well," he said, crossing his ankles. "You're a smart young lady."

I looked away, feeling the punch to my gut.

Why did guys use the word smart when giving me compliments?

I was smart, but I wanted to be more than just smart.

Maybe my sister Brianna was right. I needed to pay more attention to my appearance.

Brianna never said anything to our youngest sister about how she dressed and she rarely wore anything other than a pair of shorts.

"And," Wyatt added. "you're pretty."

Glancing back at him, I shook my head.

"That won't work," I said.

"What won't work?"

"You started with smart."

He was looking at me with that bemused expression again.

"Most girls would love to be called smart. I don't even know what you do. For all I know, you could be a heart surgeon."

"I'm not," I said.

"Then tell me one thing," he said. "Tell me why you're single."

"I'm taking a moratorium from guys."

He held up a finger. "My point exactly."

I couldn't help the bubble of laughter that escaped my lips.

Wyatt was a most perplexing man.

But that was just part of his charm.

34

WYATT

I'd never seen a girl who looked insulted by being told she was smart.

But obviously, being smart wasn't what she was going for.

But her reason for not being in a relationship made my case.

I worked with some smart women and I'd never once heard one of them claim to be taking a moratorium from men.

First off, most would just say they were taking a break and second, not too many would even admit to that. The girls I knew were always swiping left or right and doing all sorts of crazy things to try to meet men.

But Ainsley was different.

"So how long have you been on this moratorium?" I asked, curiosity getting the best of me.

"About six months," she said.

"So no dates in six months?"

She shook her head.

"Nothing?" I asked.

She smiled in that way that seem to say she was amused by me. "It's not all that long."

I shrugged. "I know some girls who can't go a week without a date."

Ainsley laughed. "I've gone for three years."

"Wow. Now that's impressive."

"I don't know if I'd call it that." She set her mug down on the floor. "What about you? How long has it been since you've had a date?"

"I don't even remember," I said quickly. Too quickly. I wouldn't call the dalliance I had last weekend a date. Exactly.

She watched me carefully.

I could only hide behind my mug for just so long.

"Okay," I said. "I've had dates, but nothing serious."

I didn't know why it was important that she know that. That I hadn't had a serious girlfriend lately.

But I didn't want her to think I was attached.

I couldn't blame my thought patterns on a frozen brain anymore.

I was watching the way she licked her lips. The way she looked at me with those big green eyes.

"So neither one of us is attached," she said.

"So it seems."

I set my mug on the floor. I didn't know where she was going with this.

"I wonder what that says about us," she said.

Before she could explain herself, her phone chimed.

She frowned at the text message.

"I have to answer this," she said with a quick glance in my direction before turning her attention to her phone.

She typed something quickly, then turned her phone over in her lap.

"Just work," she said.

I nodded.

It was almost like a game of sorts. She wasn't telling me what her work was exactly and I wasn't asking.

But I hadn't told her what I did either. I hadn't told her that I'd built and owned a multi-billionaire company.

That outside of running my company, I played video games in my spare time.

I just wanted her to like me for me.

She already knew that I not only owned an airplane, but flew the thing.

She had to be curious.

Yet she seemed to just be biding her time.

Then it occurred to me.

She wasn't asking me what I did because she didn't want me to ask her.

"We're quite a pair, aren't we?" I asked.

She smiled.

Wars had started over smiles like that.

35

AINSLEY

*I*t was a winter wonderland. That's what my father called snow like this.

I took a couple of pictures with my phone to send to him later.

For a southern boy, he had quite an affinity for winter.

Momma and Daddy had a cabin in the mountains where they sometimes spent what little down time they had.

Daddy had jokingly told us several times that each one of us five kids got our start there.

That always got him a dirty look from Momma, but she didn't correct him.

I could see how a couple could conceive in the cold weather. Staying warm could easily lead to other things.

Snow crunched beneath our boots as we walked along what Wyatt seemed to think was a sidewalk.

Personally, I couldn't tell the sidewalk from the not sidewalk.

And Beau ran ahead, darting from place to place, obviously not caring if he was on the sidewalk or not.

Wyatt held Beau's leash in a gloved hand. I noticed that we were both wearing red gloves. Not by design. It just happened that way.

As we walked along beneath the fir and spruce trees, their limbs covered in white, to me, it felt like were a couple.

Just a man and a woman taking their dog out for a walk.

But Beau didn't belong to either of us.

And that was funny because I wasn't sure which one of us had taken up with him more.

And we weren't a couple.

We barely knew each other, in fact.

We walked past a little family, a father, a mother, and two preteens dragging sleds behind them.

Wyatt and I didn't look a lot different than they did. Except that instead of kids, we had a dog.

Maybe they weren't a family either. Looks could be deceiving.

And yet they, no doubt, thought we were a happy couple.

We didn't talk much as we walked.

We seemed to have settled into a comfortable companionship.

Like any other couple.

Wyatt caught me looking at him and smiled over at me.

My heart did a flip.

He looked good no matter what he was doing.

Flying a plane.

Cooking pizza in his glass house.

Chopping wood.

Walking a dog.

We were headed to the General Store. Wyatt's friend Johnny had caved to popular request and opened his store for a few hours.

So Wyatt and I were on our way to get ice cream.

He swore that ice cream tasted best in cold weather.

I didn't believe him, but I was willing to give it a try.

Unfortunately, for me, Wyatt was one of those guys who had a way of making a girl want to do things to please him.

So off we went, walking in the cold, to get ice cream.

Possibly one of the craziest things I'd ever done.

It had started to snow again. Just soft gentle flakes that landed unnoticed on the skin, but quickly coated the eyelashes.

As we stepped onto the little bridge that crossed the river that, oddly enough, flowed freely, bubbling over rocks, I must have stepped onto a slick spot, my foot landing just right.

I felt myself sliding. Falling.

But just as quickly, I felt Wyatt's arms wrap around me, steadying me back on my feet.

"Whoa," he said. "Where are you headed there?"

I held onto his arms for dear life.

Falling and busting my head was no on my agenda for today. Or my butt. Or any body part.

Wyatt guided me away from whatever slick spot I'd stepped on and my feet found a safe place to gain purchase.

"You got it," he asked.

My heart was racing at the unexpected danger.

I could weather turbulence without a blink, but sliding on slick ice beneath deceptively fluffy snow. Not so much.

I nodded. "I think so."

But even though my feet were steady now, looking at the expanse of white ahead of us had me inexplicably nervous.

He seemed to follow my gaze and understand my reluctance to take off across what could easily be a dangerous path.

He took my glove hand in his glove hand and that seemed to steady me enough that I could let go of his other arm.

"Got it now?" he asked.

"I think so," I said, but I kept a firm grip on his hand.

Beau tugged on his leash, urging us to continue across the bridge toward the store.

We crossed the bridge, hand in hand.

Nothing had changed. At least that's what I told myself.

But everything had changed.

36

WYATT

I had to let go of Ainsley's hand to open the door to the General Store.

We weren't the only people who had ventured out.

The road might be closed down, but the people weren't staying inside.

That was the beauty of the small town.

It was actually the first time I'd been stuck in town. I'd always managed to get to my house before the roads were closed.

Of course I'd never had a green-eyed siren urging me to take her into town for last minute clothes.

The General Store also served as a cafe, ice cream parlor, and post office.

So here we were.

And I couldn't remember the last time I'd been this content to just be.

I was always working on something.

Or flying from one of my offices to another. Meeting with people.

Even playing video games was working for me.

But I had to do it. It was part of my job.

I only occasionally took a few hours for dinner. Maybe a movie.

But it was always back to work for me.

Even if I met a girl for drinks, I'd got home afterward and work.

It was what had made me successful. But I'd missed out on days like today.

Ever since that day when I had to call the ambulance to come get my sister, I'd focused on work.

Maybe I saw it as my penance for not being able to save her.

At least that's what the psychologist had suggested at one point.

Those words resonated with me.

Made perfect sense.

So I worked. Did my penance. And made more money than I could possibly ever spend.

And right now, I wanted to spend some of that money on Ainsley.

The General Store in this little town in the valley wouldn't have been my first choice of a place to take her.

There was a little Italian restaurant in Manhattan that was a good place to take a special girl.

Then there was a romantic little pizza parlor in Aspen that had a fun vibe to it.

I could think of about ten different places off the top of my head that I could take Ainsley to if we weren't snowed it.

But then if we weren't snowed in, we wouldn't be together.

Of that, I was fairly certain.

We took a seat on two of the ice cream parlor bar stools.

What was wrong with sharing some of the timeless ambience of my hometown?

After all, I had to admit that they had some of the best ice cream in the country.

Ainsley looked at my with a little smile.

"Let me guess," she said. "You're going to order vanilla."

I put a hand on my chin and studied the menu.

"Oh no," I said. "It would be an injustice to just order vanilla here. In fact, they'd probably run me out of town on a rail."

"But you said vanilla was your favorite."

"Oh no," he looked at me with a little smile. "I said I preferred vanilla over chocolate. There's a difference."

"I see," she said. "So what flavor do you recommend?"

"Well... since you like chocolate, you might like the mint chocolate chip.'"

"Always a classic," she said.

"It's especially good if you get the one with the coconut and caramel."

"That sounds good," she said. "I'll have that."

"I like a girl who makes a quick decision based on good information." I said with a smile.

"Hopefully good information," she said, returning my smile. "What are you going to get?"

"Banana caramel with almonds."

She wrinkled her nose.

"What?"

"Bananas in ice cream," she said. "sounds just awful."

"Wait. What? Have you never tried banana caramel ice cream?"

"The thought of bananas in ice cream is just not something I would order on purpose." She looked at me. "Does it have vanilla ice cream?"

I squinted toward the menu. "It comes with either. But I always get the swirl."

She smiled at me.

"I seems to me that you always get what you want."

I wasn't sure what that comment meant or whether or not it was referring to ice cream or something else.

But I was a gentleman and opted for the ice cream.

"Yes," I said. "I almost always order the same thing. The one time I ordered something different was a bit of a bad experience."

"A little OCD?" She asked.

Did nothing get past this girl?

I just shrugged. This was going to be fun.

37

AINSLEY

*M*y ice cream with mint chocolate chip, caramel, and coconut was surprisingly quite good.

Normally I would have just ordered chocolate or maybe a chocolate vanilla swirl. But instead, I went with Wyatt's recommendation. I was glad I had.

"Good?" He asked.

"Perfect," I said. "How's yours?"

"Good," he said. "You should try it."

He was holding out a spoonful of his ice cream to me.

I made a face.

"You have to at least try it," he insisted.

"Ok," I said, with a little pout. Bananas smelled bad and mixing them in with ice cream was just plain counter-intuitive.

He held up a bite of the concoction and I slid the bite of ice cream off the spoon that he held.

Quite frankly, it didn't really matter what the ice cream tasted like, it was worth it to share the moment with him.

"So?" He asked. "What do you think?"

I looked at him as I tasted. I couldn't even taste the bananas

"Well, maybe I'd smelled them just a little."

Whoever thought this mess up should be drawn and quartered.

"You like it, don't you?" He asked.

"It's okay," I said. "I like it that you like it. If that makes any sense."

"It makes perfect sense," he said with a grin.

"Want to walk around?" He asked.

"Can we do that? With our ice cream?"

This stuff was far too expense to throw out.

I'd already eaten enough calories that I was certain I'd feel it tomorrow."

Maybe I could get up and go for a jog in the morning.

But from the looks of the weather outside, that probably wasn't going to happen.

"We can do whatever we want to do," he said.

Taking our ice cream, we got up and walked around the little store, Beau at our heels.

If this were a city, we'd be doing all sorts of illegal things.

There was a little boy trying to convince his father to buy him a sled.

But several people seemed to have just come in for necessities.

We seemed to be the only people who were out just to enjoy an afternoon together.

I wasn't sure what I'd call it.

A date, maybe?

I kinda hoped Wyatt saw it as a date.

I enjoyed his company. A little too much, actually.

Fortunately, I could worry about that later.

Right now, I just focused on the moment.

Having a cup of ice cream—which I rarely indulged in—and walking around a quaint little country store in the mountains of Wyoming.

Not my usual outing by a long shot.

But the funny thing was, I was actually enjoying it.

More so than I'd enjoyed any of the my previous dates.

We stopped at one of the glass displays and looked at some jewelry lying on white velvet.

"I think they hand make a lot of things here."

"Yeah?"

I stopped to look at the jewelry. There were so many different colors to choose from.

Nothing at all like the high end jewelry stores I was used to.

The lady at the counter smiled at us.

"Would you like to see something?" She asked.

"Do you see anything you like?" Wyatt asked, looking at me.

I saw lots of things I liked.

Bracelets in copper and sapphire.

Necklaces.

I didn't wear a lot of jewelry, but especially not when I was flying.

It had been part of my training. We'd been taught to never give a potential perpetrator a weapon around your neck.

But I had an affinity for necklaces and my eyes were drawn to a lovely copper and sapphire pendent.

It looked like nothing I owned or had even ever considered owning. It actually looked like something my sister Madison would wear.

Wyatt, astutely followed my gaze.

"You like that one?" He asked.

I smiled. "Maybe."

"Can we see that one?" He asked the sales lady.

"Absolutely," she said, pulling the necklace from the glass and holding it out to me.

I set my cup of ice cream aside and took the necklace from her.

"Try it on," Wyatt said.

With a quick glance at the sale lady, who nodded, I pulled at the clasp, but my hands were trembling too much.

"Let me." Wyatt took the copper chain from me and, as I lifted my hair, he placed it around my neck and fastening the clasp.

The sales lady put a mirror in front of me.

"Pretty," she said.

And it was. The blue sparkled in the light and contrasted in a surprisingly fashionable way with the copper.

"Do you like it?" He asked.

"I love it," I said.

It just seemed to fit with Wyoming and the snow storm.

And Wyatt.

Wyatt signaled the girl and she went to the cash register, an old-fashioned machine, to ring it up.

Expecting to pay for it myself, I took one more look in the mirror. Why not? I rarely bought anything for myself. My sister Brianna would be ecstatic.

By the time I turned back, the sales lady was sliding Wyatt's credit card back toward him.

I started to say something, but instead kept my thoughts to myself.

It was never proper to refuse a gift.

"Would you like the box?" she asked.

"I think we're good," Wyatt said. "She'll just wear it."

We picked up our ice cream cups and walked away from the counter.

"That looks really good on you," Wyatt said. "I suits you."

I ran a hand along the sparkly copper and sapphire necklace.

It was so odd that he thought this necklace suited me when I'd never owned anything like it before.

Maybe I had just discovered a side to myself I hadn't known existed.

And I'd thought I knew myself pretty well.

That was one of the joys of traveling.

There was always something new to learn, not just about the world, but about oneself.

And one thing I was quickly learning was that Wyatt had my attention.

In fact, I was having a hard time thinking about anything other than him.

38

WYATT

*A*insley and I walked back to the cafe and sat at one of the little tables over by one of the front windows.

It was snowing again.

And I'd never seen snow so beautiful.

Probably because it was falling behind one of most beautiful girls I'd ever seen.

And not only was she beautiful, she was intriguing.

I knew very little about her, but I knew everything I needed to know.

It had been fun to buy her something today.

I could happily buy this girl gifts all day long if she'd let me.

I loved seeing the way her eyes lit up when she saw how beautiful the necklace looked around her neck.

If I had to guess, I'd say that she didn't own a lot of jewelry and most likely hadn't had men buy it for her.

She didn't look like the kind of girl who would buy herself jewelry.

A lot of girls were like that.

They thought jewelry was supposed to be a gift. Sort of like flowers. A lot of girls wouldn't buy flowers for themselves either.

And that made me sad.

That meant that there were so many women out there who never owned jewelry and went through life without flowers just because they didn't have a man who would buy them.

If I had a girl, she would never be without either.

At least not if that was something she enjoyed.

I wondered if Ainsley liked flowers.

It was hard to tell. But then, what girl didn't like flowers?

"Thank you," she said, smiling at me and putting a hand over the necklace.

"You're welcome," I said. "But you don't have to thank me. I'm the one who gets to see you wearing it."

My words actually brought a flush to her cheeks.

Ah hell, I was smitten.

I reached over and put a hand on hers.

She flinched, just a little, and I quickly pulled my hand back.

She was still wary of me.

That was okay. I had time to prove to her that I was one of the good guys.

"So..." I said. "I was thinking..."

"What were you thinking?" She asked, her eyes trained on mine.

"I was thinking that Beau might like some ice cream."

She looked at me blankly for a moment, then laughed. "Okay."

"But since we both have chocolate, I'll have to get him his own cup."

"Vanilla," she said.

"Wait here," I said. "I'll be right back."

I dashed to the counter and ordered a small cup of vanilla ice cream.

Beau sat next to Ainsley, but when I set the ice cream in front of him, he barked once, then lapped it up greedily.

Ainsley laughed.

"Are you sure you don't know whose dog he is?" I asked.

She shook her head, still watching Beau.

"Because I think he's your dog."

She looked up at me with confusion.

"He can't be my dog," she said. "He belongs to someone else."

"Maybe," I said. "But I think he likes you."

I liked the way her eyes lit up as she watched him lapping up the ice cream.

And the way she smiled when I suggested that he liked her.

I couldn't help but wonder... how would she react if she knew that I liked her, too?

39

AINSLEY

I'd never owned a dog.

I'd grown up around cats. My grandmother had a cat when I was growing up and we had cats at home for awhile, too.

But I'd never adopted a pet myself. As an adult.

I'd always just accepted the fact that as a pilot I traveled too much to have a pet waiting at home.

It was simply a part of the lifestyle that I'd chosen.

But Wyatt was right. Beau and I had seemed to bond in the short time we'd known each other.

"Can you find out?" He asked. "Who he belongs to?"

I shrugged.

"Probably."

I actually knew that I could find out.

I'd just didn't ask questions.

Madison had told me one time that I'd make a great hit man.

I just did the job and never asked questions.

Beau lapped up the last of his ice cream and looked over at Wyatt for more.

"You messed up, now," I said. "Now that he'd gotten a taste, he'll never be satisfied."

My words trailed off as I realized that I could be talking about something else entirely.

Something to do with me and Wyatt.

I hoped he didn't notice.

"You're right," he said. "But I don't have a problem with getting ice cream for him."

"I'll find out who he belongs to," I said. "But you may have to keep him. I can't do it."

"Why not? You have other dogs waiting jealously at home?"

And now he was doing it.

I was pretty sure we were touching on something other than just the dog.

"No," I said. "I've never adopted a dog."

"Huh." He was watching me closely as though he was trying to figure something out.

I knew what he was doing. He was trying to figure out why I possibly couldn't own a dog.

What kind of job did I do that would prevent me from keeping a dog.

I should just tell him.

It was kinda silly keeping it from him that I was a pilot.

But I'd gone this long and I had to admit it was rather fun not telling him.

And since he didn't come right out and ask me, I didn't think I had to tell him.

It was almost like he was enjoying the puzzle of trying to figure it out himself.

"So…" I said. "If I go to the trouble to find out if he's available, are you going to keep him?"

"I don't know," Wyatt said. "I still think you're the one he likes."

"I'll think about it," I said, even though I'd already thought about it and dismissed the opportunity of it even being possible.

"Okay," he said. "I'll just have to trust you."

I smiled. "Yes you will."

40

WYATT

*A*insley stared out the window at the falling snow.

She didn't seem to be just watching it. She seemed to be studying it.

Before I could sort that thought out, she turned and smiled at me.

"We should go get some more firewood before it gets too late. Gonna be cold again tonight."

I glanced over her shoulder.

"You're right. We should go ahead and do that."

"Finished with your ice cream?"

"Yes. And you know what, you were right. Ice cream is better in the cold weather.

I picked up her bowl along with mine and tossed them in the trash.

"Stick with me, Kid," I said. "I'll never steer you wrong."

We'd been skirting on the edge of talking about something else for awhile now.

We were skirting on the edge of talking about relationships and sex and all those things that had me thinking about getting her in front of the fireplace and getting her out of those clothes.

So I thought going back to the cabin was a very good suggestion.

"We need to stop by the cabin and get the little wagon to haul firewood."

"Okay," she said, sliding her chair back and standing up. "Come on Beau."

"He'd follow you anywhere," I said.

She just rolled her eyes.

"You know it's true," I said, holding out my hand for Beau's leash.

As she handed it over, our hands lingered together.

I was definitely ready to get back to the cabin now.

"Wyatt?"

The familiar voice startled me.

But surely not.

I whirled around and, Heaven help me, I was right.

Annabelle Bennett stood behind me. She looked as fresh and pretty as the day I'd met her.

"Annabelle? What are you doing out here?"

Before I knew what was happening, she'd run right up to me and put her arms around me.

"I brought my boyfriend up here and we got stranded," she said, taking a step back. "What a cute puppy." She knelt down and scratched Beau's ears.

Then she looked back up at me. "I fell in love with this place the first time you brought me up here."

I glanced quickly over at Ainsley. "That was a really long time ago." I said the words for Ainsley's benefit. No one else's.

Annabelle seemed to catch on. She always had been quick on her feet. And fortunately, our break up had been amiable.

Standing up straight, she held out a hand to Ainsley. "I'm so sorry. Where are my manners. I'm Annabelle. An old friend of Wyatt's."

Ainsley took Annabelle's hand and smiled. "It's a pleasure to meet you," she said, without a hitch. "This place is easy to get attached to, isn't it?"

"It is. Do you live in Denver, too?"

"No," Ainsley said, "I live in Houston."

"Oh. Still. You know how good it is to get away from the crowds now and then, don't you?"

"Absolutely," Ainsley said.

I wondered if I imagined the half-heartedness in her voice. She was probably ready to get back to her life in the city.

The thought automatically put me in a foul mood.

I wanted to get Ainsley back to the cabin.

Getting her back to her life in the city was the last thing I had in mind.

And besides, when she went back to Houston, it would be practically impossible for me to see her again.

And those two things together put me in a foul mood.

I didn't want Ainsley for a one night stand.

The thought wasn't even something I'd thought about until this moment.

And I wasn't even sure I had the right to think about her like this.

I didn't have the right to feel possessive of her like this.

Annabelle stood up and looked between us.

"I was just picking us up something to eat," she said. "Do you two want to join us? We're staying with Tom's cousin. No electricity though."

"Sure," Ainsley said.

"We were just leaving," I said.

Both of us spoke at the same time.

Ainsley's gaze met mine for just a flicker of a second.

She smiled in Annabelle's direction. "But we were just

leaving." She swept a hand down toward Beau. "We need to get back and feed Beau. Besides, the snow's about to get worse."

"Really?" Annabelle said with a glance outside. "Somebody said it was about to clear up."

Ainsley just smiled with a little shrug.

"We'll see," she said, letting it drop.

But I knew that she believed what she said.

And we would see, indeed. I would put my money on Ainsley before I would the weather guys. I wasn't even sure why, I just knew I would.

41

AINSLEY

*W*e walked back to the cottage in the falling snow. Maybe Daddy was right about it being a winter wonderland.

I could see the allure.

Fresh falling snow was breathtakingly beautiful.

We walked in silence, Beau walking between us.

Although I'd tried to appear okay with meeting Annabelle, I was relieved he hadn't wanted to stay.

"Sorry about that," Wyatt said.

I glanced over at him. "Sorry about what?"

"Annabelle," he said, vaguely.

"You have nothing to apologize for."

"I know," he said, looping Beau's leash tighter in his hands. "But I never wanted you to feel uncomfortable."

"I wasn't uncomfortable," I said, knowing that I was lying.

He looked at me sideways.

"At least not much," I added with a little smile.

He shifted Beau's leash so he could hold my hand.

"I guess I wasn't in the mood for catching up with an old friend, when I could be spending time with you."

"A new friend," I said.

He grinned. "Something like that."

"Were you together for very long?" I asked, hoping my voice sounded casual. Just making conversation.

If he brought her here, to his home, she must have been special.

"Most of college," he said. "Actually we had a mutual friend who was from here. We came here one summer for a visit."

"Do you think that mutual friend is her boyfriend?"

He looked surprised as though he hadn't thought of that.

"You know," he said, shaking his head a little. "That's it exactly. Son of a bitch. Sorry."

"No need to apologize," I said. "I've heard worse."

"Doesn't mean you have to hear it from me," he said. "I try to be a gentleman around ladies."

I smiled to myself. He was doing a good job of distracting me from worrying about his history with Annabelle. I had to remind myself that she had nothing to do with me.

And just because she'd been here with him before me, meant absolutely nothing.

Besides, I was merely a guest. A girl he'd rescued from the tarmac.

He was confusing the issue with the whole handholding thing.

It was making me think there was more to our relationship than there actually was.

I needed to tread carefully. I didn't want to be one of those girls who thought that just because a guy showed a little interest suddenly meant he wanted to get married.

It didn't work like that.

Since I was on a holiday from my moratorium, I was allowed to hook up with him.

And by definition, that meant no strings attached.

It was just a little holiday romance. A diversion to get us through this storm.

And the storm was about to get a whole lot worse.

And I didn't have to be a meteorologist to know it.

In fact, the meteorologists seemed to have been getting this storm wrong from the outset.

They could no longer be counted on to make an accurate forecast.

But I had something of a sixth sense about weather.

With my attention to the weather as a pilot, I'd honed that skill to the point where I was never wrong.

If I sensed a storm getting worse, the storm was going to get worse.

We got to the cabin and Wyatt passed Beau leash over to me while he unlocked the door.

I didn't really think Beau needed a leash, but he wasn't technically my dog, so I couldn't risk him running away.

We stepped inside the cottage. After I unhooked Beau's leash, he shook, sending a spray of water everywhere.

Wyatt grabbed a towel and tossed it over him.

"Too late," I said.

"Oh well. We're doing the best we can."

The newly semi-dried dog went straight to the bed and climbed up, finding his place at the foot of the bed.

I went to stand in front of the fireplace.

"I forgot. We were going to get firewood."

"Right," he said. "I forgot, too. Do you still want to go?"

"Absolutely." I turned to the dog. "Beau, do you want to wait here or go?"

Beau barked once and practically fell off the bed as he jumped off.

A minute later, he stood at my feet.

"I think he wants to go."

"Told you," Wyatt said. "That dog will follow you anywhere."

"It could be bad when I have turn him over to someone else," I said, hooking him up again to his leash.

"I'll start making some phone calls on that. Might need a little information from you."

I froze.

If I showed Wyatt Beau's paperwork, he would probably discover that I was a pilot and it would be game over.

"We can do that later," I said. "Plenty of time before the storm lets up."

It was probably silly, trying to keep my identity from him.

I just wanted him to like me for me.

42

WYATT

I had mixed feelings about going back outside, even to get firewood.

I wanted to be alone with Ainsley.

But not only would it be nice to have a fire in the fireplace, we were going to need it for warmth through the night.

The air seemed colder as we stepped back outside.

Might be because I had my mind set on being inside.

Or maybe it really was getting colder.

The snow was definitely coming down now.

The mountaintops in the distance were cloaked in clouds, so it was snowing in the high country.

Ainsley's knack with weather made me all the more curious about her and what she did besides pick up dogs from airports, but we seemed to have an unspoken truce about it.

She didn't tell me and I didn't ask.

I wondered if she'd tell me if I figured it out.

I grinned at her and took her hand as we walked toward Johnny's house where he kept his firewood.

She smiled back. So beautiful walking in the snow, her eyelashes coated in freshly fallen snow.

I wanted to kiss the snow off her lashes. To pull her into my arms and move from her lashes to her cheeks to her lips.

We turned down the path that was a short cut to Johnny's and his woodpile came into view.

"Are you sure he's okay with you taking his firewood?"

I looked at her sideways.

"Of course. He knows."

She shrugged and shivered. "Okay."

I opened the gate to his woodpile and started putting logs in the wagon.

Beau sat at Ainsley's feet. She crouched down and put her arms around his neck.

The two of them had quite a bond.

I threw two more logs onto my wagon.

I had more money than I knew what to do with.

If I couldn't find a way to buy Beau for her, my money wasn't worth much of anything after all. What was the point in having a lot of money if you couldn't make the girl you were crushing on happy?

After I had the wagon heaped with firewood, I closed the gate.

Ainsley stood up and watched as I took the handle.

"You gonna be able to pull that?" She asked.

"Sure," I said, confidently.

But as I started pulling the wagon, I was grateful that I worked out.

And maybe I should step up my workout routine a bit.

The snow started falling harder as we made our way back to the cabin.

I was probably supposed to be unhappy about the storm picking up again, but in truth I was quite pleased.

I wanted to spend more time alone with Ainsley.

And I knew that after the roads cleared and she got on a

plane back to Houston, even if I did get to see her again, it would be an ordeal.

And with the way things were right now, I couldn't see that she'd have much motivation to see me.

I was the guy who'd picked her up on a tarmac and given her a place to stay during a snowstorm.

But I wanted more from her.

I wasn't quite sure what it was I wanted, but I knew I wanted more.

43

AINSLEY

*W*e were definitely going to be here for awhile longer.

The snow was banking along the trees as we walked past.

I knew I should want the weather to clear up so I could get back to my life.

And truthfully, I had obligations to my family in Houston.

Things that I'd thought were important, but turns out they could wait after all. They had to wait. I didn't have a choice.

And even I should want to get back to my life, I didn't want to. At least not right now.

I was enjoying my time with Wyatt.

I was feeling a little guilty about not coming clean with him about who I really was, but I didn't want to think about that right now.

Right now, I wanted us to get back to the cabin, light a fire in the fireplace, and maybe have a glass of wine.

Enjoy being inside the cozy cabin while the world outside was blanketed with snow.

There were a few problems, though, that I was concerned about.

One was that my cell phone battery was almost out.

I had a back up charger, but that would only last so long.

Then I wouldn't have a phone.

I didn't see Wyatt using his phone much, so he probably still had plenty of battery.

I could use his phone if I needed to, but without my phone, I didn't have anyone's phone numbers.

There was no need to remember phone numbers when they were stored.

After we got back inside the cabin, Wyatt immediately started building a fire.

I grabbed my handbag and settled on the sofa.

While Wyatt built a fire, I wrote down three phone numbers. My father. My mother. And my sister, Madison.

Out of those three, one of them would answer. My other two sisters wouldn't be able to help me. I could call my brother Quinn if I needed to, since he was in charge of Skye Travels in Houston.

I wrote his number down just in case.

"Whatcha doing?" Wyatt asked, over his shoulder.

"Just writing down some phone numbers in case my cell phone dies."

"Good idea," he said, blowing at the little flame he had going.

"Do you need to write down anyone's numbers?" I asked.

"Nah. I can catch up after the storm's over."

"What about work?" I asked.

He shook his head. "No need. They can wait."

I thought his response was rather odd, but he'd told me he came from a small family and if work knew he was in a snowstorm, they probably wouldn't worry about him.

I almost envied him in a way. But only for a split second.

He seemed free to do whatever he wanted. I wondered what it would be like to not have obligations.

But I quickly decided that I didn't really want to know. Having family meant obligations.

And family was important to me.

The only way I could imagine not having obligations was to not have any family.

The thought made me sad. Sad for Wyatt.

He might have his own airplane and his own cabin in a valley in the mountains of Wyoming, but I wouldn't trade my family for any of those things.

Besides, having achievements like that would be hollow and meaningless without family to share them with.

I hadn't realized that Wyatt was standing in front of me, watching me.

"You okay?" He asked.

"Yeah. I was just thinking about my family."

I didn't tell him that I was also thinking about his family.

Or lack thereof.

He came and sat next to me on the sofa.

"Would you like a glass of wine?" he asked.

"Sounds good," I said.

Maybe a glass of wine would help me get my mind off worrying about things I couldn't do anything about.

44

WYATT

I had the fire roaring in the fireplace. I lit a couple of candles.

And Ainsley and I each had a glass of wine.

Under some circumstances, it would be considered the perfect romantic setting.

But Ainsley and I didn't have the foundation for a romance.

I didn't want her to think I was a blizzard romance.

Was that even a thing?

It should be a thing.

There were one night stands. There were spring break flings. There were summer romances.

Why wasn't there a name for a blizzard romance?

At any rate, even without a name to give it, I didn't want Ainsley to think that was all I wanted her for.

If I started coming on to her now, she would have no choice but to think that.

It's certainly what I would think if I were her.

So here we were in a perfectly romantic setting.

With no romance to speak of.

Beau was curled up on her bed. The dog had it made.

But I refused to be jealous of a dog.

I was pretty sure that it was getting colder.

If we were forced to used body heat to stay warm, would that count as a blizzard romance?

It didn't help that we didn't have a lot of conversation going at the moment.

Ainsley kept her cards close to her chest.

I appreciated that.

I liked being around a woman who could sometimes sit quietly and just think. Maybe think about nothing, but still, just take some time to think about that nothing.

But oddly enough, I was the one who felt the need to fill the quietness with conversation.

"If you weren't here?" I asked. "What would you be doing?"

The question seemed to surprise her.

"I guess it depends," she said. "I might be at work."

"But if you weren't at work," I said. "What do you think you might be doing?"

She shrugged and sipped her wine.

"I don't know. I might be visiting my family."

I settled back against the sofa, feeling better now that we had something of a conversation started.

"What's that like?" I asked. "Visiting your family?"

"What do you mean?"

"Well…" Maybe I shouldn't ask her things I wasn't willing to answer about myself.

"If I was visiting my parents in Florida, we'd sit on their balcony and watch the people on the beach below. My parents live on a beach, but they never walk on it. At least not when I'm there."

"That's kinda… different."

"Yeah," I said. "It's strange. And they don't drink anything other than water and juice."

"I see."

I didn't tell her that after my sister died, both of them went through several years of alcoholism.

They'd eventually worked their way out of it, but those years had left scars. Scars from both my sister's death and those years of alcoholism.

Thank god I'd never gone down that road.

If I had, I wouldn't be where I was today.

"So what do you talk about? Work?"

"Nah. I gave that up years ago."

She waited for me to explain.

"They tell me about their doctor's appointments. They talk about the neighbors. They ask me if I'm ever going to get married."

She nodded. "Are you?" She asked.

"Am I what?"

"Going to get married?" She asked with a little laugh.

"I haven't really thought about it," I said.

This conversation had not gone the way I'd intended. I'd just planned on making conversation. To get her to talk about herself, mostly.

Instead, she was delving into my private world.

Then she laughed. "You don't have to answer that. Why do people ask things like that anyway? They act like we have a crystal ball."

I took a deep breath of relief and slowly let it out.

"I don't know why they do it either," I said, talking a gulp of wine.

"Besides," Ainsley said. "It's something that just sort of happens. I don't think it's something that anyone can plan for."

"A lot of people plan on it. Especially after they date for awhile and get engaged."

She waved a hand. "I don't mean them. They don't count. I'm talking about people who aren't even in a relationship.

People will just ask, out of the blue, if we're ever going to get married."

"You're right," I said. "My parents do that. I don't know what they expect me to say."

"Maybe they think you're in a secret relationship that you aren't telling them about."

"I guess that could happen."

She smiled. "It happens all the time. But still. I don't think that's what they're asking. I think, not your parents, but other people… I think they seem to think that we've made a decision about whether or not we're ever going to get married."

"Is it something a person can predict?"

Ainsley held up her wine glass. "As the daughter of a psychologist, I can tell you with some authority that the answer to that question is unequivocally no."

"The daughter of a psychologist," I said. That was new information. "That must have been an interesting childhood."

"You have no idea," she said.

I shook my head. "No. I really can't. My parents were blue collar. They worked for the man their whole lives. Until they retired."

And that was something I had decided as young as a teenager that I was never going to do.

I think my parents still believed to this day that since I'd never held a "real" job, I was an unemployed loser.

I'd given up on trying to set them straight.

"At any rate," she said. "I guess bringing a girl home to them wouldn't be a good idea."

I laughed. "Probably not."

And I certainly wasn't going to tell Ainsley that she was the one I'd thought about taking home to meet the parents.

45

AINSLEY

$\mathcal{W}$yatt was a man of mystery.

He sat on the other end of the sofa, so we only had a couple of feet separating us.

But it seemed too far. I liked it better when we were close enough to hold hands.

Unfortunately he seemed content to sit at his end of the sofa.

He looked relaxed as he stared past me into the fire.

I sat with the heat at my back, my feet tucked beneath me.

Though I liked the heat at my back, I turned so that I could watch the flames, too.

Only now I couldn't see Wyatt.

Wyatt solved that, though, by getting up and kneeling in front of the fire.

It looked fine to me, but he took the poker and sent sparks flying.

I sipped my wine and watched him. Beau was on the foot of my bed, snoring.

Whoever got Beau would be getting a good dog.

Wyatt sat back on his heels and looked at me over his shoulder.

"What?" I asked.

"Nothing." Standing up, he replaced the poker. "Gonna get cold in here tonight."

I pulled the blanket tighter around me. I was wearing sweatpants, a t-shirt, and a sweatshirt.

"It's already cold," I said.

"Maybe we should go to the shelter," he said.

"There's a shelter?"

"Sure." He frowned. "I guess. Doesn't every town have a shelter?"

"I've never been in a shelter," I said. "We have generators."

"Yeah, me too."

But unfortunately we weren't always there to make use of them.

He pulled his phone out of his pocket.

"Do you still have a good charge?" I asked.

"Yeah, but I haven't been using my phone. I can find out if there's a shelter," he said. "I'm sure they'd have a generator."

The thought of packing up and going to a shelter didn't appeal to me. Besides, they might not take Beau.

"I like it here," I said.

He smiled. "Me too. But I'm not so sure how we're going to stay warm."

"We can sleep here. By the fire. We'll be okay."

He nodded and looked back into the fire.

"You're obviously from the south."

I bristled, just a little, though I didn't know why. Being from the south wasn't a bad thing. Especially since I was from Texas.

"What does that have to do with anything?"

"You don't hear about people freezing to death much down there."

I winced. "No. But people have a lot of heat strokes and children die in locked cars from the heat."

"Guess we don't have that so much up here in the mountains."

We sat quietly for a few minutes.

"So people really freeze to death in their homes?" I asked.

"Unfortunately more often than they should."

"Maybe we should go to the shelter," I said. Although going to a shelter didn't sound appealing, freezing to death sounded a whole lot worse.

"We have this fire," he said. "I think we'll be okay."

"You'll tell me if we're in danger?" I asked. "Right?"

I ran a hand over the little piece of paper I'd tucked in my pocket. It had all my important contacts on it. At least if I froze to death, the authorities would know who to contact. To let them know that I'd frozen to death.

"Of course I'll tell you," he said. "But a lot of people have found that body heat is the best way to stay warm."

I looked at him sideways.

"Yeah right. Isn't that just a myth?"

But he looked serious. "No. Not at all. Sometimes that's all people have. Sometimes they don't have a fire."

"Don't they both just freeze? Together?"

"I guess they could," he said. "But at least they'd be together."

"I don't know," I said, looking at him sideways. "Is that supposed to be romantic? Cause it's not working for me."

He laughed and came to sit down right next to me. Not on his side.

"Not really. But it actually does work. Haven't you ever tried it?"

"No," I said, frowning at him. "We just go inside."

"Well, when I was in high school, they made us kids go outside for recess in the dead of winter. And we had to be creative when it came to staying warm."

"Isn't that illegal or something? Sending children out in the cold?"

"Probably. But it was a small school and nobody ever said anything."

"I thought you were from Denver."

"I am," he said. "but I grew up just outside of Denver. In a little community. My parents commuted, but I went to school locally."

"Wow. That was a completely different experience than my high school years."

"I can only imagine."

"Did you even have a prom?"

"Nope," he said. "No prom."

"How did you survive high school without a prom? It sort of gives all the hard work purpose."

"Now look who's being romantic."

I just grinned at him. "I have my moments."

"I just survived. I made it until I went to college."

"Then did all the normal stuff?"

He hesitated. "For the most part."

I studied him differently now. In a new light.

Here was a man who owned his own jet. A very expensive jet. And lived in a very modern house.

How did a man get from growing up with blue collar parents who commuted into the city while leaving him to go to school in a one room schoolhouse get from there to here?

"You studied all the time, didn't you?" I asked.

He laughed. "You say that like there's something wrong with studying. Isn't that what college is for?"

"To some extent, sure. But..."

"Let me guess. You were a wild child."

"No," I said. "Actually I did study a lot. I had to live up to my family expectations. But I'd already done all my wild stuff in high school."

He sat back and finished his wine.

"Have you had your wild days?" I asked. I couldn't help it. I had to ask. He seemed so perfect. So gentlemanly. Too perfect.

He turned and looked me dead in the eyes, a little smile playing at the corner of his lips.

"Yes," he said. "I've sown my wild oats. You don't have to worry about that."

"I wasn't worried," I said, lying through my teeth. I was just curious.

But maybe worrying wasn't the right word exactly. Maybe I was asking out of selfishness.

I wanted to know if he was for real. Or if he was going to just see me as one of many conquests and forget about me.

If, of course, I let him get that close.

And if the way he was looking at me was any indication, well… I just might.

46

WYATT

I might have been something of a square in my younger days, but I could safely say that I was no longer a square.

And here I was trapped in the middle of a snowstorm with the most beautiful woman I'd ever laid eyes on.

And not only was she beautiful, she was hands down fascinating.

Everything I learned about her, just made me that much more intrigued by her.

I could just ask her outright questions that would solve a lot of the mystery surrounding her, but what was the fun in that?

I was enjoying the hell out of learning things about her as we spent time together.

There was no rush.

It was actually rather refreshing to not feel pressured to not have to compare resumes.

To just enjoy each other's company.

Ainsley made me feel young again.

Young, only better.

Because I knew so much more than I had back then.

I knew that it would be a shame to let this opportunity pass by without doing something about it.

It would be something I would regret. And I had enough regrets in my life.

I didn't need more.

"Do you think I could share your blanket?" I asked.

"Sure," she said. "Where's your blanket?"

"Beau has it."

She looked over toward the bed where Beau was curled up on our other blanket.

I hadn't left it there for him on purpose. Honest.

She lifted the end of her blanket and I scooted closer, wrapping it around both of us.

I immediately decided that this might have been a bad idea.

Now we were pressed against each other, thigh-to-thigh. Arm-to-arm.

Oh hell.

I had to put my arm around her—it was the only way to make the blanket work.

Now it was rib cage to rib cage.

She looked up at me. Maybe it was the firelight, but her eyes looked greener than they had earlier.

"I guess we can call this an experiment," she said. Though she was trying to sound flippant, I heard the little catch in her voice.

"I guess we can," I said, pulling her closer.

Now that I'd made the first move, things didn't seem so off-limits with her.

She smelled good. Like honeysuckle and vanilla.

"Are you warm enough?" I asked.

"I don't know," she said. "I think I could be warmer."

"Hmm." I nodded. "I think I can make that happen."

I picked her up and placed her on my lap.

She gasped, but didn't resist. Instead, she put her arms around me and rested her cheek on my shoulder.

"Better?" I asked.

"Perfect," she said.

Yep. Now I'd gone and done it.

Now that I had my hands on her, I was pretty sure I wasn't going to let go.

But I could be cool.

I rocked her gently.

Beau raised his head just enough so he could see us. Barked one time. And went back to sleep.

"I wish I knew what it meant when he does that," she said, her voice muffled against my sweatshirt.

"I think he's just giving his approval."

I felt her smile against me.

"My sister," she said. "And my mother would say that you're projecting."

"I don't project," I said.

"Everyone projects."

"I find it best to just put things out there in the open."

She shifted to look up at me with sheer skepticism.

"Is that so?"

"Yeah," I said. "Haven't you noticed?"

She laughed and settled back against me.

"Whatever you want to think."

"Hey, wait a minute," I said, looking down at her angelic face. "Are you a psychologist, too?"

"Not me," she said. "People aren't my thing. I prefer things that don't lie."

Things that don't lie.

So she wasn't in any kind of profession that required a lot of interaction with people.

What professions didn't require people? Researcher? Engineer?

It was almost like by narrowing things down, she'd increased the possibilities.

I'd just assumed she was a tourist or some kind of hospitality person.

Who else picked up dogs and carried them from one airport to another?

Animals.

Animals don't lie.

So she was either a veterinarian or a vet tech. Someone who worked with animals.

I decided to show my hand. Just a little. I needed to know if I was on the right track.

"Animals don't lie," I said.

"No," she murmured. "I guess they don't."

I smiled to myself. She was falling asleep right here in my arms.

I didn't mind. In fact, I liked it.

That meant she felt safe with me.

I didn't want her to sleep way over there in the bed.

At least, not unless I was with her.

I think sleeping here on the sofa was our best choice.

Sleeping here I could not only keep an eye on the fire, but we could use our body heat to supplement the warmth from the fireplace.

It was a perfect solution. Besides, I like holding her here in my lap.

I kissed the top of her head.

47

AINSLEY

*I*t was sometime in the middle of the night when I woke up.

It took me a minute to get my bearing, but I distinctly remembered falling asleep on the sofa.

And I was fairly certain that I'd fallen asleep in Wyatt's arms.

But I wasn't on the sofa anymore and I wasn't on the bed.

At least not exactly.

Wyatt had been busy.

The fire in the fireplace was blazing, sending out plenty of warmth.

In fact, it was almost too warm.

I leaned up on my elbow and looked around.

He'd brought the mattress over from the bed, along with what must have been all the blankets in the cabin.

Beau had moved over to the sofa and snored softly.

But I didn't see Wyatt.

I laid back and stared into the flames.

How had I possibly slept through all of this?

It must have been the cold.

I'd never given it much thought, but cold was as exhausting as heat.

The door opened and I sat up as Wyatt stepped inside, his arms loaded with firewood.

"You're awake," he said, dropping the wood into a bin next to the door.

"You've been outside," I said, sweeping my hair out of my eyes.

He took off his coat, shook off the snow, and went to sit on the edge of the mattress in front of the fireplace. He held out his hands.

"It's cold," he said, then turned his gaze to mine. "What do you think?"

"I think you've been busy," I said. "When do you sleep?"

He shrugged. "I don't sleep much. It takes up too much time."

Shivering, I pulled one of the blankets over my shoulders.

"I don't see how you survive without it."

He grinned. "It's how I squeeze more hours out of my days."

I nodded. I'd known people like him. People who were driven to succeed.

Most of them said the same thing.

Personally, I preferred to get my eight hours. Sometimes more.

"What do you do with all those extra hours?" I asked. "Besides rearranging furniture in cabins?"

He laughed.

"I'll show you sometime," he said. "But right now all I want to do is get warm."

He crawled under the blankets and pulled me into his arms.

I started to protest, but decided against it.

"So are you convinced yet?" He asked.

"Convinced about what?" Between being half asleep and being caught up in how good it felt to be in his arms, I wasn't doing much thinking, much less being convinced about anything one way or another.

"About the efficiency of body heat."

"Right," I said. "I don't know about warmth so much, but I am convinced that it promotes sleep."

"You really know how to pump up a guy's ego," he said, chuckling against my neck.

"I don't think your ego needs much help," I said.

"It's a good thing," he said, pulling me closer against him.

My back was pressed against him and for a guy who'd just come in out of the freezing cold, his hardness had recovered amazingly quickly.

His breath was warm against my neck as he kissed me.

"I thought you were cold," I said, but he was sending shivers up and down my spine.

"Not with you," he said, pressing a kiss to my cheek.

I wasn't supposed to be dating.

I surely wasn't supposed to be snugging up with a man I'd only just met.

But wasn't that what people did when they were snowed in?

But how many people got stranded with practical strangers?

Especially strangers as handsome and attractive as Wyatt?

I shifted just a little, turning toward him, at the same time he shifted me closer.

I was flat on my back now and he hovered over me. So close.

So close I could feel his breath against my lips.

My lips parted.

Any other guy would have already kissed me.

But not Wyatt.

He just gazed into my eyes, making me want to kiss him.

I tilted my head up just a little and closed my eyes.

If he wanted to kiss me, I was giving him every invitation.

48

WYATT

I was afraid to kiss Ainsley.

I was afraid that if I kissed her, I would never be able to stop.

She smelled so good. And her skin was soft as rose petals.

Her lips beckoned to me, practically begging to be kissed.

When she closed her eyes, her lips parted, I gave up.

I was no saint.

Never claimed to be.

Never aspired to be.

I pressed my lips against hers and savored the feel of them against mine.

There was no reason to rush.

We had all the time in the world.

The world—our world at least—was closed down for the indefinite future.

There was nothing we had to do except stay warm.

If body heat was going to keep us warm, then kissing her would produce even more heat.

I deepened the kiss and she trembled beneath me.

My cock responded immediately by straining against my pants.

Her lips were soft against mine.

As much as I wanted to ravage her body. To plunge my cock deep inside her, I wanted... needed to be gentle with her.

She wasn't someone to just love and move on from. The kind of girl that a man could fall in love with without even realizing it.

She wrapped her fingers in my hair, pulling me closer.

Her lips moved against mine, and I sucked on her bottom lip.

I groaned and swept my tongue across her lips.

Her lips parted and I plunged my tongue inside her mouth, sweeping against hers.

I cupped her cheeks with my palms.

The fire crackled in the fireplace, but we didn't need its warmth anymore.

We were creating a fire of our own.

I rubbed my cock against her, just for the sheer pleasure of it.

I didn't plan to do anything other than be an almost perfect gentleman.

But she moved her hips and parted her knees to bring us closer.

My God.

Her lips felt so good against mine.

Almost like we were made for each other.

Although it went against all my good intentions, I moved against her.

My cock nestled against the softness between her legs.

She ran her fingertips lightly along my back, sending shivers up and down my spine.

Our lips had molded together. Our tongues stroking.

I was distracted and didn't notice at first what she was doing.

She was moving against me, both of us wearing sweatpants.

The sweatpants weren't as thick as I'd expected.

The wetness had soaked through her pants and my pants, too.

Her wetness was soaking through to my cock.

She was so hot and sexy.

Being a gentleman with her was not easy.

I wanted to remove all the barriers between us.

Get her out of her sweatpants… her panties.

Just when I wasn't sure how much more of this I could handle, she leaned her head back and gasped.

I froze.

Did she just…?

Yes. She went all liquid and her hands fell to her side.

And her clit pulsed against me.

Holy hell.

I pulled her into my lap, wrapped my arms around her, and held her tightly while while she calmed.

No matter how much she tempted me, there was no way I was going to make love to a woman like this on a mattress in the floor in front of a fireplace.

She deserved so much better.

She deserved candlelight and roses and a lovely dinner.

Ainsley was a woman who deserved to be courted.

49

AINSLEY

*O*h. My. God.

      I had just come against Wyatt.

And we both had our clothes on.

Clothes that were wet now.

My body was content, but I was mortified.

We'd only been kissing and I'd gone and humped him.

I kept my face against his chest.

I couldn't bear to look at him.

What must he think of me?

When my blood started pumping at a normal rate and my brain cells started working again, I murmured against his chest.

"I apologize."

He shifted and tried to look at me, but I kept my face pressed against his chest.

"Apologize for what?"

Oh. No. He was not going to make me tell him.

Surely he knew. Didn't he? He'd held me like he knew.

"For... that."

"Oh, my love," he said. "Don't ever apologize for that."

My love.

My blood was racing again. But this time it was racing because he'd called me *my love.*

He'd inadvertently found one of my weak spots.

It was an endearment that I couldn't resist falling for.

I took a deep breath.

I couldn't keep my head buried forever.

He shifted and slid me off his lap.

"I'm going to get us some water," he said, kissing my cheek. "Don't go anywhere."

He was giving me time to get myself together.

Did Wyatt have any idea how rare he was? How much of a gentleman he was?

Most guys would have taken advantage of this situation, especially with me humping against his shaft.

Oh well.

Things would look brighter in the morning. They had to.

Because right now, I felt about as wanton as I'd ever felt.

I wasn't a virgin, but I'd only been with one other man.

And I'd dated him for a year before we'd gone all the way.

It had kind of been the beginning of the end of our relationship.

Turns out we'd been better off as friends after all.

But this thing that had happened with Wyatt was something I'd never had happen before with anyone.

I tried to think about what Madison would say about it.

Sure. She was my younger sister, but she was a trained psychologist.

She'd probably tell me to pretend it hadn't happened.

To just let it go.

That it was perfectly normal.

And that I worried too much.

And she would be right.

I laid down and stared into the fire.

In truth, it was hard to feel bad about something that had felt so good.

And anyway, I did like him.

Maybe it wasn't such a bad thing to be with a guy who could make me come just kissing me. Sure, I'd sort of humped his willie, but since he was a guy, he probably saw that as a compliment.

50

WYATT

When I woke, my arms were tangled up with Ainsley's.

And she was still asleep.

Something was different.

Something was vastly different.

It was warm.

I lifted my head enough that I could see the fireplace over Ainsley.

I'd neglected my job and the fire had gone out. There was nothing but ashes in the fireplace.

I put the back of my wrist against my forehead. I didn't have fever.

Then I heard it.

The heater kicked on.

It was warm in here because the electricity had come back on.

I laid my head back down and dealt with the disappointment.

I'd known we couldn't stay like this forever.

I'd just hoped we could stay like this for a little while longer.

A long while longer.

This meant the storm was on its way out of here.

And that meant that my days... hours... with Ainsley were limited.

I lay very still, careful not to wake her.

Life would be getting back to normal soon.

That didn't mean that I couldn't see her again.

Beau nuzzled my hand.

How long had it been since he'd been outside?

Too long, however long it was.

I carefully extricated myself from Ainsley's arms and got Beau leashed up and got myself wrapped up in my coat.

Stepping outside into the cold air was a quick way to wake up.

This was a good thing.

It wasn't snowing anymore. In fact, the sun was coming out.

The snow that had hit unexpected, was just as unexpectedly making its way out of here.

The electricity had been repaired. Now we didn't have to rely on the fireplace to keep us warm.

We could charge our cell phones and watch a movie.

We could do normal things.

Until the road cleared.

When the roads cleared, she'd find her way to the airport.

Maybe she'd let me fly her wherever to Houston or wherever she wanted to go.

I followed Beau down the sidewalk and back, not veering far from the cabin.

While Beau did his business, I took a deep cleansing breath.

Maybe the cafe would be open and I could get us coffee to start our day.

This thing with Ainsley could work.

I could make it work.

All I needed was to want it badly enough.

And I wanted her badly enough.

I wanted her more than I'd ever wanted anyone.

The problem with Ainsley was that I would never be able to get enough of her.

Still. There was no rush.

We could take our time.

51

AINSLEY

*W*hen I woke, I knew something was different.
Everything was different.

First of all, Wyatt wasn't here.

Neither was Beau, so I knew he'd taken Beau out for his morning walk.

The fire had gone out, but it wasn't cold anymore.

It was actually warm.

The heat was running.

The electricity had come back on.

I should be happy about this.

Shouldn't I?

As I always did when I woke up, I reached for my phone.

If anyone said they didn't check their phone when they woke up, I didn't believe them.

I had messages.

I checked the one from my mother first.

MOMMA: *Good morning, Ainsley.*

Momma always started off her texts like a phone message.

MOMMA: *When are you coming home?*

I scrolled up and back, but that was all she said. Her message had come in late last night after my phone had gone to do not disturb.

Then I checked Daddy's.

DADDY: *I think you should be able to fly tomorrow.*

I sat up, alert now.

His message had come in last night, too.

So this was tomorrow.

I looked out the window and blinked.

There was a hint of sunshine coming in through the window.

How long did it take ice to melt up here?

That was his only message, too.

Both he and Momma usually had more to say than that.

They were probably waiting on a response from me, but, of course, I had been… doing other things.

Other things that I would save to think about later.

My sister Madison had also texted. In fact, she had included me in a group text with our younger sisters.

MADISON: *Daddy has an appointment on Tuesday morning. I think we should all be there.*

A spurt of fear shot through me. I knew he had an appointment coming up, but with the storm and all I had forgotten that it was coming up so soon.

BRIANA: *I already have it on my calendar. I'll be there.*

WYNTER: *What time?*

MADISON: *10 I think. I'm flying in tomorrow.*

How had I missed all these messages?

If my sister was flying from Denver to Houston, this must be an important appointment.

BRIANA: *Want me to pick up you up from the airport?*

MADISON: *I'll get a car. Don't worry. I'll be there. Kade is flying me himself.*

Kade, Madison's fiancé, was a pilot. Of course he'd be flying her.

I quickly wrote back. Better late than never.

ME: *I have to see if the roads are open enough to get me to an airport.*

I waited, expected someone to write me back, but, of course, this conversation had started last night.

I was a little late.

Madison sent me private text.

MADISON: *Since you're stranded, Kade and I can swing by and pick you up.*

ME: *Not sure airport is open here.*

I saw Wyatt and Beau heading back toward the cabin.

I quickly checked the weather on my phone.

It was just over freezing outside.

There was no way Kade was going to be able to land an airplane here.

MADISON: *Kade just checked. The public airport isn't open, but if you can get to it, he has a private runway. Heated.*

A heated runway.

Wyatt has a heated runway.

I stared at the words. Then looked outside at Wyatt standing there, patiently holding the dog's leash.

Why had he not told me that he had a heated runway?

I took a deep breath. Forced myself to think logically.

Probably because the roads to his house weren't heated and we couldn't get there anyway to use the heated runway.

MADISON: *Ainsley?*

ME: *Yeah. Ok. Let me see if I can get there. The road have been impassable.*

MADISON: *We can be there just after lunch.*

Setting my phone down, I sat up. Checked the time.

Just after lunch didn't give me much time.

I was sort of a mess.

I needed a shower and I needed to put on travel clothes.
But most of all, I needed to talk to Wyatt.
He opened the door and he and Beau stepped inside.
He grinned at me.
I bit my lip.
"What's wrong?" He asked.

52

WYATT

*A*insley was absolutely beautiful sitting there on the mattress.

Her hair was tumbled and her cheeks were flushed.

But she looked worried.

I hadn't been gone that long. Had I?

I should have left her a note. It hadn't occurred to me that she'd think I'd abandoned her.

She was holding her phone. That was never a good sign.

Maybe it wasn't me that had her worried.

"Hi," I said, forcing a smile. "It stopped snowing."

"I know," she said, her brows remaining furrowed despite my attempt at levity. "We have electricity."

"I know," I said, closing the door. "It must have come on some time during the night."

Both of us had fallen sound asleep and hadn't even noticed.

"It's warming up," she said, glancing at her phone. "How are the roads?"

"I don't know. I haven't checked." I unhooked Beau's leash and he went straight for Ainsley.

She buried her face in his neck.

I was getting the feeling that my idea of us having all the time in the world wasn't holding.

Her phone chimed.

She glanced at it, then returned her gaze to mine.

"Do you think it would be okay if I took a shower?" She asked.

"Of course. You don't have to ask me that."

She just looked at me.

Of course she would ask. She was a guest.

"So would you do may a favor and check on the roads while I get cleaned up?" She asked.

"Of course."

There was an urgency in her voice that I hadn't expected and I certainly didn't like it.

She gathered up her clothes and headed for the shower.

"I'm gonna make coffee," I said.

"Okay," she said. But I had a feeling she didn't really care one way or another.

Something had definitely happened while I was out.

I measured coffee into the coffee maker and checked for creamer in the refrigerator.

I sniffed it and decided it was okay. At least I had that going for me.

While the coffee brewed, I went back out to the main room.

I didn't check the forecast or the road conditions or anything else.

Instead, I just sat on the sofa and scratched Beau's ears.

In her hurry to get to the shower, she'd left her things strewn across the bed.

Her handbag was lying open and there was an envelope sticking out of it.

I was not one to pry. I'd barely asked Ainsley anything personal at all.

And I certainly didn't snoop.

Beau barked one time.

That reminded me that I needed to check on Beau. To find out who he belonged to and offer to buy him.

So it wouldn't be prying to check for papers on Beau.

It would be helping.

And I wanted it to be a surprise.

So I would be doing a good thing by checking for Beau's papers.

The water in the shower was running now.

"Don't judge me," I said to Beau. "I'm doing it for you."

Beau didn't answer.

I walked casually over to the bed.

All the clothes she'd bought at the General Store, except the ones she'd worn yesterday and last night, were tossed here and there on the bed.

Her oversized handbag was Louis Vuitton. Understated, so I hadn't recognized the brand.

Listening for the shower and feeling like some kind of lowlife, I pulled out the envelope.

It wasn't an envelope at all. It was a folded piece of paper.

I walked to the window and carefully unfolded it.

Beau's name was there along with the name and address of someone in Houston.

Using my iPhone, I took a quick photo of the paper.

Then quickly refolded the paper and slipped it back into her handbag like I'd found it.

I went back to the sofa and opened up my photos.

I carefully read the document.

Beau was a Chinook, a rare dog breed.

I looked at Beau. "Did you know about this?" The dog just cocked his ears at me.

Feeling like I was missing something, I read the document again.

It was a contract to have Beau picked up in Aspen and flown to Houston.

The airline was Skye Travels. I'd heard of it. It had been started by Noah Worthington and grown into an empire.

That was about all I knew about it.

Flying was just a hobby for me. A way to get around to and from my own different offices.

At the bottom was a signature.

Ainsley Worthington.

Pilot.

53

AINSLEY

The hot water running over my head felt absolutely wonderful.

It seemed like it was the first time I'd actually been warm in days.

I had mixed feelings.

On the one hand I was ready to get out of here and get home to Houston.

I wanted to be there when Daddy went back to the doctor for his one month check up.

I *needed* to be there. My family supported each other with absolutely no reservations.

But on the other hand, I wasn't ready to leave Wyatt.

I'd given up my moratorium for him.

Besides, I liked him.

I liked him a lot.

I wanted to get to know him better.

To spend more time with him.

I wanted to walk to the store and get ice cream again.

But this time wasn't real.

It was like a summer romance.

A fleeting thing in a winter wonderland setting.

Maybe that's why Daddy called the snow at his Colorado cabin a winter wonderland. Because he was there with Momma—the love of his life.

I froze with a handful of conditioner.

Wyatt wasn't the love of my life.

He was just a guy.

A guy I was crushing on.

I coated my hair in conditioner.

I needed to focus on my job.

My job was to get Beau to his new owners in Houston.

I wondered if my brother Quinn had called to tell them why we were delayed.

I was sure he did. My brother may have some shortcomings, but he was good at running the Houston office of Skye Travels.

He was good with people. And very responsible.

And if he hadn't called the new owners, I was sure they'd called him.

Beau was a rare breed of dog.

I hadn't even known that I was a dog person until I'd spent some time with Beau.

I was going to miss Beau, even though he wasn't mine to miss.

He'd added to the magic of my snowstorm romance.

I rinsed out the conditioner and stepped out of the shower.

I'd gotten close to both Beau and Wyatt.

Too close.

Now I had to figure out how to pull away from both of them.

I had to get Beau to Houston and leave Wyatt here.

But first I needed to get a ride to Wyatt's heated runaway.

I didn't know what I was going to do if the roads were still impassable.

Madison didn't appear to be taking no for an answer.

She'd sent me two more texts while I was in the shower.

MADISON: *Have you found out anything yet?*

MADISON: *Kade's filing our flight plan. Let me know asap.*

I stared at the phone. This was the easiest way for me to get out of here.

If Wyatt didn't want to drive me, I could hire a car. Surely someone in this town would be willing to drive me to the airport.

Or even better, maybe I should just go to the regular airport and not Kade's. Without him being home, his runway was probably frozen over anyway.

MADISON: *I just called and checked. The roads are clear enough in town.*

Clear enough. That wasn't very comforting.

Who did she call anyway? When Madison got something in her head, she did not let it go.

Enough was enough already.

ME: *I'll be at the local airport.*

MADISON: *Great. We'll see you at about 1:15.*

Great.

I'd walk if I had to.

Madison could be a pain in the butt sometimes.

It was easier to just be there than to argue with her.

Now all I had to do was to deal with Wyatt.

54

WYATT

*A*fter her shower, Ainsley looked refreshed, but she was wearing her travel clothes.

I was sitting on the sofa with Beau when she came out.

I still hadn't convinced myself that I'd read that paper correctly.

And I definitely learned my lesson.

I vowed that this would be my one and only time at snooping into someone else's business.

"Did you get a chance to check on the roads?" she asked, heading straight for the bed.

She immediately tucked the folded piece of paper down in her handbag.

"Not yet," I said. "But there are cars on the road so I guess that means they're passable."

She nodded. "Okay." She stacked all the clothes she'd bought at the General Store into a pile and shoved them aside.

Then she came over and sat on the sofa, with Beau between us.

She tapped her phone, then glanced over at me.

"Something's come up," she said, keeping her gaze on the cold hearth. She looked so calm. Like nothing had changed.

But everything had changed.

"Anything I can help with?" I asked, trying to ignore the stab in my heart.

"No," she said with a little smile. "My sister's coming to pick me up."

Her sister. Of course. I'd been fooling myself to think that she really needed me. Now that the storm had cleared, she could be on her way. Just like nothing had ever happened.

"Flying in?" I asked, even though I already knew the answer.

"I just have to be at the airport at 1:00."

And just like that our little rendezvous was over.

I'd been looking forward to spending the day with her. Maybe getting ice cream again.

But now it seemed pointless.

What was the point of dragging out the inevitable?

"I should get home, too," I said.

"Oh," she looked at me then, allowing her gaze to settle on mine.

Her eyes looked heavy.

But this couldn't be avoided.

And since it couldn't be avoided, I intended to rip off the band-aid in one fell swoop.

Standing up, I put my wallet and keys in my pocket.

I really didn't have anything else here.

I rubbed Beau's neck. "See 'ya big guy," I said.

Then I looked at Ainsley, still flushed from her shower.

That, I decided, was how I would choose to remember her.

Bending over, I put a hand on her cheek and planted a kiss on her lips.

Then I turned and walked straight out the door without so much as looking back.

I couldn't be mad at her. I hadn't asked her what her occupation was.

Or even what her last name was.

The fact that was one of Noah Worthington's daughters shouldn't have changed anything.

According to my quick Google search, she was one the heiresses to Noah's fortune.

Whether or not she worked for her father, I didn't know.

And it didn't matter.

At least that's what I told myself.

But it did matter.

And though I couldn't explain why, it changed everything.

Even though I didn't want it to, it changed the way I saw her.

I hadn't told her who I was either.

It should not matter.

I shouldn't be mad at her.

But I was.

But even worse than being mad, was the pain that stabbed like a dagger into my heart.

I couldn't see straight, much less think. I just needed to get away from here.

55

AINSLEY

*W*yatt walked straight out the door, closing it calmly behind him, without so much as a glance back.

What the hell just happened?

I'd simply been gone for a few minutes to take a shower.

Everything had been going along just fine until I came out.

All I'd asked him to do was to check to see if the roads were open.

I pressed my fingertips to my lips.

Damn it.

I could still feel his lips on mine.

Why was it that I always went for the jerks?

It seemed like it happened every single time.

Every. Single. Time.

A guy would start out charming and all that.

Then at the flip of a minute, he'd turn into a jerk.

I crossed my arms as anger swept over me.

Beau barked once.

Then, just like it always did, my anger turned right into sadness and the tears ran down my cheeks.

I didn't even try to stop them.

I sat down hard on the sofa, wrapped my arms around Beau, and soaked his fur with my tears.

I tried to sort out what had happened.

What had changed so quickly.

Why had he kissed me before walking out the door?

I was so utterly baffled.

My tears spent, I sat back on the couch and stared at the closed door.

All I could figure was that I was a weekend diversion.

He was just a spoiled rich kid that got everything he wanted.

Then when he was finished playing with it… or it broke… which in my case was leaving, he just tossed it away without a glance back.

It certainly didn't put him in a favorable light.

But it didn't make me look good either since I was the one who'd fallen hook, line, and sinker for him.

Well. That did it.

I was done.

No more men in my life.

Maybe I'd become a nun.

Did they let nuns fly airplanes.

With a groan of frustration, I got up and went to the bathroom to wash my face.

I hated that my face was blotchy now from crying my eyes out.

By the time Madison landed at the airport, I should look normal again.

Maybe.

But only if I didn't burst into tears again.

I needed to get out of this cabin.

Get some fresh air.

I put Beau's leash on him, tossed my handbag over my

shoulder, and leaving a tip and a stack of unworn clothes on the dresser, I stepped outside into the brisk air.

I would just walk to the damn airport.

I clicked open my phone, found an address, and mapped it out.

Well, as much as I wanted to, I wasn't going to be walking to the airport.

It was seven miles away.

I quickly discovered that there were no Ubers in this town.

So I put my dark sunshades on, walked to the General Store and Cafe, ordered a coffee, and sat down at one of the outdoor tables.

I caught myself scanning the dozen or so people sitting at other tables or walking past, looking around for any sign of Wyatt.

Then I shook myself. Wyatt was not coming back.

Beau sat beside me.

He was a handsome dog with kind eyes. Reaching over, I scratched his ears.

"What have I done, Beau?" I asked.

He barked once and licked my hand. I patted my knee and he put his front legs on my lap.

I buried my face in his fur and told myself I would *not* cry again.

I was pretty sure we looked about as out of place as any woman with a dog could.

But that was the least of my problems.

I'd gone and done it again.

I'd fallen in love with Wyatt.

PART II

56

AINSLEY

The following Spring

THANK heavens Madison had chosen spring for her wedding and not summer as she'd originally planned.

The Houston heat was far too brutal, especially since she had an outdoor reception planned.

No one in their right mind would plan an outdoor reception in Houston in the middle of the summer.

Personally, if I were the one getting married, I would have done everything indoors.

The wind was going to destroy everyone's hair.

But it wasn't my wedding.

Thank God.

This morning, the day of my younger sister's wedding, she and I sat at a little restaurant near our apartment in River Oaks.

It was just the two of us for breakfast.

Madison had done that on purpose. She'd breakfast

yesterday with our youngest sister Wynter, lunch with Brianna, and dinner last night with Momma and Daddy.

We had all been together two nights ago, but it was impossible to have meaningful and intimate conversations in such a large group.

I sipped my mimosa and watched as people crowded into the restaurant.

"Ainsley?" Madison said, getting my attention. "You seem like you're a thousand miles away."

"Sorry," I said, turning my attention back to my sister.

Considering that today was her wedding day, she seemed to have herself amazingly under control.

But then she had a stylist to do her hair, a girl to do her make up, someone to help her get into her gorgeous wedding dress, and a photographer to follow her around documenting every detail.

Elopement sounded a whole lot better to me than all this.

But. Again. Not my wedding.

"You're sitting next to one of Kade's college buddies at the reception," Madison said.

"Okay." I really didn't care who I sat by.

"He's Kade's best man."

"Makes sense, I said with a shrug. "Since I'm your maid of honor."

I was just ready for this whole weekend to be over with so I could go back to flying.

It wasn't that I minded spending three days with my sisters and mother. My half-sister Danielle and her mother had flown in from California and all-in-all, it had been enjoyable, especially the day at the spa.

I hadn't felt so relaxed in…forever.

But today carried an undertone of stress, no matter how much everyone seemed to be trying to ignore it.

Madison swirled her mimosa glass and leaned forward.

"Are you okay?"

"Of course," I said quickly, hiding behind my own glass.

"It's just…" Madison was giving me her worried sister look. "You haven't been the same since you came from Wyoming."

I shrugged and set down my glass.

The server, a perky college student with a big smile, stopped at our table and put a plate of eggs Benedict in front of each of us.

"If I eat all of this," Madison said. "I can forget fitting into my wedding dress."

"Much less that little red dress you're wearing to your reception."

I took a bite of eggs and hoped that my psychologist sister would let the subject drop.

The last thing I wanted to do was to make this breakfast about me.

"There's nothing wrong with my red dress," she said.

I grinned. "Didn't say there was."

"You're just jealous," she said. "Because I'm getting married before you."

I scoffed. "Please. That's the last thing I'm worried about. Besides," I said with a shrug. "We all knew that you and Kade were going to be married."

"Is that so?"

"Sure. Just took the two of you some time to figure it out."

"You're forgetting about all the years when we lost touch."

"Minor details," I said.

Madison set down her fork. She never ate much at the time, especially not when she was nervous.

And today was definitely her day to be nervous if ever there was one.

Madison and Kade had met in high school and from all accounts, it had been love at first sight.

But then graduate school had sent them on their separate

ways. It was years later, seven, I think, when Kade had been hired as a pilot for Skye Travels by our younger brother.

It had all been rather convenient.

They'd made it all look so easy.

When everyone knew that finding that special someone was never that easy.

"So…" Madison said. "When are you going to tell me what happened in Wyoming?"

57

WYATT

I parallel parked in a spot at the Skye House, a bar across the street from Skye Travels.

"Are you sure Noah Worthington doesn't own this building, too?" I asked.

"I'm sure," Kade said. "But I bet he kicks himself every day for it."

I laughed.

"I can only imagine. They go so well together."

"And not the name," Kade said. "They both have their eyes focused on customer service."

Anytime Kade talked about his wife or even the Worthington family, his voice held such pride.

It must be something to feel such a sense of belonging to something.

Hell, sometimes I didn't even feel that kind of belonging with my own company.

Too scattered.

But Noah had planes scattered around the country.

Of course, his was a little different.

If he had a good pilot who wanted to live someplace else, he'd put a plane there.

As far as I knew, his main offices, though, were in Dallas and Houston.

We got out of the BMW sedan and walked inside the bar.

The lunch crowd filled most of the tables. Mostly pilots and a few passengers. What looked like a lot of airline staff people.

"Are you sure you want to have a drink on your wedding day?"

Kade rolled his eyes at me.

"The wedding isn't until five. What else are we going to do?" He opened the door and I followed.

"I could take you up in my Phenom."

"And that's supposed to make me feel better how?"

I laughed.

"You'd get to experience a moment of the good life."

We took a table, one of the few left, by the front window.

A server was there immediately.

"What can I get you?"

"I'll have a martini," I said. "With Grey Goose."

"Very good," the server said with a quick nod in Kade's direction before he turned.

"What?" I asked, "you don't get to order?"

Kade waved a hand dismissively.

"He knows what I like."

"Ah."

The place didn't have the look of an exclusive club.

Maybe it was exclusive just for certain people.

"Actually," Kade said, before I got around to asking him about it. "I don't think my life could get much better."

"Man," I said. "You are a besotted groom."

He laughed.

"Besotted. That's me."

The server returned with my martini and a crown on the rocks for Kade.

"Just wait," Kade said, running his thumb over the rim of the glass, his expression serious. "Just wait until you meet the right one. Then you won't be so quick to make light."

I held up my glass for a toast.

"To besottedness," I said.

As our glasses clinked together and the smooth Grey Goose made its way down my throat, I had nothing else to say.

I couldn't... wouldn't... tell my good friend that I had already found the right one. And then I'd quite simply walked away from her.

Just like I had good sense.

When it turns out, I had absolutely no sense at all.

58

AINSLEY

*L*ater, at the Cathedral, my sister was surrounded by our other sisters, my mother, a makeup artist, a hair stylist, and a photographer, finally having all the attention on her as it should be today.

Her day.

I had dodged my sister questions by deftly turning the conversation back to her. But by the time we made it to the Cathedral, I was exhausted from all that deflecting.

It would have been immensely easier to just tell her that I had met the man of my dreams, fallen in love, then the guy had literally walked out on me.

The whole thing had been so completely surreal that I hadn't spoken to another soul about it.

It was something I preferred to keep to myself.

I was not proud of it.

I had been so adamant that I could stay away from men. A moratorium according to my own words. And then I'd fallen head over heels for a stranger.

My half-sister, Danielle Johnson, sat down beside me.

She handed one of the two glasses of champagne she held to me.

"You look like you could use this," she said.

"How did you know?" I asked with a smile.

Danielle just shrugged. "Sister's intuition."

Danielle was about twenty-five years older than me.

A product of Daddy's very young first family.

I'd always like Danielle. She was a beautiful, creative woman who seemed like the girl next door.

She always had a smile. She was probably one of the happiest people I knew.

"So," she said, placing one hand on the velvet bench behind her. "When will it be your turn?"

I rolled my eyes. "No thank you."

Danielle sipped her champagne.

"Yeah? That doesn't sound like the Ainsley I used to know."

"Well…" I swirled my drink, watching the bubbles. "I'm on a moratorium."

"Is that so?" Danielle asked. "That is so very interesting." She stared past Madison and all the activity.

"What's so interesting about it?" I asked, curious now.

Danielle grinned. "We are so sisters."

I couldn't help but to smile back.

"Tell me why you say that," I said.

"I guess weddings bring these things out."

"Danielle," I said. "What?"

"I went on a moratorium once," she said.

"Really? I thought I was the only one."

"Oh no," Danielle said. "I've been there. Done that."

"But you're so happily married to Samuel."

"Exactly," she said. "That's when I met Samuel."

"You did not," I said.

Danielle nodded.

"You met Samuel while you were on a moratorium."

"Yep. And that's what I called it, too. A moratorium."

"Wow," I said, under my breath.

It was really strange that years ago, before I was even born, my half sister had done the same thing I'd done.

The only difference was the Danielle's moratorium had turned out right.

Her moratorium had a happy ending.

Mine had turned into heartbreak.

But today wasn't the day for me to be worrying about myself.

Today was Madison's day.

And I refused to dwell on something that was over and done with.

59

WYATT

$\mathcal{I}$ stood at the front of the Cathedral with one of, if not my best, friends.

There was small orchestra playing soothing music softly in the background.

The Cathedral was bathed in red rose petals and red candles.

It gave the church a surprisingly elegant look.

Kade was wearing a black tuxedo with a crimson tie.

My tuxedo was charcoal gray. My tie was a slightly less crimson color.

Not pink, but more like a light rose color.

It was like Kade was supposed to stand out in the darker, crisper colors, while his best man and groomsmen faded ever so slightly into the background.

It was an interesting concept.

But I wasn't sure Kade even so much as noticed.

He was so happy about getting married to the woman he'd loved since before I'd even met him.

I almost felt like I knew Madison as much as I knew Kade, even though I had never actually met her.

After Kade and Madison went their separate ways, I was the one he talked to about Madison.

And I felt a little guilty because I'd encouraged him to move on.

If you aren't going to at least call her, then you have to meet other girls.

It had taken the better part of a year until he'd finally agreed.

But it had been a while since I'd seen Kade.

Other than a flight training a couple of years ago, we'd barely stayed in touch.

But that's how guys were. We could go our separate ways and still be best friends years later.

Kade and I had that kind of bond that didn't break. We just picked up where we left off.

"You have the rings?" Kade asked.

"Of course, I do," I said.

That's when I saw the first sign of anxiety in Kade.

"It's all going to be fine," I said.

"I know," Kade said. "Thanks for being here."

"Wouldn't miss it for the world," I said. "This damn wedding was supposed to have happened years ago."

Kade looked at me blankly.

"I'm going to remind you of that one day," he said.

"Remind me of what?"

"Remind me that you were an ass-hole on my wedding day."

I laughed. "If I ever do let the girl of my dreams slip away, I hope you do point out to me that I'm an idiot."

The wedding music started and everyone went quiet.

The music sent an unexpected shiver up my spine.

The flower girl, a youngster I didn't recognize first, came down the aisle first, tossing even more fresh red rose petals into the air.

The girl was obviously enjoying her moment in the spotlight, bringing a moment of laughter in her wake.

Then the bridesmaids began to walk one by one down the aisle.

I hadn't met Madison's sisters, so, of course, I didn't recognize those she'd chosen as bridesmaids.

Kade had told me that they were all her sisters. And one half-sister.

Their dresses were surprisingly elegant, all in red.

Madison had a done a nice job with the wedding.

I watched Kade as he waited for his bride.

I was here for him. Not to admire his bride's sisters.

Then the music changed and everyone stood up.

Madison stood at the back of the church, a veil over her face. A lovely White mermaid dress that stood out perfectly from all the red dresses her ladies wore.

I'd never seen Kade look so proud as he did in that moment.

And I couldn't have been more happier for him.

As my eyes wandered between Kade and his bride, my gaze snagged on Madison's maid of honor.

The girl who walked in just before her.

I watched her as she walked up and stood directly across from me.

I'd always believe that it was a testament to my self-control that I kept my expression blank. Or as blank as could be expected from a man in total shock.

And why I hadn't put these two things together before now would forever be a mystery.

The maid of honor was Ainsley Worthington.

The girl I knew as Ainsley W.

60

AINSLEY

I had been in something of a daze as I walked down the aisle before my little sister.

It was a surreal moment for me.

One that I was honored to be such a big part of.

Madison could have chosen any of her sisters to be her maid of honor, but she'd chosen me.

I even liked the dress. Which meant that my sister had put a whole lot of thought into choosing something that even I would like.

I'd watched Kade as I walked toward the front of the Cathedral. He was so besotted with my sister, I was almost embarrassed for him.

Almost. Mostly I found it adorable.

I took my place at the front of the church.

I hadn't paid nearly enough attention to Madison's wedding plans as I probably should have, especially since I was the maid of honor. But she had a wedding planner for that.

I could be a follower when I needed to be. And imposing myself on my sister's wedding vision was not my style.

I turned my attention to my sister.

And watched her as she walked down the aisle on Daddy's arm.

The sight brought tears to my eyes.

Daddy was a handsome, successful man and I couldn't begin to put words to how proud and fortunate I was to be his daughter.

He looked good. Looked to be in good health and good spirits.

The treatment he'd undergone had seemed to leave him even better than he'd been before if that was possible.

I watched as he gave my sister's hand to Kade.

Kade would take care of her.

Not that she needed taking care of. She could take care of herself.

But still. It would be nice to have a man back there who could step up and take charge if need be.

Kade was that man.

He knew when to let my sister do her thing and when she needed someone to lean on.

She'd needed that someone to lean on these past few month with Daddy's treatments.

And he'd done his share of leaning on her with his own mother's dementia.

As things got started, I looked around.

With my gaze wandering past the bride and groom, I was in the direct line of sight of Kade's best man.

I blinked, bringing myself out of my own thoughts.

No.

That wasn't even possible.

I would have heard.

But hadn't I just admonished myself for not being involved enough in the planning stages.

Madison hadn't shared all the details because she knew I really didn't have all that much interest.

Like Daddy, I just preferred to spend my time in the cockpit of a plane. Especially after what had happened in Wyoming.

Flying had been my refuge from the world.

But standing right there in front of me.

Right there next to Kade Johnson, obviously as Kade's best man, was Wyatt.

Wyatt.

The man who had walked out on me in Wyoming.

The very same man who had sent my life into a tailspin.

And he had obviously recognized me.

His gaze locked onto mine and did not let go.

61

WYATT

If I ever let the girl of my dreams slip out of my fingers, please point out to me that I'm an idiot.

My own words stuck in my head like a bad song.

Ainsley Worthington was everything I remembered. And more.

She had been perfect for me.

We'd been perfect together.

Yet, in one of my worst moments of idiocy, I'd quite simply walked out on her.

I'd left her stranded in a strange place.

And for no reason other than being thrown off guard by the fact that she wasn't who I thought she was.

I'd invented an identity for her in my head and it had been wrong.

What I'd done was inexcusable.

And I admit that after I'd had time to think through everything, I had looked for her.

But I had hit a dead end while searching for someone named Ainsley W.

Even knowing she was from Houston hadn't helped.

But then I hadn't searched all that deep. It had felt wrong.

Especially when I was fairly certain that even if I did find her, she wouldn't want to talk to me.

I wouldn't have wanted to talk to me if I'd been in her shoes.

But here she was standing right in front of me.

The girl who had kept me warm in my dreams through the winter.

She was wearing a slinky red dress that showed off her curves. Curves I knew intimately.

Apparently Madison was secure enough that she didn't have to put her bridesmaids in ugly poofy dresses to make sure she was the most beautiful woman there today.

And Madison was beautiful.

But Ainsley was drop-dead gorgeous.

The moment I saw Ainsley, there were no other women in the church more beautiful. Not for me.

While the priest walked the bride and groom through the ceremony, I kept my gaze locked on Ainsley and she did the same.

She watched her sister when they said their vows, but then her gaze came back to mine.

I swallowed a smile.

I felt almost drunk on relief at finding her again.

And I knew better.

Ainsley did not look happy to see me.

In fact, I couldn't tell what she was thinking.

But if I had to guess, I'd put my money on her being angry with me.

I didn't blame her.

Not one little bit.

In fact, if we weren't standing almost face to face in the middle of her sister's wedding, I could only imagine her reaction.

She could have turned and walked away.

She could slap me across the face.

She could tell me to go fuck myself.

The weird thing was that she had the time it took her sister to get married to figure out which reaction she wanted to go with.

"The rings? Wyatt?"

I pulled the rings out of my pocket and handed them over.

And I realized that not once during the entire wedding had I taken my eyes off Ainsley.

62

AINSLEY

*W*yatt kept my gaze pinned to his.

I could barely keep up with the range of thoughts and emotions that flashed through me at seeing him.

I couldn't react.

Not in the middle of my sister's wedding.

So I didn't know how I would have reacted if we hadn't been standing next to Madison and Kade at the alter.

I do know that I wouldn't have spent the better part of half an hour having a silent stare off with him.

I hadn't expected to ever see him again.

Not that I couldn't have.

I had the distinct advantage.

I knew almost everything about him.

I knew where he lived. The plane he flew.

All the important things about him while he knew nothing about me other than my first name.

I could have shown up on his doorstep.

But there was no way I was going to do that.

He didn't know I was a pilot.

He did know I was from Houston, but Houston has millions of people.

It didn't matter.

After the way he walked out on me without an explanation, he would have no reason to track me down.

It was clear that he wanted nothing else to do with me.

And I would be an idiot to care.

Of course, I had cared.

And the whole thing had solidified my moratorium.

I was still considering the whole nun thing.

It was a little drastic though, considering how much I liked men.

I honestly didn't think that my moratorium would last forever.

I couldn't see that happening.

No. Not forever.

And now that Wyatt was standing in front of me, my body was reminding me just how much I liked men.

And that Wyatt was one of those men that I liked.

I remembered the way his lips felt on mine.

I remembered the way his hands felt on my skin.

I remembered everything about our time together in the cabin during the snowstorm.

And while my sister got married, I relived every single moment of it.

Especially that last night we'd spent together on the mattress in front of the fireplace.

That was not something a girl could easily forget.

But Wyatt had forgotten.

And even if he hadn't forgotten, he'd certainly made it clear that he wanted nothing more to do with me after that night.

I'd spent far too much brain power trying to figure out what happened.

I'd delivered the dog to the address as I'd been hired to do.

And I'd put Wyatt solidly out of my head.

I'd tossed him out of my head about a million times since that day last winter.

But now.

Tonight.

I just needed to get through this wedding and get as far away from him as I could.

I wasn't even going to admonish my sister for not telling me that Wyatt was Kade's best man.

Not today.

Maybe when she came back from her honeymoon.

No, I decided. I wasn't even going to do that.

I was just going to let him crawl back to whatever hole he'd been living in for the last few months.

I didn't have any more time to give a man who would just walk out on me like that.

He couldn't be trusted.

But, my God, he was handsome.

Unfortunately, this forced proximity was almost too much.

As much as I told myself that being near him was a bad idea, there was no way I could get away from him.

I was forced to stand here and look at him.

Well, maybe not *forced* to look at him.

I should probably be watching my sister get married.

But since I was here and he was right there, I looked at him.

It was impossible not to look at the most handsome man in the room.

Especially when he was looking at me like he wanted to eat me up.

What girl could resist being looked at like that?

Even if he was the one who'd broken my heart.

It was his loss, after all.

And he was the one looking at me.

I was just looking back.

That's all.

Nothing to worry about.

"You may now kiss the bride."

When the priest said those words, all I could do was think about kissing Wyatt.

I would have to watch the video of my sister's wedding.

Cause right now I had other things to focus on.

We were about to be set free and I needed to plot my escape plan.

Away from Wyatt.

I needed to walk away from him.

Even though every cell in my body was pulling me toward him.

Then the wedding was over.

I smiled and hugged my sister. Did everything the way I was supposed to do it.

Then I slipped away from the crowded church.

Ducked into the restroom and sat on a velvet sofa.

I frowned at my reflection. I barely even looked like myself.

With my hair

What was I supposed to do?

How was I supposed to be here—present—for my sister's wedding, when all I could think about was Wyatt?

My heart and my brain waged a battle.

My brain told me that a logical, self-sufficient woman would stay away from Wyatt.

Find another man to talk to.

After all, weren't weddings known for being hooking up breeding grounds?

This was a big wedding. There were plenty of people here that I'd never met.

But my heart was skipping around like a schoolgirl on her first crush.

It was fate.

I'd fallen for Wyatt. And here he was. What were the odds?

Wyatt had kept his gaze on mine for the *entire* wedding.

I knew because I'd only looked away from him once.

He hadn't known how to find me.

I was certain of that much and my heart chalked it up as a valid excuse.

Why did my head have to be such a hard-ass?

And why did I have to give it so much control?

63

WYATT

*A*insley managed to avoid me during the entire picture-taking event.

I admired her skill in avoidance.

Of course, the photographer and his assistant were ruthless in their organizational skills.

Then Ainsley disappeared and I didn't see her again until the reception.

Madison and Kade, looking happy as clams, took their seats at the front of the room.

Finding the seat with my name on the little place card, I took my seat and sat quietly, but my insides were coiled and alert as I watched for Ainsley.

Like the ceremony, she had to be here, but unlike the ceremony, there was nothing to keep us from talking to each other.

Except for her, of course.

I wouldn't blame her for not talking to me.

I had been a fool.

But surely even a fool deserved a second chance.

I wrapped my fingers around the stem of the champagne glass and twirled it as I watched the door.

The seats were filling quickly.

In fact, the only empty seat around me was the one to my left.

Surely not.

I'd been so focused on watching for Ainsley, I hadn't even looked at the place card at the seat next to me.

Reaching across, I nudged the place card around.

Ainsley.

I ran a hand through my hair.

Surely, Ainsley didn't hate me so much that she'd miss her own sister's reception because I was here.

I couldn't allow that to happen.

I would move. I didn't have to leave, but I could sit or stand someplace else.

I drained the glass of champagne and slid the flute, with my name engraved on it, across the table, out of the way.

I was about to slide my chair back and stand up, when I saw her coming toward me.

Taking a deep breath, I sat back as she made her way toward me.

Her red dress seemed brighter than the other bridesmaids. Maybe it was intentional because she was the maid of honor.

Or maybe it was because she was the one wearing it.

Ainsley, for me at least, lit up the room, bringing it to life.

Walking straight to her seat, she obviously knew where she was sitting ahead of time.

She sat, turning just enough that to indicate that she didn't want to acknowledge my presence.

"Thought you were going to miss it," someone said.

"There was a problem," she said vaguely.

"I hope it's all sorted out."

Ainsley smiled. "Of course."

Then there was a toast.

Ainsley lifted her glass and as she did, her gaze brushed mine.

Her flushed cheeks brought back all sorts of memories of what I thought of as *that night.*

My God, she was beautiful.

Her green eyes blazed with passion as her gaze met mine.

I would have put money on that passion being a whole lot different from the kind of passion I was thinking of.

Her particular passion at the moment was anger.

A smart man would wait and bide his time.

And although I'd been known to do some stupid things, Ainsley a case in point, I considered myself smart enough to know that this was that time to wait.

64

AINSLEY

*T*here had been a slight hiccup with the catering. Something that probably would have sorted itself out.

But I'd jumped at the opportunity to avoid the reception for a few minutes and to give myself a distraction from thinking about Wyatt.

It had helped to clear my head.

After having a thirty minute staring contest with Wyatt, then actively avoiding him during the picture taking, I was rather drained.

But it wasn't nearly over.

The reception would be going into the night.

There was no way I was going to avoid talking to Wyatt for much longer.

As I stood there at the wedding, I'd had time to put things together.

Madison had told me that I'd be sitting by the best man.

Probably would have helped if I'd bothered to ask her who exactly the best man was.

At the time, I didn't think it mattered so much.

Turns out it did matter much.

Since I wasn't one to avoid problems, I decided to get it over with.

Keeping what I hoped was a blank expression on my face, I turned and looked at him.

My breath hitched a little, seeing him so close. Close enough to touch.

If I leaned in just a little...

"Nice wedding," he said.

Wedding. Right.

I started to say something snarky. Like ask him how he knew since he'd been looking at me the whole time.

But I bit my tongue.

"Very," I said. "But I'd expect nothing less from my sister."

"She's a lovely bride," he said, his gaze still on mine.

I picked up my champagne glass and took a sip.

"How do you know Kade?"

"We were best friends when he was in flight school and I was in graduate school."

Graduate school.

Wyatt had gone to graduate school.

Wow. There were so many things I didn't know about him.

"That was a long time ago," I said. "So you stayed in touch, I guess."

"Not really," he said, with a shrug. "It's a guy thing."

"I know," I said, with a little smile. "You can talk to each other once a year and still be best friends."

Just one of the many things I knew from working in a man's world.

"Right," he said, looking at me as though he was trying to figure something out.

I glanced over at my sister, but she was engrossed in a conversation with her new husband.

"You're wondering how I know this about guys."

"Not really," he said. "I actually think I have a good idea how you know."

"You think you know," I said, sweeping a strand of hair behind an ear.

Geez. I was actually flirting with this guy. And I'd told myself I wasn't even going to talk to him.

But he didn't seem to notice.

He picked up a pretzel stick, snapped it in half, and took a bite.

"Let's see…" he said. "You work around a lot of guys."

His statement caught me completely off guard.

Then I realized that he had no doubt been talking to Kade.

I blew out a breath.

Of course, by now, he'd know I was a pilot.

"That's right," I said.

He slid another pretzel out of one of the tall glasses in the center of the table.

"These are good," he said. "You should have one."

There was something seriously messed up about Wyatt.

He was acting like he'd done nothing wrong.

Like he hadn't kissed me on the lips and walked away from the cabin we'd shared during a snowstorm.

Like it was ok to not give me an explanation for happened all those months ago.

And I wasn't going to give him the satisfaction of knowing that I cared.

Because I didn't care.

As soon as this wedding was over, I'd never have to see this man again.

65

WYATT

I owed Ainsley an explanation and an apology.

It was surprising that she was even talking to me.

That she was flirting with me like what had happened last fall didn't bother her in the least.

If it didn't bother her, then I had no reason for it to bother me.

As least not as far as she knew.

Ainsley was absolutely stunning and I could not stop looking at her.

Kade had really done me an injustice. He should have gotten back with Madison years ago and introduced me to Madison's sister.

I could only imagine how different my life could have been if I'd met Ainsley under different circumstances.

A circumstance where I didn't behave like an ass.

She took the pretzel stick I offered her and set it on her saucer.

Then she turned her attention back to the new bride and groom as the toasts started.

I would just sit back and bide my time.

If Ainsley wasn't worried about what had happened during our time together and the way I'd left her, then all I had to do was to move on past it and move forward.

And moving forward was what I was planning on doing.

I had never given much thought to fate.

But finding Ainsley here like this... The sister of my best friend's new wife was too random for me to believe it hadn't happened for a reason.

I was a brand new believer in fate.

When the toasts were finished and we were left to have our own conversations again, Ainsley held a conversation with the guy on her right.

I didn't listen.

I sipped my champagne and ate another pretzel stick.

And bided my time.

Finally she glanced in my direction.

"So," I said. "Do you hear anything from Beau?"

She looked at me sideways and made a face. "The dog?"

But I'd caught the flash of sadness that she quickly hid with that nonchalant expression.

"Yes," I said. "The dog."

"I got him to his new home," she said. "I assume he's happy."

"So you didn't check in on him?"

"Of course not," she said. "That wouldn't be appropriate."

I just shrugged and let it drop.

The lights dimmed and the music started.

That's when Madison's father, Noah Worthington, led his daughter out onto the dance floor.

I had to admit that Noah was a dashing man. Larger than life.

But with a reputation like his, I would have expected nothing less.

I glanced over at Ainsley and forgot whatever I had been going to say.

She sat straight as a statue, one hand in her lap, the other gripping the edge of the table.

Her eyes were moist and if she so much as blinked, tears would go streaming down her cheeks.

Something inside me broke into a thousand pieces.

I put a hand over hers.

At first, she didn't seem to notice, then I felt her hand relax just a little beneath mine.

I laced my fingers with hers and squeezed.

She looked down.

I wondered if maybe I should have left her alone. To let her have this moment.

But the pain on her beautiful face had been more than I could bear.

I wanted to pull her into my arms.

To comfort her and soothe away whatever it was that was breaking her heart.

And I knew right then.

I knew that I never wanted to see that kind of pain on her face again.

And there was no way in hell that I would ever be the one to cause her pain again.

66

AINSLEY

I wasn't one of those teary-eyed girls who cried at weddings.

It wasn't because I didn't have a romantic spirit. I did.

I had such a romantic spirit that I had to take occasional breaks from anything romance. Okay... maybe this time, since it was over a year, was more than a break, even if I had a little snowstorm romance in there. Did that count?

I just didn't think weddings were sad. Weddings were happy. Like a first kiss on the top of a Ferris wheel with the Autumn wind blowing against the skin.

This wedding was happy, too, of course, especially since it was my sister.

But seeing her on the dance floor, wearing her white wedding dress, with our father triggered a deep sadness.

The last year had been one of the worst in my life.

Daddy had been diagnosed with prostate cancer and underwent a round of chemo.

Subsequent tests had indicated that he was in the clear, but he had to go back for more testing every month at first, then every two months, and now he was going every three months.

Every time he had an appointment, my sisters and I were there. That was actually the reason I had to leave Wyoming so quickly. To make it in time for Daddy's check up.

I still couldn't believe that I had gotten so caught up in Wyatt's world, that I'd nearly forgotten Daddy's appointment.

Daddy's brush with prostate cancer had me questioning so much about my life.

Mostly, it had me realizing that my parents were getting older and weren't always going to be there.

That frightened me to the core.

To the world, Noah Worthington was an unstoppable, successful business man.

To me, he was the linchpin of our family.

I quite simply couldn't imagine a world without him in it.

His cancer had shaken me to the core.

Seeing him out there dancing with Madison at her wedding should have been a happy thing.

But instead, it triggered the fear and heartbreak of knowing that parents would be gone one day.

And that even if Daddy was one of the best pilots out there, he was not immune to getting sick.

I had to face the possibility that he might not be around to dance at my wedding.

He'd been at Danielle's wedding, of course, but that was before my time.

And now Madison.

But he had three other daughters to marry off.

Three other daughters that needed him to dance at their weddings.

And if I, being the most feminist of all his daughters, thought that way, that first wedding dance must be a deeply rooted tradition, indeed.

I was surprised at the strong reaction.

It was much like the reaction I'd had when I'd learned about the cancer diagnosis.

I'd dealt with it and had gotten my emotions in check. Or so I'd thought.

Wyatt's fingers laced with mine steadied me again.

And that small gesture smoothed away what was left of the hurt I'd been nursing.

Even if he had deserted me for some unknown reason, I stood by my belief that he was a good and honorable man.

And he had gone out of his way to keep me from being kicked out of the airport and stranded in Aspen.

He'd taken me into his home.

I would never forget that.

I bit my lip, took a deep breath, and closed my eyes.

Tonight was supposed to be a happy time.

Not a time to think about hurtful possibilities in the future.

I had plenty of time to think about those things. That was a good and bad thing about being a pilot. There was plenty of time to just think.

Determined to make the most out of the happy occasion of my sister's wedding, I turned to Wyatt and smiled.

67

WYATT

When I woke up this morning, I never would have predicted that I'd be dancing with Ainsley by evening.

But with the lights dim, the music celebratory, Ainsley in my arms, I was in bliss.

She was stunningly perfect.

She had one hand lightly on my shoulder and I had a hand on her waist while our other hands were clasped together.

It was all perfectly proper.

A dozen other couples danced all around us. Her sister and Kade included.

Noah danced with his wife, Savannah.

We were surrounded by Worthingtons. It couldn't be anything other than proper.

Then the music changed. Turned soft and romantic.

I lightened my touch on Ainsley's waist, just a little, then changed my mind.

Ah, what the hell.

I tightened my hold on her waist. She smelled so good. Like honeysuckle and vanilla. And something else I couldn't identify. But all three combined sent all my blood straight to my cock.

That intoxicating scent and that tight red dress made me hard as a rock.

When she laid her cheek on my chest, I lost any ability to think straight that I might have had.

She fit perfectly against me.

Looking over her shoulder, I could see the groom. Kade was not only my best friend, he was now Ainsley's brother-in-law.

I looked to my left and caught a glimpse of Quinn sitting at one of the tables.

But, most troubling, was Noah Worthington—Ainsley's father—on the dance floor with us.

I attempted, half-heartedly, to keep her at arm's length.

But Ainsley seemed to have other ideas.

She leaned closer and her soft breasts pressed against my chest.

My hand slipped across the silky material of her red dress and splayed across her back, bringing us even closer.

No one seemed to be paying us any mind. The attention was on the bride and groom. And, of course, as the night went on, people were starting to focus on themselves.

The champagne was flowing and most everyone was getting a little more relaxed.

Everyone except for me.

I was getting more and more tense.

Having a hard-on for a man's daughter right there in front of him was always contraindicated. Hell, even Wyatt, who'd just married one of the man's daughters wouldn't dare do anything to let Noah know what he was thinking about doing later.

I guided her as far away from the center of the dance floor as I could. It took a few minutes as I didn't want to do anything to draw attention to us.

But in the shadows just off the edge of the dance floor on the opposite side from the little orchestra, I could relax.

Ainsley, apparently, had the same reaction.

Releasing my hand, she slid her arms around my neck and pressed her body against mine.

Oh no. This was not a good idea.

But I was helpless against her charms.

She was the siren calling out to me and I was the hapless sailor on other side of the rocks.

A sailor with any sanity would stay away from the rocks. Ignore the siren. But I was bewitched and could not step away.

We swayed with the music.

And somehow during the next slow song she began to move against my rock hard cock.

Her fingers laced in my hair, I was helpless.

I did have enough sanity left to keep an eye over her shoulder should anyone notice us dancing like we were in a seedy bar and not at the posh wedding reception of a billionaire's daughter.

I wanted to kiss her more than I wanted to breath, but at the same time, I didn't dare neglect my watch.

I could just imagine Noah grabbing me by the ear and tossing me out the door.

And the worst part wouldn't be the humiliation, it would be not being able to see Ainsley.

The way she was moving against me was most distracting.

And it remind me of that night in Wyoming.

She was grinding her hips against mine.

Then she gasped and I felt her whole body shudder against mine.

Did she... just...?

Right here. Right in the same room with her family. Her sisters. Her brother. Her father.

Heaven help us both.

68

AINSLEY

Oh. My. God.

Soft romantic music filling the room.

The lights were low.

I was ensconced in Wyatt's arms.

He'd maneuvered us to the edge of the dance floor away from prying eyes.

Not that anyone was paying attention to us.

So much for being mad at him and keeping my distance.

And so much for any semblance of my moratorium.

I could have tried to use the excuse of being at my sister's wedding.

But there was no point in trying to pretend anymore.

I had justified my way around what happened in Wyoming.

I'd been away from home. Away from family.

Stranded in a snow storm.

But here I was. With the same guy. In my world. Literally right in the middle of my family.

No snowstorm to use as an excuse.

And right now my knees were weak.

Weak because I'd just had an orgasm against the swollen hardness that pressed against me as we danced.

Fortunately, his strong arms keep me from falling to the floor.

I was mortified.

Maybe he hadn't noticed.

But he stood there, swaying to the music, keeping me firmly pressed against him until I could breathe again.

He knew. He knew I'd just orgasmed against him.

I didn't think I could every look Wyatt in the eyes again.

But when some of the strength returned to my bones, he took my hand and led me back to our table.

He held the chair while I melted into it.

I kept my head down, wondering if I could just crawl under the table.

Or maybe...

I suddenly had a brilliant flash of insight.

Now I knew.

Now I knew the real reason Cinderella fled the ball. It didn't have anything to do with the stroke of Midnight.

If dancing with the prince was anything like dancing with Wyatt, then I understood perfectly well why she'd had to flee.

Maybe I should do as Cinderella had done and just flee the scene.

"I'll be right back," Wyatt said, leaning close.

I nodded, still unable to look him in the eyes.

I picked up the cell phone I'd left on the table and checked my messages.

Blinking, I read the message again.

I glanced in Wyatt's direction. He was halfway across the room.

Now was my chance.

And I had a legitimate excuse.

My sister would be slipping out soon.
No one would miss me.
I grabbed my phone and took off toward the door.
No one would even notice that I'd left.

69

WYATT

I stood in the restroom and tossed cold water over my face.

There was most definitely something going on with me and Ainsley.

I'd never expected to see her again, much less this.

We had some kind of magnetic attraction that was undeniable.

Even right here surrounded by her family, we couldn't keep ourselves apart.

I never should have let it go that far.

So much for being the perfect gentleman.

I respected Ainsley too much for letting this happen.

Yet it had happened anyway.

I think the only thing to do was to have an adult conversation with her.

And then I would take her on a real date.

Not a date for ice cream. But a dinner date. To a real restaurant.

It was long overdue.

We needed to get to know each other. To see if we had enough common ground to stand on. To support the physical attraction that we were having.

At least that's what I told myself.

Maybe that didn't matter.

The greatest love affairs in history were based on what Ainsley and I had.

I dried my face with one of the fresh white towels from the counter and decided that I was overthinking.

I should let things be what they were going to be.

Feeling more centered, I stepped back out into the reception area.

The music had stopped and the orchestra players were packing away their instruments. A sure sign that the party was coming to an end.

Kade and Madison were getting ready to leave.

Ainsley would need to be a part of that.

But she wasn't in her chair.

And I didn't see her anywhere.

I took a seat. I'd just wait for her to come back.

A server swept by and handed me a glass of champagne.

I twirled it in my hand, then set it aside. I needed my wits about me when Ainsley came back.

Kade nodded as his bride grabbed his hand and pulled him toward a group of people standing near the door.

I smiled and nodded back.

Still no sign of Ainsley.

Noah sat down next to me.

I straightened, my nerves going on alert.

Not every day a girl orgasmed right there on the dance floor at a wedding reception.

With her family not nearly far enough away.

"Mr. Worthington," I said.

"Noah." He looked calm. Relaxed. "You must be Wyatt."

"Yes," I said, not sure what was about to come off.

"Kade speaks highly of you."

"Kade's a good man," I said. "We go way back."

"That's what he said."

Noah stretched out his long legs and looked in the direction of his wife.

They had a legendary romance. A second chance love affair that had actually worked out.

I told myself to relax. Noah wasn't about to wring my neck. He didn't know about Ainsley and our little… episode on the dance floor.

His wife was talking with their daughter, the new bride, so he just needed a place to light for a few minutes.

And a man didn't became a legend like Noah Worthington by staying to himself.

"Kade tells me you do some flying," Noah said.

"I dabble in it a bit."

Noah laughed. "Somehow owning a Phenom seems a bit more than dabbling to me."

I laughed and ran a hand across my chin.

"I know," I said. "It was just such a beautiful plane. I knew when I saw it that I had to have it."

Noah nodded. "I understand. I've bought a few planes based off that feeling."

"It's crazy, huh?"

"It always works out. So tell me, Wyatt, what is it you do that allows you to buy an airplane like that? Especially for someone just dabbling."

It was a rather personal question and unlike most people, Noah didn't try to hide his intent to find out exactly what I did to earn so much money."

"I own my own company," I said. "I design video games."

"That sounds intriguing. Maybe we can have lunch and you can tell me more about it."

"Absolutely," I said with relief, knowing that would never happen. I lived on the other side of the country.

Noah was merely being polite.

Kade and Madison were leaving now.

Their path to the door was paved with confetti.

Madison spotted her father and stopped by his table, Kade in tow.

"Daddy," she said, her eyes moist as she hugged him.

I looked away, but I heard Noah say something, but I couldn't make out the words. Thankfully. I didn't want to hear what Noah told his daughter in this special moment between them.

That was much too private.

And I already had too much going on with his other daughter.

Then in a whirlwind, Madison and Kade left.

Without them, the reception hall seemed empty and lifeless.

It was time to go.

I still didn't know where Ainsley had gotten off to and I didn't have a way to contact her.

No one seemed concerned that she wasn't there and I wasn't about to ask.

"Nice to meet you," Noah said as he stood up. "There is one thing I'd like know, though, before I go."

"Sure," I said and stood up, too. If Ainsley wasn't coming back, I certainly had no reason to hang around.

"Was the airplane a one-time thing or do you make it a point to acquire everything that you take a liking to?"

The floor could have dropped out from under me and I would have been no less stunned than I was by Noah's question.

He was all but asking me about my intentions with his daughter.

And I'd thought that Ainsley and I had done a good enough job of keeping our attraction a secret.

Apparently good enough didn't hold water for Noah Worthington.

70

AINSLEY

I took an Uber back to my apartment.

Sitting in the back seat, I sent a message to my mother and sister, pleading a headache and exhaustion.

And that wasn't a lie. I was exhausted and I did have a headache.

It had been a long day.

One of the longest I could remember.

But Madison was married and happy.

It was done.

Life could go back to normal now.

But that wasn't the reason I'd fled the scene.

I'd had to leave.

I was utterly mortified.

I had pressed my body against Wyatt's to the point of having an orgasm.

Right there on the dance floor of my sister's wedding reception.

My parents had been right there on the dance floor, for God's sake.

Who did that?

It wasn't normal.

I could only imagine Madison's reaction if I told her.

She'd just look at me as though I'd lost my ever-loving mind.

And apparently, she would not be far off base.

I was supposed to be mad at Wyatt for ditching me in Wyoming.

Not that it had been a date or anything. But still, the way he'd left was inexcusable.

Of course, I'd had a lot of time to think.

And from my perspective, I could see where he could think I was the one who'd run off.

Maybe he'd been planning to come back, but had gotten distracted.

Then by the time he came back to the cabin, I was gone.

Maybe.

It was a possibility.

I had to give him the benefit of the doubt.

And at any rate, it was over.

And even if I'd wanted to be mad at him, my body had other ideas.

My body liked him.

A lot.

Too much.

After my experience in Wyoming with Wyatt, I should have learned to keep my distance.

But the dance floor had been so intoxicating. And he'd felt so good with his arms around me.

Besides. It wasn't all my fault.

What kind of man brought a hard on like that to his best friend's wedding?

I couldn't take all the blame for it when he'd been right there. All hard and pressed against me.

But unfortunately I did take all the mortification.

There was no way around that.

I was the one who'd had the orgasm.

I went through the front lobby of my high rise apartment complex, greeted the concierge with a wave, and darted toward the elevator.

I had a private elevator, but since I'd taken an Uber, I just used the main elevator.

While I was here, I stopped by the mail room and picked up two or maybe three day's worth of mail.

It felt odd, doing such mundane things when I'd just been at my sister's wedding.

Dancing with a man I hadn't seen in months and didn't expect to ever see again. Unless, of course, I went to him.

And that wasn't going to happen.

Despite my behavior on the dance floor, I was not what Momma would call a forward woman.

I'd learned enough about the male psyche from my psychologist mother and psychologist sister to know that relationships only worked if the male was the pursuer.

Pursuit was hardwired into their brain. They couldn't help it.

And I'd seen it play out over and over in other people's relationships. I'd never seen a male go after a woman who was pursing him.

And working in the male world of aviation, I had an up close and personal view of that happening all the time.

Women were attracted to men in uniforms—in this case pilots—and often openly pursued them. Or if they didn't openly pursue them, they made themselves available.

The only time I saw men truly interested was when the women didn't seem to give a care about them.

Especially as the men got older.

Sometimes younger men were amenable to having women pursue them, but as they got older, something switched.

Now once a man was older, it changed again and a man might show some interest in an aggressive female.

I laughed at myself as I tossed my mail on the little table just inside my front door and stepped out of my shoes.

It was funny how I seemed to know so much about men, yet I didn't have one in my life.

Unless I could count Wyatt. Which I didn't.

Wyatt and I had been in forced proximity now. Twice. And each time I'd been the one to orgasm for him.

Geez.

I berated myself all the way into my bathroom, got undressed, and slipped into my pajamas.

The best thing for me to do was to just bury myself beneath my blankets and hope that it all went away by morning.

I took my cell phone and climbed into bed.

Things always looked better in the morning, right?

I set my phone on my charger and settled into bed.

Just as I closed my eyes, my phone chimed, indicating a text message.

Thinking it was Madison giving me a hard time about not being there to see her off or Mother worrying about me. Making sure I made it home ok, I reached over and glanced at the phone.

The message from a number I didn't recognize.

307-555-3534: *Didn't get a chance to say good night... So good night.*

My heart raced and I sat up, grabbing the phone off the charger.

Area code 307. Where was that?

I did a quick good search.

Wyoming.

Had Wyatt somehow gotten my phone number?

I sat up, my blood racing through my veins.

I just stared at the message.

Then after a few minutes, it occurred to me that it wasn't going to answer itself.

ME: Good night.

I waited. Watched as the little bubbles came up, indicating another message. But then they stopped.

So that was it?

He wasn't going to write back?

After going to the trouble to get my phone number, all he had to say was good night?

So much for getting any sleep.

71

WYATT

I sat on the edge of my bed in the hotel room and stared at the little napkin with a number scrawled across it.

I replayed my conversation with Noah.

After basically asking my intentions, he'd leaned forward, picked up a napkin, and pulled a pen out of his jacket pocket.

He'd scrawled the number across the napkin and slid it across the table toward me.

"If you like my daughter," he said. "Do *not* do what I did. Don't make her wait and wonder."

I picked up the napkin, but didn't look away as Noah continued to speak.

"Not everyone gets a second chance like I got with Savannah."

He sat back then and ran a hand through his hair.

"My God. I have so many regrets about those lost years. Years I could have spent with her. I wasted them on a life I didn't belong in."

I didn't know what to say. THE Noah Worthington was telling me personal things I shouldn't know.

I held the napkin in my hands.

"Thank you," I said.

Noah shook his head. "Don't thank me." He nodded toward the napkin in my hands.

"That number gives you a choice I didn't have. Decide what you want to do. Then do it."

"Yes sir," I said, still not sure what I was supposed to say to him. His gaze on mine was intense.

I had a feeling that I did not want to tangle with this man.

"You'll make the right decision," he said, then with a quick clap on the back, he left me standing there.

So I'd put the number in my phone. A phone number I'd wanted for some time.

409-753-7593.

But since her father was the one who'd given it to me, it held more importance than it might otherwise have held.

Maybe.

I was intrigued by Ainsley.

So it probably wouldn't have mattered where I got her phone number.

I still wouldn't have known what to say to her.

It was kind of odd that she didn't ask who I was.

Maybe she recognized the area code.

Whatever the reason, I took heart in the fact that she had responded at all.

She could have easily just blocked my number and that would have been that.

That was part of the reason why I'd gone ahead and texted her. To give her the chance to block me and get it over with.

But no matter what, her father's words echoed in my head.

That number gives you a choice I didn't have.

He was right.

I might not have had a choice before this wedding, but now,

not only knowing who Ainsley was and holding her phone number in my hand, I most definitely had a choice.

And I already knew what I would choose.

72

AINSLEY

I had to be at the airport the next morning.

I had a passenger to drop off in New Orleans.

An easy flight.

And the the passenger was a businessman who'd flown with me several times. His name was Mark Miller and he was a good-looking man in his mid-thirties, maybe early forties. He never asked for anything special.

Of course, the flight was short and he was on business, so there wasn't much he could possibly need.

I had a feeling that he just wanted to get there and get back.

I had to wait for him. It was usually a couple of hours. Sometimes three.

Usually just long enough for me to grab some lunch.

But today he broke routine.

"Mind if I sit up front?" He asked as he stepped inside the plane.

It wasn't a request I got very often, but it certainly wasn't out of the ordinary.

"Of course not," I said. "Glad to have the company."

I wasn't sure that was entirely true, but it wasn't like we'd be able to talk much anyway after takeoff.

After we got harnessed in and cleared to prepare for takeoff, Mark struck up a conversation.

"Any idea when you might start flying for your Father?"

The question caught me off-guard.

Most of the time I forgot that my father was well known in the community. Not just the aviation community, but he was well-known in some circles of Houston.

"I don't know," I said. "I haven't spoken to him about it lately."

"Well, don't wait too long," he said.

"What do you mean by that?" I asked, checking the computers.

"Nothing really," he said. "I've been flying with you for what? A couple of years."

I nodded. That was about right.

Mark grinned. "I've watched you grow into a top-notch pilot. One of the best if you ask me."

I checked gauges and got confirmation for takeoff.

"That's a very kind thing for you to say."

"Wouldn't say it if it wasn't true," he said.

I put Mark out of my mind as we left the ground and achieved ground effect.

Airborne. That was my favorite part of flying. That first feeling of being off the ground.

After we were in the air and had a straight shot for New Orleans, I relaxed a bit.

Mark started talking again.

"If Noah isn't going to hire you on at Skye Travels, I'd like to hire you on for my company."

I watched him out of the corner of my eyes.

"I didn't realize your company needed a pilot."

"We do," he said. "We have someone flying out at least two

or three times a week. I'm the only one who flies private. Our accountant ran the numbers. Suggested we'd be better off buying a small aircraft and contracting pilots."

"Wow," I said. "That's an unexpected offer."

He shrugged and sat back.

"Just think about it," he said, pulling his sunglasses over his eyes and settling back for the flight.

Just what I needed. Another thing to think about.

I had my father to think about. And Wyatt.

And now I had a job offer.

I really didn't want to work for anyone.

My father had given me this little plane the day I'd graduated with a degree in aviation.

And I understood why he hadn't hired me yet.

He required a minimum number of flight hours and I just didn't have that yet.

I would though and when I did, I didn't anticipate any problem going to work for Skye Travels.

But I'd be giving up a chunk of my freedom to do that.

It would be more flying and more business than I was getting right now, but my schedule would be made by someone else.

And that was my barometer. If someone else was setting my schedule, I was doing something wrong.

Setting my own schedule was the most important thing to me about working.

Sure, I made concessions for passengers all the time, but if wanted a day to do something else, I just didn't schedule anything for that day.

I already knew what I was going to tell Mark.

But the offer was kind. And I appreciated it.

It was actually what I needed today.

An affirmation that I was doing at least one thing right.

I hadn't heard back from Wyatt last night since that quick good night message.

And I'd been obsessively checking my phone since.

That annoyed me just a little.

I was annoyed that he'd given me a reason to check my phone and I was annoyed that he hadn't written back anymore.

Maybe it was his way of saying good-bye.

It was more than I'd gotten last time.

Last time I'd gotten a kiss though.

And, I reminded myself with a blush, this time I'd gotten an orgasm.

It definitely made Madison's wedding something I would never ever forget.

Even if I didn't see Wyatt again, I had a vivid memory of that dance we'd shared.

That wasn't something a girl could ever forget.

73

WYATT

*T*he best thing about owning my own company was that I had complete control over my own schedule.

I'd planned on flying out this morning. After the wedding.

But after reconnecting with Ainsley, I decided to stick around.

I hadn't texted her again.

I wasn't sure what I would say to her.

I really wanted to see her in person.

So I got an Uber and headed up to the airport.

If there was one place to find a girl like Ainsley, it would be the airport.

And besides, I needed to check on my airplane.

At least that's what I told myself as I got out of the Uber and walked toward the hangar where my airplane was housed.

I'd already called, so they knew not to expect me today, after all.

As I finished up a quick inspection, someone came up behind me.

"Nice plane," Ainsley said.

Just the sound of her voice sent my blood racing through my veins.

She was wearing her uniform, including a little hat, and she looked like she'd gotten a good night's sleep.

I was glad she had because I certainly hadn't slept much.

I'd lain awake for what seemed like hours trying to figure out how to approach her without coming across as a stalker.

I didn't say anything. Just put my hands in my pockets and waited to see what she would do.

"Heading back to Wyoming?" She asked, keeping her expression blank.

"Not yet," I said. "There's something I wanted to do here first."

"You got Kade married off," she said with a little smile. "What else could you possibly need to do in Houston?"

"Well," I said. "There's a girl I know who happens to live here. I thought I might look her up."

She nodded. "That could go either way."

I grinned. "I'm hoping it goes well, actually."

She shrugged.

"Want to take the Phenom out for a spin?" I asked.

Her eyes widened.

"Maybe."

"You can drive."

"I'm not trained on the Phenom," she said.

Good to know that she took her job seriously.

"You could copilot."

I knew that look on her face.

Ainsley was a true pilot.

And I knew that there was no way she was going to be able to resist.

Unless she already had something scheduled.

"That is, if you're not on your way to another flight."

"I'm just getting back," she said.

"Already?"

She shrugged. "It was an early flight and it got cut short."

"I see. Then it sounds like you're available. If you're up to it."

"Where do want to go?" She asked, still looking at me suspiciously.

"The sky's the limit."

She seemed to consider.

"Let me make a quick phone call." She pulled her phone out of her pocket and walked out of my hearing range.

While she was on the phone, I walked around the plane again, double-checking everything. If I was going to have Ainsley on board, I couldn't take any chances of anything going wrong.

A few minutes later, she came back.

"I'm all good to go," she said.

I felt like a teenage boy who'd just gotten the girl to say yes to the Friday night dance.

"All right, then," I said, keeping my voice even.

We climbed aboard and I stashed her bag.

I kept everything I needed on the plane, so I didn't need a bag.

"Have you decided where we're going?" I asked as we harness up.

"Surprise me," she said.

74

AINSLEY

I didn't consider myself to be a spontaneous person. And everyone in my family would agree.

To just hop on an airplane with no place to go, leaving the destination up to someone else was not at all in my nature.

But it was nice to just sit back and let someone else make the decisions.

Besides, it was a beautiful day for flying. Not a cloud in the sky.

And the Phenom handled like a dream.

Daddy was definitely going to have to get one of these.

I didn't know our final destination, but I did know that we were traveling north east.

It was interesting to try and figure it out while I let Wyatt handle the airplane.

I'd had my taste, now I wanted to just ride in peace.

I closed my eyes to the gentle sway of the airplane.

It wasn't until I felt the wheels touch down on the ground that woke up.

It was an odd feeling to wake up on an airplane and not know where I was.

I did not sleep on airplanes.

But apparently today I did.

"Where are we?" I asked as the plane came to a stop.

Where were in the middle of nowhere.

The airport was a simple strip. Trees all around.

Wherever we were, the Phenom must have barely rated for this runway.

Someone riding a horse and buggy came forward and sat waiting for us.

Wyatt turned to me and grinned.

"Welcome to Mackinac Island."

"Mackinac Island?"

The only thing I knew about Mackinac Island was that Daddy housed a plane up here.

And it was definitely up here.

It was amazing how quickly the Phenom had gotten us to the northernmost part of Michigan.

"Our chariot awaits," he said.

We gathered up our things and Wyatt lowered the steps.

As he secured the plane, I pulled out my phone and made a quick Google search.

Mackinac Island allowed no cars. None.

And it was where the movie *Somewhere in Time* had been filmed. I distinctly remembered that there were cars on the island in that movie.

So apparently they occasionally made exceptions.

After we climbed into the wagon, the driver draped a blanket over our laps.

"It's still cold up here on the island," he said. "But it's wonderful romantic weather for a young couple."

Then he climbed into his own seat and we headed away from the airport.

He thought we were a couple. And Wyatt hadn't corrected him.

Of course, I hadn't either.

But I was the one who was out of my element.

"How many times have you been here?" I asked.

He put an arm around my back and pulled me toward him.

"It's my first time," he said.

When I turned and looked at him, he just shrugged.

"It's on my bucket list," he said.

"Your bucket list," I said, but I relaxed against his chest.

If it was on Wyatt's bucket list, it must not be too bad.

Besides. I was curious.

And Somewhere in Time was one of my favorite old movies.

I smiled.

This could be fun.

75

WYATT

*A*s we made our way along the road, riding in the little horse drawn carriage, I knew I'd made a good choice.

One of my employees, a young lady by the name of Misty, had just returned from her honeymoon a few days ago and she'd raved about how much she'd loved Mackinac Island.

Since I was born and bred in the west, I'd never heard of it. So looked it up and filed it away for one of those someday things to do.

I didn't have an actual written bucket list, but maybe I should work on that.

It was good timing because I had a tendency to forget things like this.

Unless, of course, something made a lasting impression on me.

Ainsley had most definitely made one of those lasting impressions.

Her and Beau.

I still had the information, but I hadn't called about the dog.

That was something I'd do when we got back to Houston.

"I hope you have a reservation," the carriage driver said over his shoulder.

Oh shit.

"There's some kind of event going on right now," the driver continued. "and I heard all the rooms were booked."

We had to stay the night.

Both Ainsley and I both had our go bags, so there was no reason not to.

Unless we couldn't get a room.

"Are we staying the night?" Ainsley asking, her breath brushing against my ear.

Definitely.

"That's up to you."

"Maybe. Did you make a reservation?"

I looked over at her and grinned.

"You might recall that it was a spur of the moment trip."

She nodded and looked ahead.

The Grand Hotel was coming into view and it was indeed grand.

"I guess we'll take our chances," she said.

"I guess we will."

The driver took us straight up to the front door and waited with our bags while we got out of the wagon.

I pressed a tip into his palm and took our bags from him.

At least I'd had the presence of mind to have a carriage waiting for us.

I remembered Misty talking about how the carriages were like taxis on the island.

Another detail about the island that had stuck with me.

I hadn't known that such a place existed in this country.

The Grand Hotel porch was so long that we couldn't see the other end of it.

We went inside and were greeting by a concierge who directed us to the front desk.

"Welcome," the young man behind the counter said. "How can I help you?" He was tall and slim and seemed to be nearly bouncing with energy.

I glanced at Ainsley.

She just lifted an eyebrow and shrugged.

"We'd like a room," I said.

"Of course. What name is the reservation under?"

"Unfortunately we don't have a reservation."

"Oh dear," the young man said. "It's a busy night for us."

"We heard," I said, pulling Ainsley closer. My excuse was that maybe if he thought we were newlyweds, he'd take pity on us.

The young man tapped on the computer keys, frowning the whole time.

"No need to worry," he said, but his expression suggested the opposite.

Then he looked at us, from me to Ainsley and back again.

"Is this your honeymoon?" He asked, hopefully.

"Yes," I said, without giving myself time to second guess myself.

"Congratulations," he said. "We get a lot of honeymooners."

He continued to click on the keys. "But they usually have reservations." He looked up and grinned again. "No need to worry."

The more he said that, the more worried I became.

"Can you wait right here for just one moment?" He asked.

"Sure."

Ainsley looked at me sideways. "Honeymoon? Really?"

I pulled her closer and kissed the top of her head.

"He seems like the kind of guy who would help out a hapless guy like me who was so excited to be with his bride, that he forgot to make a reservation."

Ainsley rolled her eyes.

"Seriously?"

But as the young man came back, she put an innocent smile back on her face.

I was more and more impressed by her with every passing moment.

The young man grinned at us.

"You're in luck." He practically sang the words.

I liked the man's enthusiasm.

"We had a last minute cancellation due to weather." He stopped typing and looked up. "I'll need to see some identification and a credit card."

While I pulled my license and credit card from my money clip, I added just one more thing to the list of things I liked about Ainsley.

She didn't make a big deal out of trying to pay for everything.

I was the one who'd brought her here, so of course I would pay.

Some women made too much out of trying to prove that they could take care of themselves.

And maybe they could, but where was the fun in that?

I handed the young clerk my credit card and finally caught up to what he had said.

"You said there's weather coming in?"

"Yes," he said. "A rain storm is coming in later this evening. You definitely don't want to be out in that."

"No. We wouldn't want that."

"What was it about me and Ainsley and storms?

First we'd been stuck together during a snowstorm. And now a thunderstorm.

What were the odds?

It was almost like fate was trying to make sure we spent time together.

And who was I to argue with fate?

A night with Ainsley.

And there was only one room left.

Apparently I'd done something right to deserve such good fortune.

76

AINSLEY

*T*here was something about Wyatt that put me at ease. I didn't feel like I had to prove anything with him.

I didn't know what it was, but I didn't try to analyze it.

The feeling was too far and far between.

I probably should have asked for two rooms.

But it was clear that we were doing good to get one room at all.

Besides, Wyatt and I seemed to be past the whole charade of pretending that we didn't want to be together.

Of course we wanted to be in the same room.

He didn't react, one way or the other. Just handed the clerk his credit card.

As the clerk tapped on the computer keys, Wyatt looked over and winked at me.

A little thrill of anticipation shot through my system.

Wyatt had a confident charm about him that both attracted me to him and made my wary of him at the same time.

Though he wasn't technically a pilot by trade, he was a pilot.

And since my experience with pilots was rife with bad memories, I had a lot of conflicting emotions about him.

Maybe we should just take it slow.

"Dinner is about to be served," the clerk said as he handed Wyatt his credit card. "Coat and tie are required for gentlemen and a dress for the ladies."

Wyatt glanced down at my go bag sitting at his feet.

"Did you happen to bring a dress?"

As strange as it may seem, I actually did usually have a dress with me. But not today.

I shook my head.

"No need to worry," the clerk said. "There's a rental shop just down the hall."

A rental shop for formal attire.

Whoever came up with that idea was no less than brilliant.

"Thank you," Wyatt said. "We'll stop by there."

"Very good," the clerk said. "Here's your room key."

And it was actually a key. A large, old-fashioned key.

"You don't want to miss dinner. I highly recommend the experience."

As we left the desk and walked through the lobby.

"What do you think?" Beau asked.

The hotel lived up to its name.

Grand.

First of all, it had a mile long wall of windows.

The walls and furnishings were decorated in deep colors. Velvet drapes.

Elegant sofas.

And plants. Lot of brightly flowering plants.

Mother would know what kind of plants they were.

She knew a lot about lots of things.

She was good at finding out what mattered to people and using that to connect with them.

She claimed it was a skill she'd learned during her years as a drug rep before she decided to go to graduate school to become a psychologist.

"I like it," I said.

The shop the clerk had mentioned was there on our right.

Wyatt lifted a brow and looked at me.

"Why not?" I shrugged. "We're here."

"I like your attitude," he said. "That you can take the time to have fun."

We'd no more than stepped into the shop when an elegantly dressed middle-aged woman stepped from behind the counter to greet us.

"Welcome to the Grand Hotel," she said. "Is this your first visit?"

"Yes," we both said.

According to her name tag, her name was Bridgette.

"And you need something to wear to dinner." Without waiting for an answer, she lowered her glasses and peered at us over the rims.

"I have just the thing. Come with me. Dinner is so much better when we're dressed up, don't you think?"

Wyatt and I exchanged a look.

"I agree completely," he said.

When I narrowed my eyes at him, he just shrugged.

"For the gentleman," she said, pulled a suit and tie, already matched from a rack.

"Right size?" She asked, handing the suit to Wyatt.

"Actually, yes." He seemed surprised.

"Good," Bridgette said. "You can get changed in one of the dressing rooms."

"I'll be back," Wyatt said with a little shrug. "Don't go anywhere."

"Where would I go?"

"And now for the lady," Bridgette said, ignoring our exchange.

I followed Bridgette across the shop to the lady's section.

She went straight to a section of dresses in my size.

"Can you wear a six?" She asked.

"Usually."

She sped through a section of clothing, hangers sliding easily on the rod.

Obviously looking for something.

"Ah ha," she said, stopping when she reached a taupe colored dress.

It looked a bit like what I thought of as a flapper dress.

Straight lines that fell to just below the knees. And tasteful fringe.

It had short sleeves and a tasteful neckline.

She held it across her arms for me to examine.

"What do you think? I doesn't look like much on the hanger, but it's one of those dresses that comes alive when you put it on."

I reached out and ran my hand along the soft silk.

"I'll give it a try," I said.

"Very good," Bridgette said. "What good is life if you can't have a little bit of fun, right?"

"Right," I said, taking the dress from her.

"You can take the other dressing room. And while you're doing that, I'll find you some shoes."

"I'm good on shoes," I said, pointing to my red bottoms.

Bridgette held up a hand. "Trust me," she said. "You've got to give this a try."

"Alright," I said, ducking behind the curtains of the vacant dressing room.

It was little unsettling knowing that Wyatt was just across the hall, also changing clothes.

Since he had a head start, he got dressed before me.

"What do you think?" Bridgette asked as he came out of the dressing room.

"I think it's perfect," he said.

As I slipped my jeans off, I thought about this whole thing. Bridgette was obviously a very hands on clerk.

I wasn't sure how I felt about that.

My younger sister Briana would have wanted to look through everything before making a choice.

But sometimes just going with the simplest was the best way.

I stepped into the dress and after fastening the back as best I could, I took a look in the three way mirror.

Beatrice was right.

The dress did come alive once it was on. Though it looked taupe on the hanger, it had a silky red layer beneath it that showed through as I moved.

I absolutely loved it.

Beatrice came to the curtain. "I have your shoes," she said, setting them down at the bottom of the curtain.

The shoes were actually little boots.

With a shrug, I changed out of my red bottom shoes into a pair of little lace-up booties.

Dressed, I stood straight and examined my reflection.

All good, I opened the curtain.

Wyatt was standing there, leaning against the wall.

My breath hitched as I realized he'd been waiting for me.

He pushed off the wall and smiled at me.

He was heart-poundingly handsome in his black tuxedo and red tie.

Beatrice had matched his tie to the red undertones of my dress.

Wyatt took my hand and led me to a big mirror at the end of the hallway.

Putting his arm around me, he studied our reflections.

"We look good together," he said.

I smiled back at his reflection.

He was right.

We did make a good looking couple.

77

WYATT

*T*he moon was full and hung low over Lake Huron. I couldn't have asked for a more beautiful night.

Soft piano music drifted from the lobby. The pianist had been playing nonstop all through dinner.

Old music. Jazz from the Roaring Twenties.

It was all quite impressive.

I'd made a good choice in bringing Ainsley here.

"Will you take a walk with me?" I asked. "Along the world's longest porch?"

"That sounds lovely," she said.

I stood and took her hand in mine.

As we walked through the dining area, heads turned.

We made a striking couple, if I did have to say so myself.

I tucked her hand in the crook of my arm in a subtle statement claiming her as my girl.

Of course, I would never tell her that.

Ainsley was much too elusive and independent to allow herself be claimed.

As we stepped out onto the famous porch, I wondered how she was still single.

Beautiful and intelligent. Yet she carried an elusive air about her that probably allowed her to keep men at bay when she wanted to.

She hadn't done much to keep me at bay.

First in the cabin in Wyoming. Then last night at the wedding reception where she'd danced scandalously close. So close our bodies had become intimate.

It wasn't something we'd talked about and I doubted that we ever would.

Ainsley and I seemed to have established a tacit level of privacy.

As we walked along the porch overlooking Lake Huron, I decided that I wanted to change that.

I wanted to delve beneath her layers of privacy and discover the true girl beneath.

"Tell me, Ainsley Worthington," I said, startlingly her out of whatever path her thoughts had taken.

"Tell you what, Wyatt Beaufort?" She glanced up at me with a raised eyebrow.

I grinned at her.

"Tell me one of the many things I don't know about you."

Even in the moonlight, I could see the blush that stole over her cheeks.

"I think you know quite a bit about me," she said.

"Oh no. You don't get off that easy." I lifted her hand and kissed the back of her fingertips. "You are one of those still waters run deep kind of girl."

"I haven't heard that expression in a long time and I don't think I've ever been described that way."

"But you have to admit that you hold your cards close to your chest."

She nodded.

We walked past rows of white rocking chairs and flowering plants.

A horse and carriage drove past, carrying a young couple only interested in each other.

"I could say the same about you," she said.

"You're right," I admitted. "I haven't told you much about me."

We walked in silence, leaving the piano music behind like a distant echo.

"So if I go first, will you tell me something about you?"

She looked at me sideways.

"Sure," she said. "Why not?"

I smiled to myself. I didn't know how to describe our relationship. We weren't dating. Yet we had a connection. And we were more than a casual hookup.

"Alright. I'm not just a pilot."

"I knew that."

"I also design video games."

"And?"

"And I own my own company."

"Sounds like that could be a long story."

She didn't seem the least bit surprised. I wondered if someone had told her. Maybe Madison. Or if she just expected no less. It wasn't like I tried to hide my wealth.

"It is," I said. "But it's your turn.

"Well," she said. "I don't own my company. But I do work for myself."

"Kind of the same thing?"

"Not really." She shrugged. "I fly one of my daddy's planes. And one day, when I have enough experience, I hope he'll hire me on at Skye Travels as a pilot."

"I'd think you'd be a shoe in."

"Daddy has really high standards."

"Well, I'm sure that he'll figure it all out soon enough."

"Do you have any siblings?" She asked, quickly changing the subject.

"I have a sister. We aren't close."

"I'm sorry about that. I'm sure you figured out that my family is close."

"Hard to miss that one."

We met another couple coming toward us, walking in the opposite direction.

"So you're where you want to be?" She asked. "In your career?"

"Right now, I guess I am. I have enough to keep me busy."

"So you run your company? Or do you actually design the video games?"

"Both," I asked. "I run the company because I have to. It allows me to design video games. In my free time."

"And where exactly do you find this free time?"

"Here and there," I said. "I guess it's not exactly free time, is it?"

"We make time for things we really want to do. Right?"

"Right." I squeezed her hand. "But right now I'm exactly where I want to be. Doing exactly what I want to be doing."

"Me too," she said.

We reached the end of the porch and stopped to gaze over the lake.

"This place is amazing," she said. "I can't believe I've never been here."

"Me either. Doesn't your father have planes here?"

She nodded. "He has planes in a lot of places."

"He's a true business man."

"I guess," she said, her voice quiet again.

If I had to make a guess, I'd say that there was something going on with Noah that the family wasn't telling.

I didn't have to be a psychologist to figure that out.

But I wasn't going to be the one to bring it up.

In fact, I needed to distract her.

"So…" I said. "they say the best way to see the island is by bicycle."

She lifted an eyebrow and looked at me.

"And?"

"So I was thinking we could get up early, rent some bikes, and watch the sunrise in the morning."

She nodded slowly.

"I'm beginning to see how you get so much done."

"How so?" I asked.

"You don't sleep."

I just grinned and she rolled her eyes.

But I saw the smile that played about her lips.

78

AINSLEY

*S*tanding on the longest porch in the world, watching the waves of Lake Huron beneath the moonlight.

When I woke this morning, this was not how I pictured my day ending.

Not by a long shot.

I planned on having a glass of wine, watching something on Netflix to unwind, and going to bed early.

I'd had an early flight this morning, so I was exhausted.

I'd never been a stay up late and party kind of girl.

And I'd never felt like I'd missed anything.

I actually felt fortunate that I feel the need to partake in that world.

People called me serious.

And I owned it.

I was serious.

But I had goals.

I wanted to be a pilot that my father could be proud of.

To live up to his standards.

Not that he ever pressured me.

But he hadn't hired me yet either.

With his illness, I was pretty sure I'd fallen off his radar.

And it didn't seem right to pester him while he still convalescing.

Wyatt squeezed my hand.

Unlike him, I required my full eight hours of sleep.

But watching the sunrise with Wyatt sounded like a whole lot more fun than sleeping in.

He pulled me into a hug and everything else faded away.

Somehow we'd ended up back together.

What were the odds?

I wasn't a gambler, but I knew the odds were immeasurable.

Then again, the aviation world was overall a small community.

So maybe the odds weren't as impossible as they seemed.

"Penny for your thoughts," he said.

"I was just thinking," I said. "This isn't quite what I had planned for my evening."

"And what did you have planned for your evening?"

I wasn't about to tell him about my date with Netflix and an early bedtime.

"Well, I guess it doesn't much matter now, does it? Someone swept me away."

"I always liked that song." He started humming something.

"What song is that?" I asked.

"I'll give you a hint," he said. "Frank Sinatra."

I listened to his soft humming for a few more minutes, just enjoying the moment.

"Fly me to the moon," I said.

He stopped humming and kissed the top of my head.

"I knew I loved you," he said.

My heart skipped a beat.

And I almost forgot to breath.

He kissed the top of my head again and pulled away.

"Come on," he said. "Let's get you some sleep."

As he led me back down the longest porch in the world, my mind raced.

Had he accidentally said it?

Did he mean it?

Whatever the reason, I was no longer sleepy.

79

WYATT

I had to admit that I wasn't always a gentleman.

Usually, but not always.

My grandmother had instilled gentlemanly ways in me when I just a boy.

Always walk on the edge of the sidewalk by the road, keeping your lady safe on the inside.

Never let a lady pay for anything when you're together.

Always hold the door for her.

Those were just the basics, of course.

Something about being with Ainsley brought my grandmother's words to mind.

I wanted Ainsley to see me as a gentleman and I wanted to treat her as a lady.

Even when we'd been in Wyoming, I'd had the utmost good intentions before I'd allowed things to get intense and then I'd been an ass.

And at the wedding reception, I didn't know she was going to… react the way she had.

And even with all that we'd done together, I still wanted to treat her as a lady.

I wanted to take care of her. To make sure she was safe and healthy.

She needed rest and I wasn't going to be the one who kept her from it.

We didn't talk as we walked through the lobby of the brightly decorated Grand Hotel.

We didn't talk as we waited for the elevator or as I unlocked the door to our room on the third floor and we stepped inside.

Our bags, such as they were, had already been delivered to the room and sat just inside the door.

The room, decorated all in blue, had two rooms in one. There was the main room with a little alcove that had its own smaller bed.

A little bit disappointing in some ways.

With two rooms in one, I had no excuse to sleep in the same bed with her.

"Which bed would you like?" I asked.

"The little one is fine," she said, going to the little alcove with the twin bed.

"Good choice," I said. "Looks cozy."

The curtains were open and there was a lovely view of the moonlight over the lake.

She sat on the edge of the bed, her eyes heavy.

"Do you want me to wake you up in the morning?" I asked.

She winced. "Sure."

"Good night, sweet princess."

"Wyatt?" she asked, before I could turn away.

"Yes?"

"Thank you."

"For what?"

"It's just... there's been a lot going on in my life lately and I needed to get away."

"You're welcome," I said.

She smiled that genuine and rare smile that she had and my heart swelled.

Out on the porch, I'd said words to her in a casual way.

But they were words that I meant from the bottom of my heart.

I'd known when I first saw her standing there in the airport, Beau at her side that she was someone special.

And that feeling hadn't gone away.

I'd been so afraid to break the spell that I'd created a wall between us.

A wall of misconceptions and misunderstandings. So when she'd had to go home all of a sudden, I hadn't taken it well.

I'd been disappointed and hurt and done what my grandmother would have called tossing the baby out with the bath water.

I'd pushed her away simply because I didn't want her to go.

Ainsley inspired feelings in me that I honestly didn't think I would even have again.

Leaving her there to sleep, I went to the other bed, but not to sleep.

I took my computer bag with me and pulled out my iPad.

I had some work to do.

80

AINSLEY

I woke the next morning to the sound of a ferry horn.
Not a normal sound.

I was used to the distant roar of cars on the freeway far below my penthouse condo.

Sometimes the steady roar was interrupted by street racers or a string motorcycle riders out for a group ride. Sometimes there were even sirens that blended into the background.

The neighbor below me had a Husky that he'd let out on the deck when there was cool weather.

Mostly the dog was quiet, but sometimes he'd find something to bark about. Not that there was much excitement on a balcony that high up. No squirrels to chase. Or even other dogs to keep away.

But a ferry horn was something new.

It took my brain a few seconds to connect the sound of the ferry horn with yesterday's events and to remind me that I was not in my penthouse condo.

I was in a bedroom at the Grand Hotel on Mackinac Island.

And Wyatt was here in the same room.

Or at least I thought he was. Right now, I couldn't hear him.

It was curious how we'd gone from being intimate to sleeping in our own beds.

And yet…

He'd said he loved me.

Had he been being flippant when he said that?

As in *I love pizza.* Or *I love sleeping late.*

Wyatt was such a mystery.

He was gentlemanly and affectionate one minute. Then the next minute, he'd kiss me goodnight and go to his own bed.

My tortured thoughts had kept me awake for all of about five minutes before I'd fallen asleep.

But the torture picked up again right where it had left off.

Maybe he'd left again.

With my heart in my throat, I tossed the covers back and put my feet on the cool wood floor.

I just wanted to see if he was still here or if he'd slipped out like he had in Wyoming.

I tiptoed over to the edge of the alcove and peeked around at the other bed.

He was still there.

I let out a sigh of relief and buried back to my bed.

I grabbed my phone and burrowed back beneath the warm covers.

Wyatt had said he wanted to get up early and watch the sun rise.

He must have changed his mind, since he was still asleep as the first tendrils of light were breaking the dawn.

I didn't mind.

My phone automatically went to do not disturb, so I turned that off first, then checked my messages.

I had two messages.

The first was from Madison.

My sister was supposed to be on her honeymoon, not worrying about me.

MADISON: *Are you okay? Not like you to disappear like that.*

Although she'd sent the message last night, I sent back a quick response.

ME: *I had an early flight. All is well.*

My fingers hovered over the keys as I debated adding the simple statement that it had turned into an overnight.

I decided against it.

Madison was on her honeymoon. If she knew I was out of town, she'd be worried.

So I left it alone.

The second message was from the scheduling person at SkyeTravels. The girl, Mary, was new and sometimes got things confused.

For example, she sometimes seemed to think that I worked at Skye Travels.

MARY: *Mr. Worthington wants you to do a pick up. Are you available today?*

I groaned and closing my eyes, leaned back against the pillow.

No. I'm not available. I don't even work for Skye Travels. But I answered appropriately.

ME: *Sorry. Not available today. Maybe tomorrow.*

As soon as I hit send, I realized that she'd written the message yesterday.

So today was tomorrow.

ME: *Make that Tuesday.*

I put my phone aside.

I wasn't awake enough yet to be making sense.

It was best to keep my fingers off the keys.

I needed coffee.

And a hot shower.

Though preferably in that order, I opted for the shower first.

The hot water felt heavenly and was exactly what I needed to shake off the cobwebs.

I thought about waking Wyatt up so we could go for our daybreak bicycle ride.

Then I thought better of it.

It would give me time to go downstairs and search for coffee.

Take a look around the old hotel.

I'd been to a lot of places in my travels, but this was by far one of the most interesting.

And peaceful.

Not that I'd want to live here all the time.

I preferred the sound of cars on the freeway to random ferry horns.

I quickly blow dried my hair, then pulled it back in a high, messy ponytail.

There was a stack of stationary on the coffee table, so I scrawled a quick note just in case Wyatt woke up looking for me.

Then I slipped out into the hallway.

The hotel walls were painted in a bright yellow on one side and a bright green on the other.

It was a long walk to the elevator.

After waiting for couple of minutes for the elevator that didn't come, I decided to take the stairs.

It felt good to move around.

When I reached the bottom floor, I followed the scent of coffee to the little cafe.

It was early enough that I was the only person up moving around.

I ordered a latte and wandered out to the porch.

The early morning air was chilly, but the sun was pleasantly warm.

I curled up on one of the sofas and looked out over Lake Huron.

It was like looking out over an ocean.

There were a couple of boats on the water. A yacht and a ferry carrying tourists.

I wondered what it would be like to come onto the island on a ferry boat instead of an airplane.

Although I considered myself lucky, I often wondered if I missed things that other people experienced.

After wandering around a bit, my brain wound its way back to Wyatt.

It had been such a shock to see him standing across from me at my sister's wedding.

I still didn't know what had happened that had caused him to walk away from me that day in Wyoming.

We both tended to hold our cards close to our chest.

But maybe that needed to change.

Maybe I needed to do something to change that.

Wyatt had told me he loved me.

It didn't matter that he'd said it in an off-hand, casual way.

He'd still said it.

And I knew that I was falling in love with him.

And he'd brought me all the way up here to Mackinac Island to fulfill one of his bucket list items.

I didn't even have a bucket list.

Sometimes I felt like I just went through my days with no particular goals in mind.

But now wasn't the time for an existential crisis.

Now was the time to figure out what to do about Wyatt.

81

WYATT

I found Ainsley on the grand porch. She was sitting alone, sipping a cup of coffee.

The early morning wind lightly tousled her hair and her expression was unguarded.

I wondered what she was thinking about as she sat there staring out toward Lake Huron.

I'd stayed up far too late last night, but I'd gotten a lot things done.

When I made a decision, I didn't hesitate.

Sometimes a decision was based on research and required time to explore.

But some decisions didn't require that kind of hesitation.

Some decisions were from the heart.

And when a decision was from the heart, I saw no reason to wait.

Life was too short to wait on the important things.

I moved so that Ainsley could see me walking toward her.

I didn't want to startle her.

Her face lit up when she saw me. I took that as a good sign.

"Good morning," I said.

"Hi." She tucked a strand of hair behind an ear and balanced her coffee cup in her lap with both hands.

"You're up early."

"I slept well," she said. "You?"

I sat down beside her and balanced my own cup of coffee on my knee.

"Stayed up too late," I said.

She nodded slowly, watching me as though trying to figure out why I'd stayed up late.

"Work?" She asked.

"Yeah. I had some things to do."

I watched one of the ferries slowly make its way toward the island.

It would be full of tourists.

"I guess we missed our bicycle ride," she said.

I sipped from my cup.

"We can still go," I said.

"I didn't want to wake you."

I smiled to myself.

It had been hard to sleep through her shower and the ensuing hair drying.

"You didn't," I said.

I'd actually been awake before she was, but I'd decided to let her sleep in.

After she left the room, I jumped in the shower myself.

She was like a magnet that I couldn't resist.

"Did you get all your work done?" She asked.

"I did actually."

"Working on a game?" She asked, with a little smile.

"Not this time. I had some business to take care of."

I had the sense that she wanted me to say more about my work. Maybe she was feeling the same thing I was feeling.

That we needed to talk more about our personal lives.

I was okay with that, but I wasn't ready to talk about the work I'd done last night.

Even though I'd made my decision and wasn't going to back out, it wasn't time to tell her about it.

"So…" I said. "What do you say? Ready to take a spin around the island? See what we can see?"

"I'm ready when you are," she said.

I nodded toward the boatload of tourists coming in.

"We should get going then. The island is about to get a whole lot more crowded for the day."

It didn't really matter to me how crowded the island got.

As long as I was with Ainsley, I would be content.

And as far as I was concerned she was the only person who mattered.

82

AINSLEY

"*A*re you sure you've ridden a bicycle before?" Wyatt asked.

I shot him a look.

"Of course I have," I said. "It's just been a long time."

A really long time.

My younger sister Wynter was the athletic one in the family. She'd take her bicycle to Memorial Park and ride for hours.

But me, I preferred to spend my time in the air.

We'd had to take a horse and buggy taxi downtown to rent the bicycles. And Wyatt was right. The little Main Street was crowded with day tourists by the time we got there.

It didn't seem to matter that we were tourists. Since we'd gotten here last night, it felt a bit like we had edge over the wide-eyed tourists as they admired the little town and its view.

But as we peddled side by side along the lake away from downtown, the crowds thinned out.

It didn't matter to me one way or the other. Crowded with tourists or not.

All that mattered to me was that I was with Wyatt.

I didn't know how long we were staying here on the island.

There were so many things we didn't talk about.

It was almost like if we didn't talk about things, we could stay in our own little fantasy world.

But a text message from Daddy popping up on my watch had me rethinking the practicality of living in that fantasy world.

I put on the brakes and brought the bicycle to a stop. I had to slide off the seat to put my feet on the ground.

Wyatt stopped, too.

"Everything okay" he asked as I pulled my phone out of my pocket.

"I have a message," I said absently and unlocked my phone.

DADDY: *Can you take a flight for me in the morning?*

Damn it. Sometimes Daddy had the worst timing.

ME: *Let me check. Back in a few.*

I secured the phone back in my pocket and got the bicycle going again.

Wyatt followed suit.

I watched Wyatt out of the corner of my eye.

He seemed quite content with not a care in the world.

It didn't seem to bother him that we had no plan whatsoever.

But... I had plans to make.

I couldn't just run away from my responsibilities like this.

Squaring my back, I decided it was time to open up the lines of communication.

"When are you planning on us flying back?" I asked.

"I haven't really decided yet," he said. "Was going to talk to you about it."

Well, that was an unexpectedly good sign.

At least he had plans to talk to me about things.

"I kind of need to know," I said, steering past a man traveling the road on foot.

It was interesting that the island had roads, yet there were no cars. It was about eight miles around the whole island and it was supposed to take us about an hour to bike the whole way.

But Wyatt had brought food for a picnic, so it would be some time in the afternoon before we got back.

Then if we flew out, it would put us back late.

"I was thinking we could stay at least tonight," he said.

I took a deep breath.

"Daddy wants me to take a flight in the morning."

If I wanted Wyatt to be upfront with me, I needed to be upfront with him.

"You're working for Skye Travels now?" He asked.

I couldn't tell if he was genuinely asking or if he was being snarky.

"No," I said. "But sometimes I fly for him."

Wyatt nodded.

"Okay. So you want to go back today?"

The way he asked, matter of factly, as though he didn't care on way or the other was hurtful.

"It's not that I want to," I said. "I just need to."

Wyatt put stopped and balanced on his bicycle.

I made a wobbly stop and slid off the seat to put my feet on the ground.

"What?" I asked. "Surely you have responsibilities, too. It's not like we planned this trip."

He looked at me for a moment.

"You're right. We didn't plan it. But I took the week off."

"See," I said. "I didn't."

"It's okay," he said. "I've got a ton of things to do anyway. Want to turn around?"

"No," I said.

And damn it. This was why I hadn't wanted to ask.

I didn't want to ruin the fantasy.

"I want to finish our ride around the island."

"Alright," he said. "But you should know that there's supposed to be a storm later tonight."

Well hell.

I shifted my gaze away from Wyatt to look out across the lake. Another ferry boat was coming in.

More tourists.

People without a care in the world.

It would be nice to have that luxury once in a while.

So Wyatt was saying that we needed to either leave right now or wait until tomorrow to leave.

"Are you sure?" I asked. It was such a beautiful day. Not a cloud in the sky.

He smiled a little.

Of course he was sure.

He wouldn't make something like that up.

83

WYATT

$\mathcal{I}$t seemed like Ainsley and I couldn't get any time together without life intruding on us.

I had to remember that just because I had a flexible schedule didn't mean she did.

And I hated that it irritated me whenever she had responsibilities.

But it did.

I wanted her all to myself.

I didn't want to share her with her family or the world. At least not all the time.

It didn't seem like too much to ask for just once.

Here we were in one of the most fascinating places in the country and already she was being called back to work.

I told myself it wasn't a big deal.

We both had airplanes. We could come back anytime.

Some people commuted in their cars for longer than it would take us to fly back up here.

It was silly to be upset that she needed to go.

"I'm sure," I said. "I checked before I reserved the room for another night."

She pulled out her phone and sent a quick message before climbing back on the bicycle.

The bicycle was really too big for her.

I would have to look into buying her a bicycle more her size before we came back up here.

It would be no problem to throw a couple of bikes in the plane and bring them with us.

In fact, it made perfect sense.

Now that we'd been here once, next time we knew more about what to expect.

We knew to bring formal clothes with us for dinner.

And we knew to bring our own bicycles.

I considered that to be a win.

We'd discovered an awesome place to visit.

A place neither one of us had ever been to before.

It could be our place.

All couples had a place, right?

The only thing missing was Beau running alongside us.

We rode in silence, the lapping of the water's waves mixing with the steady clicking of the bicycle wheels.

It was relaxing.

Even when a couple of other riders zipped past us, we just kept up our leisurely pace.

I couldn't think of anywhere else I'd rather be right now.

And I certainly couldn't think of anyone else I'd rather be spending my day with.

I didn't know if we were returning to Houston today or tomorrow.

But it didn't matter.

We could come back.

And next time I would have things planned out a lot better.

Ainsley glanced over at me with a little smile, then pulled ahead.

Pulling myself out of my disappointed train of thought, I took off after her.

84

AINSLEY

*A*s much as I hated to admit it, Wyatt was right.

I didn't work for Skye Travels.

And I didn't work for Daddy.

I wanted to.

I wanted him to hire me on at Skye Travels.

But the last time we'd talked about it, he said I didn't have the hours.

And I knew he was right.

He shouldn't make an exception for me just because I was his daughter.

But that had been, what? At least a year ago and I'd been flying my ass off these past few months.

It was time Daddy and I had another discussion.

Being his favorite daughter should carry some weight, after all.

I'd make a point to talk with him when we got back.

It just hadn't seemed right bringing it up when he was dealing with being sick.

This was one of the few times I'd turned down a job he'd asked me to do.

I'd always thought that if I took all the jobs he offered, it would put me that much closer to being hired full-time.

It just didn't seem to work out that way.

So I determined to put work out of my head at least for the rest of the day.

I was here on Mackinac Island. One of the most beautiful places in the country with the man I was crushing on.

All I had to do was to be in the moment.

I peddled as hard as I could and pulled ahead of Wyatt.

The cool wind felt good blowing over my skin.

I liked going fast.

Guess that had something to do with flying airplanes.

I liked to get where I was going quickly.

Driving certainly wasn't my thing. Why drive when you could fly?

And though riding bicycles had never been my thing, I could appreciate the speed of zipping past people who were walking.

I spotted a little picnic area up ahead nestled in the trees.

Looked like a good place to stop and have that lunch Wyatt had brought.

I rode over to an empty table and, stopping the bike, slid off the seat.

Wyatt was right behind me.

"Good place to stop for lunch?" I asked.

"Looks great to me," he said, sliding off his own bike and unbuckling the basket off the back of his bicycle.

I stretched and looked out over Lake Huron.

The view was dotted with sailboats.

"You like it here?" Wyatt asked.

"It's beautiful," I said, turning to him with a smile. "There's just one thing missing."

"Yeah?" He looked at me, holding two tuna sandwiches in his hands. "What's that?"

"Beau," I said. "He'd love it here."

Wyatt set the sandwiches on the table with an odd expression on his face.

"It's funny you would say that," he said.

"Why's that?" I asked, coming to slide onto the picnic table bench.

"Because I was just thinking the same thing."

I grinned. "Because it's true."

"Why are you suddenly in such a good mood?" He handed me a bag of potato chips.

I opened it and popped one in my mouth.

"Because…" I said. "I like it here. And we get to stay here another night."

Wyatt sat down across from me and, opening a bottle of water, handing it to me.

"Thought you had to get back to work."

"Nope," I said. "You were right. I don't work for Skye Travels. Daddy can get one of his other pilots to take the flight tomorrow."

Wyatt smiled. "Good for you."

"Don't get used to it, though," I said. "I do have bills to pay."

"Don't worry," he said, unwrapping his sandwich. "You'll find that I'm actually quite the workaholic."

"You?" I leaned forward on my elbows and looked into his clear blue eyes. Bluer than Lake Huron.

"Since I've known you, I've never seen you work. You hardly even ever check your phone."

"You see," he said. "that's where being the boss comes in handy.

I knew that Wyatt ran his own company, but I hadn't thought about it quite like that.

About just how freedom that must give him.

He obviously wasn't just starting out. If he had been, he

wouldn't have that kind of freedom. He'd be working his ass off trying to get his business going.

No. Wyatt was definitely successful already.

That was pretty obvious, though, since he owned his own plane.

I slowly ate my sandwich and chips, wondering what kind of man Wyatt would be when he wasn't on vacation.

I planned to take my time and find out.

After all, we hadn't just found each other again for no reason.

There had to a bigger purpose behind it.

Like Momma said, everything happened for a reason.

85

WYATT

*A*fter our bike ride around the island, we walked up to the Mackinac fort and watched as reenactors fired off a cannon.

It was interesting to hear about the history of the island, but even more, it was nice to spend time with Ainsley.

Truth was, I couldn't get enough of her.

Just looking at her.

And when she smiled at me, my heart did flips.

She didn't smile all that much, but when she did, it lit up her face.

And today she'd been smiling enough to throw me completely off guard.

By the time we left the fort and started the hike back down to the town, it was starting to get dark.

And true to the weather report, the storm was coming in across the lake.

"I guess you didn't make up the bad weather after all," Ainsley said as we neared Main Street along with a hundred other tourists.

"Why would I make that up?" I asked, taking her hand so we didn't get separated.

She shrugged. "I don't know. Maybe you weren't ready to go back."

"Yeah, well. I wasn't. But I'd just tell you. I wouldn't make something like that up."

"Okay," she said, looking at my sideways.

"You must have been hanging out with some shady people in your day."

She looked away as we sidestepped a group of teenagers walking toward us.

"Not really," she said, looking all serious.

"I was just teasing."

Her eyes were misty again.

I never knew what was going to bother her.

It would have been helpful if I knew a little bit more about what she was going through.

I knew that her father had been sick, prostate cancer, but by all accounts, he was recovering well.

I didn't know anything about her mother, except that she was a psychologist and had five children later in life.

The only other thing I knew was that Kade was madly in love with their daughter, Madison. And now happily married.

I knew that Ainsley was kind and loyal to her family. Perhaps loyal to a fault.

I knew that when I spent time with her, I was content. Happy.

Ainsley made me happy.

We passed by a fudge shop with a line out the front.

She grabbed my arm.

"Hey," she said. "I heard about this place. We have to get some fudge."

"Look at the line," I said. "There's a bunch of places to get fudge on the island."

"I know," she said, flashing me that smile that sent my heart racing. "But this is supposed to be the best. It's got to be." She shrugged. "That's why there's a line."

And so we spent the next thirty minutes in line to get fudge.

Leaving with a box of signature fudge, we sat on a bench outside the little shop and tried it out.

"Okay," I said. "I guess crowds don't lie."

Ainsley cut off a little piece of chocolate. "You like it, don't you?"

"What's not to like?"

She nudged me with her shoulder.

"Told you," she said.

"Yes, you did."

And I knew then that I was wrapped around her little finger.

I'd known it before, but this just solidified it.

I'd made the right decision.

86

AINSLEY

"*I* don't think I can go to dinner," I said, sitting on the sofa in our room.

"Why not?" Wyatt asked, looking up from his iPad.

"My legs are killing me."

I tried to keep the pain out of my voice. To sound strong and brave.

But that bicycle ride had totally caught up with me.

"Really?" Wyatt came over and sat next to me on the sofa.

"Yes." I sat back and closed my eyes. "What's wrong with me?"

I opened my eyes just enough to see Wyatt smiling at me.

"Why are you laughing? I'm dying."

"You're not dying. It's just delayed muscle soreness."

"You're a doctor, too?"

I was being testy. I couldn't help it.

This didn't make sense. I jogged three or four times a week on my treadmill.

I should not be this sore.

"I can help," he said.

"How?"

I was wearing blue jeans and a sweatshirt. I hadn't brought any leggings. I might have been more comfortable if I had. Blue jeans weren't the best outfit for an active day of riding and walking.

"May I?" He asked, putting his hands on my sneakers.

"Okay."

He laughed as he untied the laces of my sneakers.

"I can see that you have very little faith in my healing powers."

I scoffed. "Healing powers. If you have healing powers, now just might be a good time for you to use them."

"Okay," he said, dropping one shoe to the floor, then the other.

He didn't massage my toes like I expected.

Instead, he started by massaging the backs of my shins, just above the ankles. Front and back.

I leaned back and took deep breaths.

This might actually work.

If nothing else, it would be a good distraction from the muscle pain.

He gently but firmly massaged the backs of my legs.

Then he stopped.

I opened my eyes and looked accusingly at him.

"You stopped."

"I can't do what I need to do with you wearing these jeans."

"You're just trying to get me out of my pants."

"And is that such a bad thing?"

"Maybe not," I admitted. "Turn around."

"Seriously?"

"Yes."

He turned around.

"Okay," I said, unzipping my jeans and slipping out of them.

My shirt was long enough that my modesty was preserved.

"You picked a weird time to develop modesty," he said, but

since he continued to massage my legs, I didn't care how much he complained.

"Is this helping?" He asked.

"A little," I said.

He stopped. "Just a little."

"No," I said quickly. "A lot. It's helping a lot. Don't stop."

He was laughing at me, but I didn't care.

I'd never had such bad post-workout pain.

And his hands on my skin was better than any medicine.

Of course, I also knew that it was a dangerous, slippery slope.

After all, he already had me out of my pants.

And on top of that, his hands were all over me.

"Does this feel good?" He asked, skipping over my kneecaps to press his fingers against my thighs.

"Yes," I said.

"Do you want me to stop?"

"Please don't."

He was enjoying my pain a little too much.

But I didn't care.

I was enjoying his hands on my skin a little too much, too.

87

WYATT

*A*insley, as usual, was making it difficult to be a gentleman.

I knew that my massage was helping her leg pain.

I also knew that riding a bicycle like that could be quite painful if a person wasn't used to that kind of exercise.

So I had a lot of empathy.

I'd actually been there.

But I hadn't had anyone to massage my legs for me. Instead, I'd subjected myself to ibuprofen, ice, and heat.

And a whole lot of rest.

Unfortunately, if I didn't get her past this crazy pain, we were going to miss our evening out.

I kicked myself for not thinking about this possibility.

Ainsley was brilliant, for sure. And she was an airplane pilot.

But other than for being a pilot, she was a city girl.

She dressed like a city girl.

Carried herself like one.

Even her hair was obviously kept up in a salon. She had stylish highlights, purposely darker at the roots.

She didn't spend a lot of time outside.

I didn't mind that. Not in the least.

It just hadn't occurred to me.

I'd seen an opportunity for us to do something together and I'd jumped on it without thinking.

And she'd agreed.

That actually told me a lot about her.

It told me that she liked me enough to get out of her comfort zone to do things I wanted to do.

Well, from now on, I was going to think about her when I made crazy plans.

In fact, I just might even let her do the planning.

Because it really didn't matter to me what we did. As long as we were together.

I'd given her some ibuprofen.

Still. I was surprised when her eyes grew heavy.

I kept massaging her legs, even as I knew she was falling asleep.

I didn't matter.

It didn't matter that I had planned on us going to dinner again.

Last night's dinner had been elegant, but tonight they were doing a little live play based on the movie *Somewhere in Time*.

Ainsley had mentioned that *Somewhere in Time* was one of her favorite movies and I was looking forward to surprising her with the play.

Oh well. There I went again. Making plans without her.

The rain had settled in to a steady patter against the window.

And the storm was coming in, too.

Already flashes of lightning were coming in across the lake and the thunder followed in its wake.

It was a perfect night for sleeping.

A perfect night for cuddling up and sleeping together in the Grand Hotel.

But Ainsley was asleep.

I took a blanket and tucked it around her.

The bed would be more comfortable, but the sofa wasn't bad and it wasn't worth waking her up to move her to the bed.

With the storm roaring outside, I went to my bed and climbed in.

I had some promising emails.

And some text messages to answer.

From all accounts, everything was going as planned.

Better even than I had hoped.

88

AINSLEY

I woke on the sofa.

My legs had hurt worse than they ever had.

We'd ridden completely around the island, then we'd walked miles up to the fort and back again.

Wyatt hadn't seemed to think anything of any of it.

He was obviously in much better shape than I was.

I might need to increase my morning workouts.

There was a storm in the distance. I didn't know if it was coming this way or if it had already passed.

Wyatt had given me something. Ibuprofen. And it, along with the exhaustion of the day, had knocked me out.

Well, that and Wyatt's massage.

Amazing enough, my legs didn't hurt anymore now. A little sore, maybe, but a normal kind of sore. Not that intense work out pain that I'd had earlier.

It was dark and I could hear Wyatt lightly snoring in his bed.

I smiled to myself. It wasn't really a snore so much as it was just the way he breathed when he was sleeping.

It was funny because I'd spent enough time sleeping in the

same room as him to know what he sounded like when he was sleeping.

There weren't all that many men I could say that about.

One maybe. But I never even thought about him anymore.

Wyatt had tucked a blanket around me.

He had a kind heart.

Even when he was frustrated, he was kind.

And he had to have been frustrated. He'd seemed especially excited about dinner tonight.

And I'd gone and slept through it.

I didn't know where my phone was, so I didn't even know what time it was.

I thought about getting up and getting into my own bed.

And I thought about climbing into bed with Wyatt.

Moving to my own bed would take too much effort.

And climbing into bed with Wyatt would not only wake him—which I did not want to do—and... it would have me making assumptions I wasn't ready to make.

Our relationship was too new. Too fresh.

I didn't want to change the way it was going.

I liked the way it was going.

Slow and easy.

There was an obvious attraction. He could definitely satisfy me and we didn't even have to be in bed for that to happen.

But it seemed, to me at least, like there was more to it than that.

But again. Coming off my moratorium, this was a good pace.

I wasn't about to through off the balance we'd established by climbing into his bed.

Not that I would mind spending the night with him.

But that could wait.

By the time I sorted all that out in my head, my eyes were

heavy again and the steady rain falling against the window lulled me back to sleep.

And I slipped into a pleasant dream about a handsome pilot who smiled at me with beautiful blue eyes.

And then he kissed me.

89

WYATT

I woke early the next morning.

The sun was barely even up.

My phone, set on do-not-disturb, for the night was blowing up with messages.

Ainsley was still asleep on the sofa.

I wondered if she had woke at all during the night. If she had, surely she would have gone to her bed.

I hoped she was in less pain today.

I felt bad for being the one responsible for putting her through such hell.

But we'd both learned from the whole thing.

And all in all, I had enjoyed my first visit to Mackinac Island.

I was especially pleased that it was a memory I had with Ainsley.

After a quick shower, I got dressed and made my way downstairs to the lobby.

Armed with a strong cup of coffee, I found a secluded spot to set up a workspace.

The lobby was as long as the porch, so it wasn't hard to find a secluded place.

Besides, it was early in the morning and not all that many people were up.

I'd made an unconventional business decision.

Most would have called it impulsive, and it even felt a bit like it to me, but I'd been thinking about it for a long time now.

So it wasn't really all that impulsive.

A normal person, without people, wouldn't have been able to pull it off as quickly as I could.

But I had people.

That was the thing about having a lot of money. Instead of doing the work myself, all I had to do was to pay someone else to do it.

Nonetheless, some of the decisions were big, so I took some time to look over some options that had been sent to me overnight.

Fortunately, I knew what I liked, so it only took about an hour to sort through everything and make some choices.

Another hour to relay those decisions and answer questions.

I leaned back in the chair and stretched.

It was just now time for breakfast and I'd gotten more done than most people got done in a week.

There were definitely advantages to having people.

It expanded work time exponentially.

Now that my work was done, I got a refill on my coffee and went out onto the veranda.

I logged into my iPad and filed a flight plan.

Now all I had to do was to get Ainsley back to Houston, make a quick trip to Wyoming, and then tell her what I'd done.

But for now, all I had to do was to take a few minutes to relax.

The first ferry bursting with tourists floated up toward the island.

Just another day for the islanders.

It would be an interesting place to live.

To see the tourists come and go while trying to live a normal life.

It would definitely put a curious spin on life.

Watching others on vacation while going to work every day and doing normal things. Trips to the post office. The dry cleaners. The grocery store.

It had been a little like that for me in Wyoming, except that I'd lived out in a secluded area.

But all that was about to change.

I was overdue for a life change.

And now I had the motivation to do it.

Ainsley was my motivation.

90

AINSLEY

*W*yatt was being quiet today.

It wasn't so much that he was being quiet since he wasn't a very talkative person to begin with. It was like he was preoccupied.

I buckled myself into the passenger seat of his plane and prepared myself for take off.

I felt out of sorts.

I liked it here on Mackinac Island. It was definitely a place I wanted to visit again.

And I would have liked to stay a little longer.

But it wasn't just that.

It was that we were leaving and I felt like something had changed in my relationship with Wyatt.

We were leaving here and going back to our ordinary lives.

The trip had most definitely not been what I'd expected.

Wyatt had been a perfect gentleman.

I'd thought we'd moved past that point where we slept in separate beds. But apparently not. That was precisely what we'd done.

Actually I'd spent last night on the sofa.

Fortunately, it had been a very comfortable sofa. Probably just as comfortable as I would have been in the bed.

I wouldn't have minded sharing a bed.

Just our luck that the one room had two beds.

But if Wyatt had decided to keep me at arm's length, then it was for the best.

I watched Wyatt out of the corner of my eyes as he went through the preflight checklist.

Just from watching him, I would have thought he flew his plane every day.

He definitely knew what he was doing.

He saw me watching him and shot me a quick grin.

I smiled back, but it didn't do anything to lessen the sense of loss I was feeling.

We were going back to reality. Which meant that I was going back to my life in Houston and he would be going back to his life in Wyoming.

He'd said he had the week off, but he hadn't said anything about what his plans were past getting me back to Houston.

Not that we ever discussed plans all that much. I'd thought we were doing better in that department.

But now I wasn't so sure.

Maybe it just wasn't in the cards for us to be together.

According to my psychologist sister, the people we were friends with and the people we dated were all about proximity.

And it made sense.

Long distance relationships didn't work. Not even for pilots who had access to the quickest form of transportation.

I'd seen it happen too many times.

The people we see every day end up taking precedence over the ones who live off.

I leaned back and looked out the window as Wyatt took the plane into the air.

It would work out the way it was supposed to.

It always did.

I'd done quite well by myself these past few months and I could continue to do it.

I'd chalk Wyatt up to being a momentary dalliance and tuck him into my memory bank of past loves.

After last night's storm, today was a beautiful day for a flight.

Wyatt flew us around the island before heading south.

The Grand Hotel was just that. Grand. It was most definitely a gem in the list of tourist destinations.

I watched as the island disappeared below us, then closed my eyes as it disappeared into the distance.

Another chapter closed.

But this had been a good one.

91

AINSLEY

wo weeks later

I STEPPED off the elevator at Skye Travels, and nervously smoothed my skirt.

Other than seeing him at family dinner last Sunday, I hadn't talked to Daddy since I'd turned down the job he'd offered while I was on Mackinac Island with Wyatt.

I'd been surprised to get his text asking me to come to his office.

Surely if something was wrong, like with his health, I would have already heard.

I couldn't, in fact, remember Daddy ever asking me to meet him at his office.

I was wearing my uniform. It was what I almost always wore when I was flying. One of the rare exceptions had been my trip to Aspen on that day I'd met Wyatt. I was even wearing my pilot's cap. The only thing missing way the Skye Travels logo on the jacket.

But since I didn't work for Skye Travels, I wouldn't have it.

Daddy hadn't asked me to take any other flights either since that day I'd turned him down, but that wasn't unusual.

"Hi Betty," I said to the receptionist as I passed her desk.

"Noah's in his office," she said. "He's expecting you."

I smiled and kept walking, but inside I was shaking.

Anytime I stopped by Daddy's office, I just walked in. There had never been a summons and the receptionist had never been so formal.

I reached his open door and stopped.

He looked up and smiled.

"Come in, Ainsley," he said, standing up.

"Is everything okay?" I asked, walking up to his big desk and sitting down in one of the two chairs.

He walked around and sat in the other one.

"Everything is great," he said, adjusting his tie.

I clasped my hands together to keep them from shaking.

"You wanted to see me," I said.

"Yes."

But he just looked at me.

I shifted uncomfortably.

"Ainsley," he said. "Out of all six of my children, you're the only one who took to flying."

"Well…" I said. "Madison married a pilot. And Danielle did, too."

That meant that out of the six married children, the two that were married had married pilots.

"I'm not discounting that," he said. "But it's different when it's your own flesh and blood. You'll understand one day when you have children of your own."

I must have made a face that reflected the skepticism that I felt at that comment.

"You will," he said. "You just have to give yourself time."

"Is that why you wanted to see me?" I asked, with a little smile. "To talk to me about children?"

"No," he said, with a half smile. "But if you have anything to tell me, I'm listening."

"No, Daddy," I said. "I don't have anything to tell you."

"Well," he said, with a grin. "Now that we got that out of the way, there is something I wanted to talk to you about."

My momentary relief turned back to anxiety.

"Okay," I said, straightening. Whatever it was, I could handle it.

"I don't think I've told you lately just how proud I am of you."

I didn't say anything. I just kept my gaze locked on his.

"And I'm very impressed at the level of commitment you've shown in getting your flight hours. Most of them on your own. And all your passengers have had nothing but good things to say about you."

"Thank you," I said.

"At any rate," Daddy said. "I've been distracted and put off something that was long overdue."

"It's understandable."

"Ainsley," he said. "I want you to come to work at Skye Travels."

My heart stuttered in my chest.

This was what I had wanted since the first time Daddy had taken me up in a plane.

Or at least the first time I could remember. By all accounts, he had all of us in airplanes before we could walk.

"You mean it?" I asked.

I'd wanted to hear him say these words so long, it felt surreal that he was actually offering to hire me.

"Yes," he said. "And I admit that I've been harder on you than I am on anyone else. But since you're family, I didn't want anyone to question my decision."

I smiled. "Daddy. I don't think anyone ever questions your decisions."

He smiled back. "It's your turn, Kiddo. Maddy has all the paperwork for you to fill out. You can start whenever you're ready."

"I'm ready right now," I said.

Daddy stood up and held out his arms. I went in for a hug.

Daddy gave the best hugs. His hugs always said that everything was going to be okay.

Five minutes later, I walked out of Daddy's office, on top of the world.

This day couldn't possibly get any better.

I'd just gotten my Skye Travels wings.

Life was good.

92

WYATT

*L*iving in the city wasn't as bad as I'd expected.

The traffic, actually, wasn't as bad as the traffic in Aspen. Just different.

As long as my car had GPS, I could get anywhere I needed to go.

The biggest difference was that I had to plan my outside walks.

I lived on the twenty-ninth floor of an apartment complex. It was temporary housing, but I was looking into another high rise.

I kind of liked having my own private elevator and I like being high above the city.

It was a little bit like living in an airplane.

Or about as close as humanly possible.

I had been biding my time. Waiting for the right time to let Ainsley know that I was living in Houston.

Although I was trying to find the perfect time, I was getting antsy.

Seeing her was long overdue.

But I was a man of big surprises.

I hadn't exactly known that about myself until I'd met Ainsley, but somehow she brought that trait out in me.

And, hell, I didn't even know if she liked surprises.

Just another thing to find out about her.

There was plenty of time.

Maybe today would be the day.

I walked into my apartment, dropped my keys on the counter and went out on the balcony, taking my Starbuck's latte with me.

It was a beautiful day. The sun was warm and there wasn't a cloud in the sky.

A good day for flying.

It was interesting that I'd been thinking more about flying since I'd reconnected with Ainsley.

Before that, flying had just been a quick way to get from place to place.

I had a car and a truck, but I would be content to not have to drive anywhere.

Of course, now that I lived in Houston, that would be next to impossible. Houston was most definitely a driving city.

The only other option would be to hire a driver, but that was too confining.

Going back inside, I glanced over at my desk. I had a brand new game I was right in the middle of conceptualizing. A game that involved, no surprise, airplanes.

It was a little different than what I normally did, but I just went with whatever my muse dictated.

It was an odd juxtaposition being an artist of sorts and running a million-dollar business. But I did what I wanted and that made all the hard work I'd done worthwhile.

I hadn't planned on moving to Houston until I met Ainsley, but that came from a lesson I'd learned a long time ago.

Go where your girl is.

Or she won't be your girl for long.

Now all I had to do was to convince her to be my girl.

Instead of sitting at my desk, I jumped in the shower.

While I was in the shower, a text came in.

NOAH: *Are you ready?*

That was all the impetus I needed.

I'd waited long enough.

Today was the day.

93

AINSLEY

I filled out all the paperwork that made me an official Skye Travel pilot.

I couldn't help but think that something was missing.

Sure, I had my family to celebrate with. And celebrate we would.

But it would have been nice to be able to tell Wyatt. To celebrate the achievement of my lifelong dream with him.

I stood at the elevator, waiting.

And put Wyatt out of my mind.

It had been two weeks since our trip to Mackinac Island and I hadn't heard from him once.

And he knew where to find me now.

So there was no excuse.

I stretched to my full height.

It was okay. I was okay. Or at least I would be.

The elevator dinged and the doors slid open.

A dog stepped out.

Beau?

The dog barked once, then started licking my hands.

I knelt down and rubbed his neck.

I laughed when he licked my chin.

"Where did you come from?"

Beau sat back and barking once, looked back over his shoulder.

I looked up, expecting to see the young man I'd delivered the dog to.

Beau was supposed to be trained to be a service dog. Knowing that he was going to be serving others was the only way I was able to leave him without a fight.

I stood up, keeping one hand on Beau's head.

Wyatt stepped out of the elevator.

The very one I'd just been thinking about.

Had I conjured him?

A fanciful notion, Momma would say.

But Daddy would understand.

Daddy and I were of kindred spirit.

"Ainsley." His voice was soothing. Like a balm I'd been missing.

"What are you doing here?"

He smiled. "I brought you a friend."

"I'm not sure which one of you I'm more surprised to see."

He grinned.

"My guess would be Beau. You'd have to know I couldn't stay away."

I was speechless.

So I just looked at him, my brow creased.

"So Beau had a hug. Can I have one?"

When I didn't move, he stepped forward and, wrapping his arms around me, swept me literally off my feet.

I held onto his arms and giggled.

He set me on my feet and kissed me on the lips.

Beau nuzzled our clasped hands.

I couldn't process what Wyatt was doing here, so I tucked it into the back of my mind to work on later.

"So, really, what's Beau doing here?"

Wyatt looked quite pleased with himself.

"He's yours."

"What?" I rubbed Beau's ears. "What do you mean?"

"I guess technically he's our dog. He's been living with me for a few months now."

"I don't understand."

"I tracked him down and bought him."

"So you tracked down the dog."

What I didn't say was that he tracked down the dog, but he didn't bother to track me down.

But he seemed to know exactly where I was headed.

"I saw Beau's address, but I only knew your first name."

I tried to remember back.

I'd had Beau's papers in my bag.

And I hadn't told Wyatt my last name.

What he was saying was plausible.

Not exactly what I'd expected, but definitely possible.

"Okay," I said. "I think we need to start communicating a little better."

"Agreed," he said quickly.

I heard Betty talking in the background.

The sound of a jet engine preparing for takeoff.

Normal sounds.

But things had changed. For me.

"I'll start," he said. "I live here now."

"Here?" I tucked a strand of hair behind an ear. Now I was completely confused. "Here where?"

"Here Houston." He said it like he was talking about the weather. Like it was a normal thing for him to just up and move from Wyoming to Houston.

"What about your job? Your company?"

He grinned.

"I brought it with me."

"You… brought… it."

He did own his own company.

"Why?" It was the only coherent word I could come up with.

He shook his head.

"It would be hard to court you from Wyoming."

"Court?" I put my fingertips over my lips to keep from laughing out loud. "An odd phrase."

Beau nuzzled his hands, trying to draw his attention.

"Let me rephrase. I don't like the odds on a long-distance relationship."

"A long distance? Relationship?"

My blood was pounding dangerously in my ears.

Wyatt wanted to be in a relationship?

And here I'd thought I'd never see him again.

This was the second time we'd been down this road.

But this time he'd found me.

Intentionally.

94

WYATT

When I'd moved my business to Houston and even when I'd tracked down Beau and took him to Wyoming to live with me with the intent of buying him for Ainsley, I'd known that I ran a risk.

I ran a risk that I'd burned a bridge with her.

Or even worse that I'd merely been a snowstorm diversion.

She could have someone in her life already.

Or she might just not want me.

But it was a risk I'd been willing to take.

Because she was the woman I wanted.

And I was willing to take whatever risk was necessary to show her that I had no doubts.

Despite the way I'd left in Wyoming. I'd been an asshole.

And that was odd because I wasn't an asshole kind of guy.

And, yes, I'd tipped things in my favor by letting Noah know my intentions.

Another big risk.

But Noah had gotten on board without any problem.That had been a pleasant surprise.

But just because the Father was on board didn't mean the daughter was.

Ainsley knelt down again and was scratching Beau on the ears.

They were happy to see each other, that much was clear.

Even if she didn't want to date me, I'd done the right thing by bringing her Beau.

"Maybe I should back up," I said.

She looked up at me from beneath her dark eyelashes with a look that probably made most men squirm.

Ainsley Worthington was a force to be reckoned with.

A man had to be brave to pursue a girl like her.

"We had a good time in Mackinac, right?" I asked.

She shrugged. "It was nice."

"So I thought maybe I could take you on a date."

"Wait," she said, standing up, but keeping one hand on Beau's collar. "You moved here so you could ask me on a date?"

When she put it like that, it made me sound a bit insane.

"Sort of," I said. "I'm living in temporary housing."

"Oh."

I took heart that she sounded disappointed.

It had to be a good sign.

"So," I said. "Will you go on a date with me?"

She looked down at Beau.

"Well, you did bring me Beau," she said. "So I can hardly say no."

Just then Noah Worthington strode toward us on his way to the elevator.

"Wyatt," he said. "Good to see you again. Ainsley. Why aren't you out celebrating?"

"I've got a flight," she said.

"Did she tell you?" Noah asked me.

"Tell me what?" I asked.

"She's now an official pilot for Skye Travels."

"You don't say?" I looked over at Ainsley. She just shrugged. Noah hadn't told me that.

"We are definitely going to celebrate," I said.

"I have a flight," Ainsley said again.

Noah looked at her then.

"I'll get someone to cover it," he said, pulling his cell phone out of his pocket.

He sent off a quick text, then pressed the elevator button.

"There," he said. "You're free for the day. Go celebrate."

The elevator dinged and the door slid open.

Noah stepped inside.

"Coming?" He asked, holding the doors.

I looked at Ainsley. "Ready to take Beau home?"

I handed her the dog's leash.

"Okay," she said. "Apparently I've been outmaneuvered and overruled."

The three of us, four counting Beau, rode down to the first floor.

"Oh," Noah said as he headed toward his BMW. "Your mother is planning a dinner for Saturday. To celebrate. You should bring Wyatt."

Before either of us could respond, he strode to his car, opened the door, and got inside.

Ainsley just looked at me.

"Why do I get the feeling that you two have conspired against me?"

"Never against you," I said. "For you."

She just rolled her eyes.

"Is Beau riding with me or you?"

95

AINSLEY

*A*s I made my way through the mid-morning traffic, Beau sat quietly in the backseat.

Wyatt followed me in his own car. Instead of the old truck he'd driven me around in up in Wyoming, he drove a fire engine red Tesla.

In the last two hours my life had completely changed.

I had a job with Skye Travels. The job I'd worked toward my whole life.

And now I had a dog.

Wyatt had been right. I'd gotten quite attached to Beau while I was in Wyoming.

That wasn't supposed to happen. I was supposed to just pick up the dog and drop him off at the training facility.

But Wyatt had intervened. So that meant Wyatt had had Beau all along.

That meant that Wyatt had been thinking about me all along. He just didn't know how to find me.

I suppose that was plausible, though I still wondered why he hadn't put everything together.

And on top of all that, it seemed I had a boyfriend.

Daddy had just invited him to our family celebration for my new job.

If that didn't put him in the boyfriend category, I didn't know what did.

Not only that, but Wyatt had moved to Houston. And he'd brought his company with him.

Surely not his whole company. Just his part.

Despite our agreement to communicate more, there were a whole lot of things we didn't know about each other. Or at least that I didn't know about him.

Apparently he'd been talking to my father and Daddy hadn't even told me.

I'd have to think about that later.

I pulled into my private parking space and Wyatt pulled in beside me.

He was wearing his dark shades and just watching him get out of his car sent my heart rate into overdrive.

He was a handsome man that no red-blooded woman would be immune to.

Myself included.

And he wanted to date me.

The truth was, I wanted to date him.

He was there to open my door before I'd barely turned off the motor.

Taking my hand, he helped me out of the car.

"Ainsley," he said. "I'm willing to spend the rest of my life making up for the way I left you in Wyoming."

I opened the back door and Beau spilled out, all gangly legs.

"The rest of your life seems like a long time to make up for that." I grabbed Beau's leash.

I was not only responsible for him, but he was my dog.

And this was the city.

That meant I had to be extra careful to keep a hold on him.

As we rode up the private elevator to my apartment, Wyatt leaned back against the mirrored wall.

Beau sat down and waited. Either he'd had some training, or he had an innate sense of how to behave.

"You're not going to believe this," Wyatt said.

"What's that?"

As the elevator dinged and the doors slid open, Wyatt looked at me.

"We're neighbors."

96

WYATT

"There's no way you didn't know that," Ainsley said as we stepped off the elevator into my apartment.

It was a huge apartment. A penthouse with views in three directions.

Larger than mine and most definitely higher in the air.

I had to admit I liked hers better.

"I didn't know," I said, going to stand at the nearest wall of windows.

Now this I could get used to. If I could live like this—in the air—I could be more than content in Houston.

I rarely went outside in Wyoming anyway. If I wasn't glued to my computer screen, I was flying my jet to Aspen or to Denver.

Ainsley crossed her arms.

"Then how, in this city of a million people with a million apartments, did we end up being neighbors?"

I turned and shrugged as I faced her.

"One of my assistants found it for me. I didn't have a clue where it was until I typed the address in the GPS at the airport."

She shook her head, but I could tell she believed me. Almost.

It was a lot to ask of a coincidence.

"Anyway," I said. "It's temporary. She's looking for something else. Actually…"

I pulled out my phone and sent off a quick text to that assistant to make sure to find a high floor.

ME: *The higher the better.*

MANDY: *I already knew that. But hard to find.*

Ainsley watched me with a raised eyebrow as I slipped the phone back into my pocket.

"My assistant," I said.

Ainsley dropped her keys and handbag off on the kitchen island and went to the cabinet to find a bowl for water.

Beau, still at her heels, lapped thirstily.

Then she pulled out her own phone.

"We should get him some dog food," I said. "I have some at my place."

She held up a finger and finished what she was doing.

"It'll be here in less than two hours," she said.

"Delivery for dog food?"

She smiled devilishly. "You're not in Wyoming anymore."

"That's the truth."

Now that Beau was taken care of, she went to the edge of the island and leaned against it.

"Since you're here, what are we supposed to be doing to celebrate?"

"What would you do if I wasn't here?"

She pushed off the island went to sit on her neutral colored leather sofa. One of the few pieces of furniture in the room.

"I have that family thing this weekend."

"No," I said, going to sit on the other end of the sofa. "Today. What would you be doing today?"

When Beau jumped onto what was no doubt a very expensive sofa, she didn't bat an eye.

"I'd be flying," she said without a hitch.

"You're idea of celebrating is working."

She smiled. "How do you think I got this job?"

When I didn't answer, she said. "Never mind. Don't answer that."

"Ainsley," I said. "I know how you got this job. You worked your ass off."

She looked blankly at me for a moment, then smiled.

It was one of those rare smiles. Delightful like when a butterfly lands on someone's fingertips.

Rare and special.

Yes I'd moved my business to Houston on a whim.

A whim named Ainsley Worthington.

97

AINSLEY

*H*aving Wyatt in my apartment felt surreal.

After our time in Wyoming, I'd thought about him constantly.

But I hadn't thought to see him again.

Not really.

I imagined all sorts of chance meetings.

A coffee shop.

An airport.

Usually an airport. Probably somewhere in Colorado since he had no reason to fly in my typical flight direction.

But then he'd shown up at my sister's wedding.

As the best man.

And then after I'd embarrassed myself on the dance floor and flown off to Mackinac Island with him, he'd disappeared again.

He was truly an enigma.

I'd almost call him flighty. Except that was a term usually used to describe a woman.

Maybe he was just a scatterbrained creative person. A bit like my younger sister who had trouble actually landing her attention on anything for any period of time, unless, of course, it was doing something creative that she was actually focused on.

The real question was what was I going to do with him?

I didn't know what he expected.

Some of the things he said led me to believe that we had a future together.

But his actions didn't quite line up with that.

"Is there some place we can take Beau out for a walk?" He asked.

I actually had to think about that for a minute.

"There's a park not far from here."

"What do you think?" He asked. "Want to take him for a walk?"

"Sure."

It was either that or we could sit here and look at each other.

But looking at him made me think about other things that we could do. And after the wedding reception, I didn't trust myself to get that close to him.

This time, instead of going in separate cars, I drove. Beau sat in the back seat.

As I pulled out of the parking garage onto the street, I remembered something that Wyatt had said.

"What did you mean when you said Beau was *our dog?*"

He shrugged. "I bought him for you, but I've been taking care of him for six months."

"Oh," I said, still not sure where he was going with that.

We rode in silence the rest of the way to the park.

It was that late morning time when there were very few people out taking walks.

Beau ran to the end of his leash, stopping just in time for it to catch, then ran back in the other direction.

"You've been working with him," I said, surprised.

"A little," Wyatt said.

"So, tell me, what were you going to do with him if you didn't see me again?"

"I'd just keep him," Wyatt said. "The girls at work really took to him."

"You took him to work?" I tried to ignore the stab of jealousy at the thought of other women taking to Beau... not to mention Wyatt.

"Of course. I couldn't very well leave him home alone."

"Right."

Beau came back and walked between us.

Was this something he was used to doing? Walking between Wyatt and someone else?

"Just because you bought him for me, doesn't mean that maybe you shouldn't keep him."

Wyatt scoffed. "I can't keep him," he said.

"Why not?"

"Because he's your dog."

I didn't know why Wyatt insisted that Beau was my dog.

I'd merely found him. And if not for the snow storm, I could have simply delivered him and forgotten about him. I did a decent job of not getting attached to pets or passengers.

Or other pilots.

And right now, I suddenly realized, Wyatt was acting like a pilot.

That was the thing that had been bothering me about him.

He was acting like a flighty pilot.

Here today. Gone tomorrow.

Exactly the kind of man I vowed to stay away from.

98

WYATT

"I'll be back in a minute," Ainsley said, mumbling something about changing clothes.

Her expression told me she wasn't going to *change into something more comfortable* as they said in the old movies where the leading lady was getting ready to seduce the leading man.

In fact, I listened closely to make sure she didn't actually head to the elevator.

Even Beau stayed with me.

"What do you think, Beau?" I asked. "Where do you think I screwed up?"

Beau tilted his head and looked at me.

If the dog could talk, he'd probably tell me that I'd screwed up in Wyoming when I'd left Ainsley in the cabin.

He'd probably also wish me luck in making up for that.

Apparently Ainsley wasn't inclined to let that go.

Sometimes she seemed to forget and forgive, then other times, like just now, she'd give me a look that told me she'd just remembered.

Did she know that I'd tracked down Beau and bought him for her? For her. Not for me.

All I'd said was that I took Beau to work with me.

And that the girls there took to him.

Leaning back on the sofa, I put a hand over my face.

Damn.

That was it. She was jealous.

I didn't know if she was jealous because of me or because of Beau. Or both of us.

That was something that I hadn't expected.

Ainsley Worthington had everything.

The career.

The family.

The look of a model.

She was perfect.

And she was jealous.

Surely not.

I hadn't taken Beau to work impress other girls. I'd taken him to work so that he wouldn't have to be alone.

The dog had obviously remembered Ainsley, so he must not have been all that impressed with the other women.

I watched the traffic below as I waited.

A few minutes later, Ainsley came from the back wearing blue jeans and an oversized sweater.

She'd let her hair down and it flowed around her shoulders.

I swallowed, my throat suddenly dry.

Without meeting my gaze, Ainsley stepped into her kitchen.

"Want something to drink?" She asked.

"Just some water," I said.

She nodded and pulled two bottles of water from the refrigerator.

Handing me one of them, she took the other and sat across from me.

"We need to talk," she said.

99

AINSLEY

*E*ven as I said the words, I knew that those words could strike fear into the heart of anyone in a relationship.

The look on Wyatt's face told me he wasn't immune.

And we weren't even in a relationship.

Yet here he was. Sitting on my sofa next to the dog he'd bought for me.

Just because I'd taken to the dog didn't mean that I wanted to be a dog parent.

He should have asked me.

I sipped my water and tried to figure out what it was I wanted… needed to say to him.

I didn't want to come across as being petty.

That wasn't my style.

I appreciated the gesture.

It was just… I *liked* Wyatt.

I'd been seriously crushing on him since that first day we'd met.

And I didn't like the way he seemed to feel free to come and go.

If I was going to be in a relationship, I wanted communication.

It wasn't my fault.

Both my mother and my sister were psychologists.

Communication was what we did in my family.

Except now Daddy had gone and conspired against me with Wyatt.

I decided that was a good place to start.

Maybe the safest anyway.

"How did you and Daddy get to know each other?"

He looked a bit surprised by the question. He'd probably expected the worst and I didn't blame him.

"At the reception. After you left." He sipped his water, then turned his blue eyes back to mine.

"You weren't there," he said. "And we talked."

"But you stayed in touch."

He nodded. "I asked him not to tell you I was coming to Houston."

I didn't say anything. If Daddy didn't tell me, he had a good reason.

"I told him I wanted to surprise you."

"He knows I don't like surprises," I said, mostly to myself.

"He told me that," Wyatt said. "But then I told him about Beau and he seemed to be okay with it. We set up a time when I could bring him to the office."

That sounded like something Daddy would do.

It wasn't like he'd given Wyatt my address. Right?

"He didn't tell you where I lived?"

"Are you kidding? When it comes to you, Noah is a closed book. And he let me know in no uncertain terms what would happen if I were to do anything that might hurt you."

I smiled to myself. That was my father. He had a heart of gold. But the one thing he didn't tolerate was anyone hurting his family.

Beau laid his head in my lap and all the anger I'd been trying to brew dissipated.

It was impossible for me to stay mad at Wyatt. Even when I thought I should.

"So," he said, with a little grin. "Can you forgive me?"

I scratched at Beau's ears. "I don't really have a choice, do I?"

"You always have a choice, Ainsley."

I looked at him. It was hard to tell who's side he was on anyway.

I told him so.

He laughed.

"I'm on your side. And if you tell me to take Beau and walk out that door right now, I'll do it."

I kissed Beau on the head.

"You can't have Beau," I said.

I looked at Wyatt from beneath my lashes.

"And I guess you can stay, too."

"Anybody ever tell you that you really know how to boost a guy's ego?" He asked.

"I didn't realize you needed any help in that department."

He laughed.

"I thought you worked around men."

I smiled.

And that was exactly why I knew that Wyatt's ego was just fine.

More than fine.

100

WYATT

"So," I said. "Back to your celebration."

She sat on the sofa with her feet under her and Beau's head on her lap.

Lucky dog.

"The one on Saturday?"

"No, Silly," I said. "The one today."

"Oh," she shrugged.

The more I learned about Ainsley, the more I discovered that she wasn't what she seemed.

She seemed like an incredibly successful and confident woman.

And she was all those things, but she was also vulnerable. And I had a feeling she had put her own needs behind those of others.

She'd worked so hard to gain her father's approval. To be a pilot worthy enough for him to hire for his company.

Noah must have been harder on her than he was on anyone else he hired, at least from what I'd seen.

It occurred to me in that moment that I hadn't actually

flown with Ainsley. She'd flown with me, but not the other way around.

And when I'd asked her how she wanted to celebrate, she'd said she wanted to fly.

I'd dismissed that, thinking that she was like other women. That maybe she'd want to go to dinner or some other such traditional celebratory activity.

That was the problem with being a geek.

I didn't always have a good idea of what other people needed.

I forgot that they didn't see the world the same way I did.

"I have an idea," I said.

"What's that?" she asked, obviously wary.

"First of all, I need to know if you like ice cream."

"You know I do," she said.

"Hmm." I just wanted to make sure I wasn't assuming that she liked something just because I did."

"What's your idea?" She asked.

"There's this ice cream shop in Silverton, Colorado named Smedley's. It's my favorite ice cream place in the whole world."

"You're wanting ice cream?" she asked with a little smile.

"Only if you do. It's your celebration."

"I wouldn't mind," she said, but Colorado is a long way from here."

"I know." I grinned. "I was thinking we could take my plane."

I saw a shadow cross her features, but it was so brief most people would have missed it. That told me I was on the right track to understanding her.

"Okay," she said, still rubbing Beau's ears.

"But I want you to fly it."

She froze and stared at me. Then shook her head.

"I can't."

"Why not?"

"I'm not licensed to fly a Phenom."

"You are if I'm right there with you." I grinned.

She just looked at me for a moment and I would have given anything to know what was going on in her head.

Then she smiled.

One of those beautiful rare, true smiles.

"Okay," she said. "Let's get some ice cream."

101

AINSLEY

*T*he Phenom handled like a dream.

It was sort of like the difference I'd noticed when I'd traded in my first car, a Toyota, for a BMW. It just felt different.

My takeoff from Houston was smooth and steady.

Wyatt was right there in the copilot's seat, watching everything, but so far, he'd been silent.

I was pretty adaptable when it came to flying.

Sometimes Daddy took me with him to trainings and I got to try out some simulators that were normally off-limits for someone at my level.

As we approached what passed as an airport in Silverton, Colorado, Wyatt did all the communicating.

But I was the one who took the plane down for what I considered a perfect landing.

"You're good," Wyatt said as the plane came to a stop. "Better than good."

I grinned. "Thanks."

"You should have been flying for Skye Travels a long time ago."

I pulled off my headset. "Daddy made me work twice as hard for it. He didn't want anyone to ever question it."

"Who questions Noah Worthington?"

"Exactly," I said. "And that's why. He's above reproach."

Wyatt nodded. "Well, I'm impressed."

"Okay," I said, looking around. There were no cars waiting. Not even a horse and carriage. "How do we get to town?"

Wyatt checked his phone. Then frowned.

"The car is late."

"Actually," I said. "I think we're a little bit early."

And just then a car came toward us.

"There they are," Wyatt said with obvious relief.

"It's not that far," I said. "I'm surprised you didn't want to just walk or take a bicycle."

Wyatt winced. "Am I that bad?"

"Sometimes," I said.

"It's okay if you tell me," he said. "Sometimes I forget you're a girl."

My jaw dropped. "You did not just say that."

"I don't mean it like that."

"Wyatt," I asked. "Are you gay?"

Wyatt rolled his eyes. "And you did not just ask me that."

I laughed. "I kind of need to know if you are."

"Is that so?" He asked. "Why is that? Do you have designs on me?"

The car stopped outside our door and we unhooked our harnesses.

"Wyatt," I said. "Sometimes you use strange language."

"Sorry," he said. "I'm working on a fantasy game and I'm learning a lot of new phrases."

I didn't say anything as we stepped went down the steps. Beau went down first with Wyatt holding onto his leash.

This was the first thing Wyatt had told me anything about his work.

He really was trying to communicate more with me.

We climbed into the back of a car and Wyatt took my hand. I sat in the middle of the back seat, close to him, because Beau sat on the other side of me.

It was Wyatt's idea to bring him.

Since apparently Beau had been flying a lot since he'd gone to live with Wyatt.

Silverton wasn't so much a town as it was a street.

We passed the railroad tracks of the Durango-Silverton narrow gauge railroad.

"That looks like fun," I said.

"It is," Wyatt said. "We'll go sometime."

It was the strangest thing.

Just that simple phrase *we'll go sometime* did strange things to my heart.

102

WYATT

*A*insley's hand fit perfectly in mine. Such soft skin.

This was why I'd picked up and moved to Houston.

Just to be near her.

I had to treat her carefully though.

I'd been an ass to her in Wyoming. Strike one.

Then, although I hadn't realized it, I'd hit strike two when I hadn't contacted her after our trip to Mackinac.

In retrospect, I could see how my attempt at being a gentleman could easily have been interpreted by her as being disinterested.

But I was most certainly not disinterested.

On the contrary, I was infatuated with her.

I just had to be very careful not to hit strike three.

Sometimes getting me out of my own head was difficult.

But with Ainsley it was easier than with most people.

I wanted to do everything with her.

I want to take her on the Durango-Silverton narrow gauge railroad.

Unlike Mackinac, it was something I'd done before and I wanted to share it with her.

I wanted to share things I liked and I wanted to have new experiences with her.

I was besotted by her.

We reached Main Street in no time and the driver pulled straight up to Smedley's Ice Cream Parlor.

"Why do they call it Smedley's" Ainsley asked. "Is that the name of the family who owns it?"

"That's an excellent question," I said, opening the door and holding out a hand to help her out on my side.

"I actually asked them that question."

Beau jumped out after Ainsley and shook himself as though he was adjusting his hair.

"It's actually the name of their cat."

"Their cat?" Ainsley asked. "How cute."

"I thought it was pretty cool that they named their business after their cat."

"It is," she following me toward the door. "My father named his company after my mother."

"Skye Travels? How so?"

Ainsley smiled. "My mother's name is Savannah Skye Richards Worthington." She shrugged. "So he named it Skye. Most people think it's just a unique way of spelling sky, you know for the sky."

"I thought that, too," I said and held the door as Ainsley stepped through.

She stopped. "Wait. Can Beau come in here?"

"This is Silverton," I said. "Anything goes." Then I lowered my voice. "We probably don't want to be here after dark."

She looked around at the families sitting at the tables and shot me a skeptical look.

"You have to trust me on that one," I said.

We went up to the ice cream display.

"You want your usual?" I asked. "Chocolate and vanilla swirl?"

"You remembered? I'm impressed."

I grinned like a schoolboy, but shrugged nonchalantly. "Not all that hard," I said.

"Sure," she said. "that sounds good."

As we waited for the girl, probably a college student, to scoop our ice cream into bowls, a little boy, not more than ten walked up to the counter.

"Can I get a an ice cream cone?" He asked the girl.

"Sure," the clerk said. "What flavor do you want?"

"Vanilla," he said. "It's for my little sister." He pointed over his shoulder toward a little girl, about seven sitting alone at a table.

"That'll be four dollars and thirty-five cents," the clerk said.

The little boy reached into pocket, pulled out a crumpled dollar, and placed it on the counter.

"This is all I have," he said.

The clerk frowned at him. "I'm sorry," she said. "I can't sell you an ice cream for a dollar."

"But—" The boy looked distressed.

"Sorry," the girl behind the counter said.

The little boy took his dollar and walked back to the table with the little girl.

"Do you see his parents?" Ainsley asked.

"I don't know."

Our ice cream was ready, so I put the little boy out of my mind and took our ice cream from the clerk.

But instead of taking her ice cream from me, Ainsley stepped up to the counter and ordered two vanilla ice cream cones.

"Changed your mind?" I asked, at a loss as to why she'd be ordering something different.

She paid for the ice cream, then waited patiently while the girl filled two cones with vanilla ice cream.

At that moment, I knew what she was doing.

103

AINSLEY

I watched calmly as the clerk filled two cones with ice cream.

Calmly on the outside anyway.

I didn't know what the little boy's situation was, but I saw no reason to deny him or the little girl something so simple as an ice cream cone just because he didn't have the money to pay.

The girl smiled as she handed me the cones, but I kept my expression blank.

Then I marched right over to the table with the two children and handed an ice cream cone to each of them.

The little girl continued to look sad, even as she took the ice cream, but the little boy's face lit up.

"Thank you," he said.

"You're welcome."

Wyatt stood silently behind me, holding our two cups of ice cream.

There was no way I would have been able to enjoy my ice cream knowing that two children were sitting right there doing without.

"Are your parents around?" I asked.

The boy shook his head.

"Nah. My mom is here with our stepdad. He left us here while they went to eat some lunch."

"Oh," I said, forcing a smile. "How did you get here?"

"We rode the train," the little boy said. "It was so awesome. Did you ride it?"

"No," I said. "Not yet. But I've heard good things about it."

"You should definitely ride it," the boy said.

"I will," I said. "Enjoy your ice cream."

I turned back to Wyatt and took my cup from him.

We found a private table near the window.

"What kind of parents leave their children alone like that?" he asked.

"The kind who don't want to be bothered," I said, taking a bite of ice cream. "This really is good."

He didn't say anything. Just ate his ice cream in silence.

I wondered what he was thinking, but it didn't really matter.

I'd only done what any decent person would have done.

I'm sure even Wyatt would have done it if he'd seen what was going on.

A few minutes later, Wyatt sat his ice cream bowl on the floor in front of Beau.

The dog lapped it up in seconds.

Wyatt had only eaten about half his ice cream.

I held my plastic spoon in the air. "Something wrong with your ice cream?" I asked.

"Nah," he said.

Wyatt seemed preoccupied.

I found it rather odd that he was the one who'd wanted to fly here to Silverton just for ice cream. And then he'd barely eaten any of it.

"Something bothering you?" I asked.

"No," he said, picking up the bowl and taking it the trash.

I watched him walk away and back.

I'd never seen him like this. He seemed... edgy.

I didn't care what he said, something was bothering him.

He sat back down next to me and we watched as the children's parents come into the ice cream parlor.

I couldn't understand what the mother said, but the children pointed in my direction.

I just gave them a quick nod of acknowledgement.

The man, supposedly the stepfather walked in my direction.

Oh no.

He did not look happy.

As he reached our table, he opened his wallet and pulled out a ten dollar bill.

"We don't take charity," he said, laying it on the table in front of me.

"Charity?"

I was confused. How was buying children ice cream charity?

Wyatt stood up and moved in front of me.

"We don't want your money," he said, picking the money up and holding it out to the man.

"Fine," he said, jerking the money from Wyatt's hand. "But don't be buying other people's kids ice cream."

The man started to turn around on his heel.

"Wouldn't have to if the parents didn't leave them alone."

Though he spoke the words under his breath, the stepfather heard him and turned around.

I couldn't see what happened next, but I heard the sound of flesh making contact with flesh.

Then Wyatt was on the floor.

104

WYATT

"*D*o you want to press charges?" the Silverton police officer asked.

I shook my head. "No." I held the cold compress against my jaw.

I hadn't seen the man's fist coming. If I had, I would have at least ducked.

But then fist fighting wasn't something that happened in my world. Ever.

All I knew was that the man had threatened Ainsley.

All she'd done was help out a couple of neglected children.

When she did that, my heart had swelled with pride.

It was such a little thing, all in all. But it wasn't something most people would take the time or effort to do.

I'd been processing that information when that asshole had walked up and offended her by trying to give her money.

The last thing Ainsley needed was money. All he'd had to do was to say thank you.

If he'd just thanked her like a normal person and not insulted her, I wouldn't be sitting here on the floor holding a cold compress against my jaw.

The young lady behind the counter had seen the whole thing and had called the police.

I'd known that Silverton was a rowdy place, but typically the tourists weren't the ones being rowdy.

The children had left with their mother and stepfather.

"Well," the policeman said. "I'm going to question him anyway."

The man who'd clocked my jaw was sitting outside, a policeman at his side.

The woman and children had left already.

"How am I supposed to get back to Durango?" I heard the man ask as he was ushered outside.

"Not something for you to worry about," his escort had said.

Ainsley sat quietly, watching.

After the policeman walked away, I looked into her eyes. Eyes that I couldn't read at the moment.

"I'm sorry," I said. "I didn't mean for that to happen."

Her eyes were full of moisture.

Strike three, my gut said.

I wasn't sure if it was because I'd made a comment that had made the man come after me or if it was because I hadn't found back.

Truth was, by the time I figured out what had happened, I was seeing stars.

Ainsley put a hand over mine.

"Don't apologize," she said with a little smile.

"That never should have happened," I said. "I should have kept my mouth shut and let him just walk away peacefully."

"There was nothing peaceful about that man," she said.

I agreed with her one hundred percent.

I glanced over at where the police were questioning him.

That man was trouble. If he didn't have a police record, I predicted he would.

"You were just trying to protect me," Ainsley said. "Thank you."

I shifted my gaze back to hers.

She didn't look disappointed in me. And she didn't look like she saw this as the third strike.

She put a finger lightly against my lips, then leaned over and kissed me.

"That's going to hurt later," she said.

"I don't know about later," I said. "But it doesn't feel so good right now."

Actually it hurt like hell, but I wasn't going to tell Ainsley that.

"I have some Tylenol," she said, digging in her handbag.

My heart swelled with admiration for this woman.

She was one of the most kind-hearted people I'd ever met.

It wasn't that she made grand gestures to help people. It was that she took the time to help the little person.

To do something special that made someone's day. And she didn't ask for recognition or even thanks.

And it was almost reflexive for her. She didn't have to think about it.

She just did it.

It was hard to think past the pain in my jaw, but the feelings I'd been having earlier were back.

And I realized that hadn't been thinking about my sister.

Instead of dwelling on the past and the loss of my sister, I'd been focused on Ainsley and the future.

All this had happened and I hadn't even realized it.

Now all I had to do was figure out how to do what I needed to do.

Without hitting strike three.

105

AINSLEY

a simple situation had gone from bad to worse.

I should probably be upset about the whole thing, but I was actually rather impressed.

Wyatt was the first man who had ever stood up for me, much less to the point of taking a punch for me.

Being a man, he thought he should have punched the guy back or at the least ducked to avoid being knocked to the floor.

But instead, I fell a little bit more in love with him.

After the police left, he decided he didn't need the ice pack anymore.

"We should at least go walk around town a bit before we have to fly back to Houston."

"Okay," I said.

We hadn't brought our overnight bags, so we have a repeat of our spontaneous overnight trip to Mackinac.

I was fine with that, especially since I'd gotten a notice that I had my first flight with Skye Travels in the morning.

It was just a simple flight to Dallas to drop off a passenger, but it was my first flight as an official employee of Skye Travels, so it held a high level of importance for me.

I glanced at my watch.

"Okay," I said, "but I need to get back early so I can be rested for my flight in the morning."

"Understood," he said, taking my hand and leading me out the door of the pizza parlor.

It was nice to get outside into the fresh mountain air.

We'd been inside the pizza parlor far too long, much longer than we'd expected.

The crisp mountain air had a slight invigorating chill to it that cleared my head.

Wyatt and I walked hand in hand down the street until we came to a little park.

The park had two wooden benches in a grove of aspen trees.

"Mind if we sit?" he asked.

"Or course not," I said, thinking that his jaw must be bothering him.

We sat next to each other on one of the benches.

"You really like the mountains," I said.

He let go of my hand and, putting his arm around me, pulled me close.

He laced my hands in his and kissed my cheek.

"I do like the mountains," he said, his breath warm against my ear.

"Yet you moved to Houston," I said, the words catching at the back of my throat.

"Yes," he whispered against my ear. "I found something that I like more than the mountains."

"Yeah?" My heart was racing.

I was overwhelmed with emotion at the possibility that he was talking about me.

"Yeah," he said. "You see. I bought this dog named Beau for a girl who lives in Houston and while I was keeping this dog, I got so attached to him, I didn't think I could live without him."

"I see," I said with faux seriousness. "So you uprooted your business and moved to across the country. To a place without mountains. For a dog."

He chuckled.

"Pretty much."

I turned so that I could look into his clear, beautiful blue eyes.

"I think it was a good move," I said.

My eyes fluttered closed as Wyatt kissed me on the cheek, then the corner of my mouth.

That kiss sent shivers down my spine.

I turned and touched my lips to his.

"Ainsley," he said, his lips close to mine. "I don't want to live my life without you."

"I feel the same way," I said, my heart full of joy.

He held me close. So close.

He held me like he would never let me go.

EPILOGUE
AINSLEY

Three weeks later

I made a perfect landing, my wheels touching smoothly against the Houston airport runway.

No one seemed to notice, except maybe Beau who sat right behind me. But I didn't care.

I was pretty much on top of the world right now.

I had a date with Wyatt later.

We'd seen each other every day since our trip to Silverton, but this was different.

He'd said to wear something formal.

So I'd gone shopping with my fashionista sister, Brianna, yesterday and bought a new sexy red dress.

So far we'd stayed in, ordered delivery, and even done some cooking, so this was something different.

Although I knew exactly what time it was, I glanced at my watch. I had just enough time to get home, shower, and get dressed.

All I needed was for the traffic to hold.

I taxied down the runway to the Skye Travels terminal. I

still felt a sense of pride that I got to wear the Skye Travels logo on my uniform.

After securing the plane, I snapped on Beau's leash and we climbed out of the plane.

The hot Texas air hit me slap in the face.

Maybe Wyatt and I should have flipped it around. Maybe we should have moved to Wyoming instead of Houston.

But looking up, I saw the Houston skyline spread out in front of me and I knew we were in the right place.

This was home.

This was where my family was.

I didn't want to live anywhere else.

But I wasn't opposed to visiting places with cooler climates, whether they were Wyoming, Mackinac, or Silverton, Colorado, especially in the middle of summer.

Since I didn't have time to go inside, I went straight to my car.

While I waited, I got a text from Daddy.

DADDY: *Can you come up for a minute?*

I groaned. Daddy must have seen me land.

Well at least somebody saw that smooth landing I made.

ME: *Kind of in a rush. Can it wait til morning?*

DADDY: *Just take a minute. Important.*

Well, damn.

If Daddy said it was important, I couldn't ignore it.

I went inside and pressed the elevator button.

Looking at myself in the mirror, I wondered if I could skip washing my hair. I had it pulled up beneath my pilot's cap. With a few strands escaping, it didn't look so bad. Maybe I'd just wear a hat. There was probably one somewhere around the apartment.

Maybe in Madison's room. My older sister had left a lot of her things when she'd moved to Denver.

The elevator dinged and I hurried toward Daddy's office.

My heels against the wood floor were the only sound in the quiet office space.

Betty lifted a hand in greeting as I passed, but she kept her eyes glued to the computer.

As I reached Daddy's office, I stopped.

Wyatt stepped out his office.

His was wearing a black tuxedo and a smile that would melt any girl's heart.

And since this girl was already madly in love with him, it was almost more than I could stand to look at him.

"What are you doing here?" I asked, thinking back quickly. He'd said to meet at my apartment. I was certain of it.

"Decided we should get a head start," he said.

"A head start for what?" I took two steps toward him. "I got a text from Daddy."

"I know," he said, looking guilty. "I enlisted his help."

"You could have just told me," I said.

"And ruin the surprise?"

"I don't like—"

"I know. You don't like surprises."

I shrugged, but couldn't help but smile.

"I'm not dressed," I said. "Was heading home."

"You don't have to," he said, stepping back and sweeping a hand toward Daddy's open door.

Walking slowly, I went to Daddy's door and looked inside.

My red dress was draped over one of Daddy's chairs and there was a bag, no doubt with my other things.

"How did you…?"

Then I saw my sister, Brianna, standing across the room.

She was grinning.

"I helped a guy out," she said.

I looked at the three of them, one by one. Then my gaze stayed on Wyatt's.

"Okay," he said. "It was supposed to be a surprise, but I'll go ahead and tell you. We're having dinner at the Grand Hotel."

"Why?" I asked.

Wyatt looked at Noah. Noah just grinned and shrugged.

"Can you wait that long?" Daddy asked.

Wyatt blew out a breath. "I don't think so."

"Then now seems like as good a time as any."

Wyatt stepped forward and took my hands in his. His hands were trembling.

"What's the—?

Then Wyatt dropped to one knee.

"Ainsley?"

My breath hitched. There was only one reason a guy would be on one knee.

And if he was doing this in my daddy's office, he was indeed the bravest man I'd ever met.

"I was going to wait, but… well… I'm not good at waiting."

He kissed my fingertips.

Then looked into my eyes.

"Will you marry me?"

"Yes," I said, falling into his arms. "On one condition."

"Anything," he said.

"No more secrets."

**Keep reading for a preview of Brianna's story,
First Time Charm…**

FIRST TIME CHARM PREVIEW

Brianna Worthington

*A*fter zipping up the side of my lipstick red pencil skirt, I stepped into my black red—bottomed heels.

I pulled a black cashmere sweater from a shelf in my walk-in closet and pulled it on over my white silk button down blouse.

I turned this way and that in front of the full-length mirror propped on the floor of one end of my closet.

At five seven, I was the tallest of my four sisters. Two older sisters and one younger sister in my immediate family and one much older half-sister who already had kids of her own.

In fact, the half-sister, Danielle, was the only one of us who had any children and she lived in California. My oldest sister Madison was married and my next oldest sister, Ainsley, was engaged.

Ainsley lived here in Houston, but Madison had moved to Denver for a university professor job.

Madison took after Momma. Both of them were psychologists.

Ainsley took after Daddy. They were both airplane pilots for Daddy's company Skye Travels.

Then there was me.

I was an odd combination of both Daddy and Momma.

I had Daddy's passion, but I preferred to keep both feet literally on the ground. Daddy lived and breathed aviation. Me. I didn't fly simply because I had no reason to.

I was quite content driving around Houston in my 2022 fire-engine red Maserati Quattroporte.

Yes. Daddy bought it for me.

And anyone who had a problem with that could take it up with somebody who cared. Because I didn't.

I didn't have time in my life for judgmental people.

Besides, I had a thick skin.

I'd been dissed by the best of them. Perfect strangers felt compelled to give me their opinions of everything from my lifestyle to my career choice to the color of my lipstick.

So I went with what made me happy.

I had Momma's fashion sense and breezy personality.

Momma could walk into a room and charm anyone.

She was a drug representative turned psychologist.

From what I'd heard Daddy say, never in a critical way, the psychology training had taken some of the natural shine off that innate charm.

What he actually said was that she was a lot more serious now than she had been before.

But after giving birth to five children, all after the age of thirty, she'd earned the right to be as serious as she wanted.

I walked through my living room, stylishly furnished in neutral tones and turned on all the lights as I went.

I straightened the blue vase filled with pale pink roses and dark pink daisies on the table in my foyer.

Stepping into my home office, I pulled my MacBook from the desk draw, powered it on, and logged in.

I quickly opened my template, typed in the date and a working title.

Then I hit record and sat on a little stool in front of my desk.

"Hello lovelies," I said into the camera. "Welcome back to my channel. If this is your first time here, my name is Brianna Worthington and I'm going to talk to you today about creating your very own capsule wardrobe. It's not hard. And there are two important things I want you to take away from today's video. One is that a capsule wardrobe does not have to be boring."

I stepped away from the camera to show off my red pencil skirt and high heels.

"Seriously?" I asked with an impish grin. "Does this look boring?"

I turned this way and that so the camera could capture my full outfit.

"And second, a capsule wardrobe doesn't have to last forever. The guideline is that it lasts for about three months. For those of us who love shopping, that's awesome news."

"But…" I held up a finger and sat back down on my stool so I could look directly into my camera.

"You can start anywhere and your capsule wardrobe can last as long as you want it to. In fact, when I started my capsule wardrobe, I started simple. I started with this shirt I'm wearing. And guess where I bought it?"

I paused for effect.

"No. Not Nordstrom's. I bought this blouse from Target. And two years later I'm still wearing it. I wear it all the time. With everything.

"And it's so basic, no one even notices. Then I built around it."

I swept a hand down my skirt.

"A year later I bought this skirt at Nordstrom's. It was on sale. I admit. But it's good quality. I'll put the link below so you can look it up if you want to. And, yes, it's so basic and not trendy that they still sell it after almost a year."

I leaned forward into the camera.

"But... and this is very important. If you're going to buy new pieces for your wardrobe, buy things that fit you perfectly on the day you walk out of the store with them. Do not buy something that you hope will fit in a few months when you lose ten pounds. And another thing."

I paused again for effect.

"Buy things that you feel comfortable wearing. Something that is you. Not something that your fantasy you would wear. You know. The one where you're outgoing and carefree. Trendy.

"If the thought of wearing a tight red skirt sets your nerves on edge and you know you'd never put it on and walk out your front door, pick something more basic and add something like a scarf for color."

My phone chimed and a text message popped up on my screen.

I hit pause on my recording.

Editing was part of the process and was to be expected.

I didn't even mind editing.

But I rarely shot a video more than one time.

If I got interrupted. Like right now. I'd just edit out the interruption and keep going.

MOMMA: *Good morning.*

It was funny because not even having five children had gotten Momma out of the habit of thinking she had to communicate a normal conversation through text messaging.

She didn't seem to understand that greetings weren't required.

You could simply pick up a conversation you'd been having days ago as though no time at all had passed.

But I'd given up on trying to change that about her. I was just happy she texted at all at the ripe old age of fifty-five.

ME: *Hi.*

MOMMA: *Don't forget. Dinner on Sunday.*

ME: *I know. It's in my phone.*

MOMMA: *You should keep a paper calendar, too. It's easier to maintain. And keep up with.*

ME: *Okay.*

Another thing I'd given up on. Making Momma go digital was a lost cause. Not worth the fight.

But even though I left her alone about her paper calendars, there was no way I was going to start writing my appointments down on paper and Momma knew it.

There was no sense in reminding her, though, of the many ways the two of us were different. There were far too many ways that we were alike.

And those things were what mattered.

I didn't have to be a psychologist like her and my oldest sister to know these things.

Thinking that Momma was finished with the current conversation, I played back the last of my recording to orient myself back to what I'd been talking about.

MOMMA: Did you remember that you're picking your sister up from the airport today?

Damn. Damn. Damn.

I unlocked my phone and checked my calendar. I'd forgotten to set an alert and it had completely gotten overlooked.

ME: Of course not. I'm on my way out the door now.

Damn it. I hated it when Momma was right about her paper calendars.

I logged out and closed my computer. Tucked it back into the drawer and slid the stool back under the desk.

In my defense, picking my sister up from the airport was a most unusual request.

She was flying in on one of Daddy's planes. By one of Daddy's pilots. Probably Madison's husband if he was available. And I couldn't imagine why he wouldn't be. The two of them were stuck like glue.

Most people would just get an Uber or in my family's case, they'd schedule a car to pick them up.

But this was Madison's first time home since her wedding to her college sweetheart Kade. You'd think she was freaking royalty the way everyone was acting.

Madison and Kade had been college sweethearts only to break up for several years before they finally got back together, apparently by accident, and finally got married.

Anyway, apparently, I was the only person available to pick up my sister from the airport.

They would go down the list. Daddy had a flight. Ainsley had a flight. Momma had a patient. Quinn had a meeting. My younger sister was in class or whatever she did.

So that left me. The one who worked at home.

Somehow the *worked* part of the phrase *worked at home* was silent.

Like the P in psychology.

And, like always, I told myself it was okay. Because I was happy to see my sister and we could have lunch together before she was swept up in everyone else's activities.

I grabbed my charcoal wool coat, shrugged into it, and dragged my hair out of the collar.

I'd pull it back, but there wasn't time.

I was seriously late.

Next time, maybe, my sister would schedule a driver to pick her up.

A real driver.

Jackson Fleming

SEEING the skyline of Houston again brought back a lot of memories.

I'd grown up in Houston, but college had taken me away.

I always figured I'd find my way back there some day.

And I'd always thought of Houston as home even though I hadn't lived there in twelve years.

I was what people called an easy-going person.

I liked flying. And as long as I was flying, I was content.

My buddy, Daniel, had been the one who convinced me to join him in Denver after college.

We'd progressed from college roommates to apartment roommates and we'd lived together for the sum total of two months before he'd moved in with a new girlfriend.

To his credit, they were still together, though, for the life of me, I didn't know how a man could meet a girl and move in with her in just two months.

There were too many variables.

Anybody could be on their good behavior for two months.

Hell, I'd known people who could hold it together for over a year before they showed their true colors.

But I was glad my buddy had had good luck with his whirlwind romance.

I still lived in the same apartment we'd moved into back then.

Occasionally I considered looking for something else, but then I'd get a call for a flight and that would go out of my mind for the unforeseeable future.

As I approached the runway of the Houston airport, it occurred to me that I probably saw Denver as a temporary stopover. One that had lasted seven years.

The problem was I had established connections in Denver. I didn't work for any particular airline.

I did private contracting.

And damn if it didn't keep me busy.

More business than any regular job.

They said sitting was the new smoking. Well, I might as well hang it up. I kept waiting for somebody to make an airplane with room for pilots to stand up while they navigated the plane.

Surely someone out there was working on that.

I heard my passenger, Madison Worthington, talking on her cell. Technically she was Mrs. Kade Johnson, but since she was Dr. Worthington, she'd kept her own last name.

I didn't much see the point in that.

But I was an old-fashioned guy.

I figured that if two people were going to get married and become a family, the least they could do was to share a name.

I didn't even care if I had to be the one to change my name.

Kade could have changed his name to Kade Worthington.

There would have been nothing wrong with that, at least not in my book.

Unfortunately, that was one of those things that could get a man-card revoked.

So they kept their own names.

Not my problem.

And the whole thing was more than I needed to know.

I just needed to know when to pick her up and where to drop her off.

All the other personal stuff really wasn't my business.

I also knew that this week was Madison's birthday and that her husband was going to be flying in later in the day.

They had a whole family thing planned for Sunday.

Just knowing all this information made me uncomfortable.

The more I knew, the more I had to interact and the more I had to keep up with.

I didn't have to have the plane back until tomorrow so instead of flying straight back like I normally would—just so I could take another flight job, I was planning to spend the night in Houston.

Drive around a bit and see how things were holding up.

Maybe revisit some of my old stomping grounds.

I didn't really know anyone from here anymore, so I didn't have any plans past that.

That suited me just fine.

Other than planning my work flights, I preferred to let things happen as they fell.

Life seemed to move a whole lot smoother when a man didn't jerk on the steering wheel too much.

KEEP READING First Time Charm...

Kathryn Kaleigh is the author of over seventy novels, over one hundred short stories, and many collections.

kathrynkaleigh.com